"Dark night!" he shouted as the M60 ripped a burst along the cliff

"Why are we driving this way?" J.D. yelled again. "We're triple-fat targets down in this nuking ditch!"

"Business!" Marcus answered. "That's what makes Trader Trader. He's willin' to take risks others ain't."

The M60 snarled. J.B. approved of the way the gunner was firing in measured bursts. It was a way to minimize overheating the big weapon and to maximize the shots between barrel changes.

And then the big blaster fell silent.

J.B. frowned. He could see muties popping up on the gully walls ahead. It should be a target-rich environment.

Mebbe the barrel melted through, he thought. Sooner or later heat caught up with a machine gun.

"Damn!" the assistant wrench roared. "The sixty's jammed! And it's the only top-mounted blaster on War Wag One."

There was no hesitation. J.B. moved out, heading for the big blaster. Without it, Trader's convoy would be overrun.

JAMES AXLER

DEATH LANDS®

Storm Breakers

A GOLD EAGLE BOOK FROM

W❂RLDWIDE®

TORONTO • NEW YORK • LONDON
AMSTERDAM • PARIS • SYDNEY • HAMBURG
STOCKHOLM • ATHENS • TOKYO • MILAN
MADRID • WARSAW • BUDAPEST • AUCKLAND

Recycling programs
for this product may
not exist in your area.

First edition July 2013

ISBN-13: 978-0-373-62621-2

STORM BREAKERS

Printed in U.S.A.

Life is a series of natural and spontaneous changes. Don't resist them; that only creates sorrow. Let reality be reality. Let things flow naturally forward in whatever way they like.

—Lao Tzu

THE DEATHLANDS SAGA

This world is their legacy, a world born in the violent nuclear spasm of 2001 that was the bitter outcome of a struggle for global dominance.

There is no real escape from this shockscape where life always hangs in the balance, vulnerable to newly demonic nature, barbarism, lawlessness.

But they are the warrior survivalists, and they endure—in the way of the lion, the hawk and the tiger, true to nature's heart despite its ruination.

Ryan Cawdor: The privileged son of an East Coast baron. Acquainted with betrayal from a tender age, he is a master of the hard realities.

Krysty Wroth: Harmony ville's own Titian-haired beauty, a woman with the strength of tempered steel. Her premonitions and Gaia powers have been fostered by her Mother Sonja.

J. B. Dix, the Armorer: Weapons master and Ryan's close ally, he, too, honed his skills traversing the Deathlands with the legendary Trader.

Doctor Theophilus Tanner: Torn from his family and a gentler life in 1896, Doc has been thrown into a future he couldn't have imagined.

Dr. Mildred Wyeth: Her father was killed by the Ku Klux Klan, but her fate is not much lighter. Restored from pre-dark cryogenic suspension, she brings twentieth-century healing skills to a nightmare.

Jak Lauren: A true child of the wastelands, reared on adversity, loss and danger, the albino teenager is a fierce fighter and loyal friend.

Dean Cawdor: Ryan's young son by Sharona accepts the only world he knows, and yet he is the seedling bearing the promise of tomorrow.

In a world where all was lost, they are humanity's last hope....

Chapter One

Ryan Cawdor's sixth sense suddenly began to tingle. Something was about to go down.

Flanked by a pair of hard-faced chillers, Deke Sogram, a long, lean bastard in a wolfskin coat, stretched out a scarred hand toward the sealed document the gaudy-house owner had given Ryan back in Cole, a ville in the hills of what some still called New England. The companions had gotten free meals, lodging and some local jack in return for delivering the envelope to the gaudy owner's acquaintance here at the crossroads.

The snow was falling heavily from a sky so dark it made it hard to tell if the early sunset had happened yet, though Ryan knew it was a couple of hours off. The wind was brisk rather than driving. It swirled, throwing up the newly fallen snow almost to chest level, adding to the tricky viewing conditions.

Pine woods rose on all sides, fading to dark, obscured spike palisades. The roads that crossed at this point were roads only by virtue of people calling them so. They were, in fact, a couple of deep ruts slashed through by what seemed little more than a double-wide game trail, both so buried under snow that the only way to know they were there was that they made furrows lower than the surrounding snowfields. But the ground lay clear here for a good thirty or forty yards in every direction, which gave the companions a certain sense of security from ambush.

Sogram's right hand secured the heavy envelope of coarse gray-brown paper, whose lumps suggested it was predark-made. It was sealed with a blob of hard blue wax stamped with a signet ring made out of a copper coin that Ryan knew from his education as a baron's son was called a penny. Sogram let the envelope fall into the drifting snow between him and Ryan. The one-eyed man realized in a flash that he and the companions had been set up by the gaudy owner, that the envelope was bait.

Both of Sogram's men had their right hands out of sight. And while the coldheart was making his move with his left, it was slow and deliberate, so as to avoid alerting his target.

He failed.

Ryan was under no such restriction, automatically shouting, "Trap!"

His left hand was already under his own heavy coat. It came out swinging the long, broad blade of his machete-like panga at the coldheart's prominent Adam's apple.

Sogram was good. He instinctively leaned back and dropped his chin to protect his gullet from a sure chill-shot.

Ryan's blade chopped like an ax into Sogram's lower jaw. The man's shout came out as a gargling scream of blood and teeth, a couple still held together by a chunk of bone. He fell over backward, vanishing almost instantly into a low snowdrift.

Ryan was already dropping flat in place. As he did, a blaster shot almost shredded his right eardrum.

KRYSTY WROTH HAD read the flamboyantly mustached coldheart's evil intent in the narrowing of his dark eyes.

To see danger was to act. It was a skill that her mother, Sonja Wroth, had taught her, long before Krysty and the tall, dark and handsome one-eyed Ryan Cawdor had crossed paths. Association with her love and life-mate Ryan had certainly sharpened those skills.

Along with many others.

She opened her mouth to cry a warning. As she swung up her Smith & Wesson Model 640, she dropped to one knee in the same motion.

Before the warning left her lips, Ryan had roared his and chopped at the lower half of the coldheart's face with his panga. Already cleared to fire past Ryan's right shoulder—the main reason she'd taken up position a step to the side as well as one back—Krysty lined the rudimentary sight of the short-barreled revolver on the nearest available target as the leader went down spewing gore that was black in the half-light.

That was the burly bastard who looked like a bear, and not just because he wore a coat of brown bear-hide. He was an older guy, heavier set. He had a shaved dome like his boss's, Asian eyes and a much neater mustache running down past the corners of his mouth. He opened his mouth as he brought up the wired-together Remington 870P pump shotgun to blast apart Ryan's head at muzzle-flame range.

"Remember!" he bellowed as he tracked his dropping target with the scattergun's short barrel. "Grab the bitches, chill the pricks!"

Slavers, she thought grimly. Her little blaster roared with much more doom than its 158-grain .38 Special slug actually carried. The muzzle-flame was huge and yellow and almost dazzling in the gloom. That was the curse of the short barrel of her blaster: recoil made it rise. But she knew how to handle her little piece. Krysty controlled the kick as best she could, dropped it back down to the center of the brigand's broad chest and fired again.

This time she didn't wait for the blaster to fall back online. Instead she blasted a third time as the nub front sight of the little wheelgun passed the man's broad chin headed north.

It was a trick from predark that Mildred Wyeth had taught her: the Mozambique Drill. Two in the chest and one in the head/Make sure the bad guy is thoroughly dead! Mildred had taught her the chant. That seemed more than a bit cold-blooded for a trained doctor, not to mention one who still struggled sometimes with the values and morals she'd carried with her through her century-plus sleep as a twentieth-century freezie.

But when the hammer came down, the stocky brown-skinned woman with the beaded plaits had the icy practicality of a battlefield doctor, which was why she survived and fit in so well with the rest of the companions.

Krysty's last bullet hit the shotgunner square in the middle of his broad forehead. From the geyser of matter that blew out from more or less the top of his head, she guessed the bullet had passed through to blast out a piece of skull and a fistful of brains.

The shotgun erupted in thunder and fire. Her heart froze in her chest. *Ryan!*

RYAN'S SIG-SAUER P-226 handblaster was in his fist a heartbeat before he landed in the snow, which cushioned his flat fall. His impact shot up a cloud of powdery white that masked his vision like a smoke gren.

His right ear rang from the blaster shot that had gone off as he went down. Through the tinnitus's whine he heard more shots erupt. And then, as the fallen snow began to settle, it was lit up as if somebody'd opened a gate straight to hell, then slammed it shut. The sight was accompanied by about the same amount of noise.

Shotgun, he knew. He didn't even bother thinking, it missed.

Ryan's face was caked in cold. He blinked his one eye clear of snow. He already registered the shadow-form of the chiller on the leader's left going down. He switched aim to his own left, where the second flanker stood. He had a semiauto blaster holstered on his left hip. Even through the thinning snow-smoke and an annoying tiny ice-flake clinging stubbornly to his eyeball, Ryan could tell he was only now drawing the weapon.

That's just too bastard bad, he thought, firing three quick shots, center-of-mass.

As the guy went down, he heard the ripsaw roaring of J.B.'s Uzi machine pistol.

When the first burst ended, the Armorer shouted, "They're all around us! Comin' out of the snow!"

FIGURES REARED UP out of the snowbanks to either side of the ruts they'd followed to the meet. Snow cascaded from their bodies and the crusty old tarps they'd been buried beneath.

And the nearest man to J.B.'s left promptly fell back down with a couple of 9 mm hardball rounds in his gut.

J.B. heard the crack of a .38 handblaster, which meant Mildred, who'd been pulling tail-end Charlie as they trudged to their rendezvous with the man they'd been charged to deliver a message to, had cut loose with her heavy Czech-made wheelgun. Then came a more authoritative roar from a .45 behind him, and a similar noise from Doc Tanner's big .44 LeMat.

J.B. almost smiled even as he loosed another blast that made two more figures fall down—though he was fairly sure he'd missed them, at twenty yards or more. They were just ducking away from sheer reflex.

While J. B. Dix was a man who swore by precision in everything he did, there was also a thing called fire superiority, and it was also as real a thing as a compound fracture. Translated loosely, that meant, *If you can make the other bastard flinch first, you double your chances*.

And right now, every chance they could get might still be too few.

The reason he grinned was that the big handblaster doing its thing meant that Doc was in the fight, and that the Armorer's young protégé, Ricky Morales, had likely scored his *second* chill. Because the first .45 round would have been fired from the youth's DeLisle carbine whose whisper-quiet report he'd missed in the general fireworks.

Then Ricky had plainly let the longblaster with the fat stub of barrel and its built-in silencer fall to the extent of his carrying sling. Because fast as its Enfield-style bolt action was to throw, he could fire the big double-action Webley revolver, rebored to shoot the same .45 ACP as the carbine, even faster.

J.B. had gone to one knee. He looked for targets, moving his head side to side while keeping the other guy who'd gone down at his second burst in the soft focus sides of his vision-field. He wasn't sure he could spare a short make-sure burst to him yet, since he might *not* be playing possum.

There was still shooting behind and on both sides. Then he heard Ryan bellow, "Go, go, *go!*"

That was why he'd gone to a knee rather than flopping full prone. He couldn't afford to make too fat a target for the ambushers. But he didn't want to make it too slow to get back into action, either, since the best way to bust an ambush was to assault right straight into it.

More coldhearts had come out of the trees, half-obscured by the falling snow, and more than half from belly down by the stuff they kicked up. J.B. already knew that Ryan would drive straight forward, past the trio who'd stood to meet them, which meant running the direction the coldhearts had most likely come from. Meaning they might just run into a whole bunch of other coldhearts.

But it wasn't as if they had any *good* choices. J.B. recalled a saying of his and Ryan's old mentor, Trader: when you're caught in an ambush, your survival depends entirely on the incompetence of your ambushers.

He loosed a quick blast at the nearest of the oncoming coldhearts as he drove himself back off his knee into a run to the west. They hadn't opened up yet.

Fortunately this gang of coldhearts had two strikes against them from the get-go. First, they knew their quarry was walking into a trap—meaning they were overconfident, sure of getting the drop, or at least the telling first shots.

Second, they were slavers. The one man's shout had confirmed what J.B. already suspected when he saw Ryan chop the coldheart boss. The whole point of the ambush was to grab the women, Krysty and Mildred, not just alive but undamaged.

The men—strong and healthy specimens—could fetch a good price, too.

He saw one fall, thought he'd hit him. Muzzles flashed from the shadowy pursuers. They mostly seemed to be coming from north and south of the road from the west—Ryan and the rest's backtrail.

Meanwhile, a flash look up front showed the way ahead was clear, as far as J.B. could see through the rad-blasted snow. The slavers had buried eight or ten chillers in the snow, then sent about a dozen around east to cut off the quarry's escape. They hadn't left a reserve to the west. That might have been cockiness, too—likely that played its role, as it so often did—but mostly J.B. just reckoned the boss didn't trust his men with cocked blasters *behind* him. With coldhearts keyed up like jolt-walkers on adrenaline by the prospect of dealing pain, accidents happened. Sometimes things happened that weren't accidents.

J.B. slowed to wave Mildred past him. She gave him a hard look in passing.

The slavers were firing on the run, usually piss-poor practice in J.B.'s opinion. While there were exceptions, the Armorer always figured that when the time was to shoot, you shot, and when the time was to move, you moved; you didn't divide your intent and action mixing up the two. Also, they were probably afraid of hitting the women.

He started to run again, his boots sinking out of sight at every step. The Armorer could feel the cold wetness the snow-pack left on his trouser legs where they were bloused into the boot-tops. The snow made it hard to run—not as bad as slogging through soft sand, but bad enough.

Then a big yellow muzzle-flash blossomed from the pine woods to the north. A heartbeat later, a slam of sound hit J.B.'s ears that was even harder and sharper than the coldheart longblasters.

He grinned as the new pack of pursuers faltered and called out to each other in dismay.

Another fire-bloom. This time, a figure and the weapon he held dropped out of sight in the ground-cloud of snow. The coldhearts either threw themselves down or backpedaled to the safety of the trees.

Jak Lauren, the last member of the party, had circled around to cover his friends from concealment.

His .357 Magnum Colt Python revolver wasn't exactly a longblaster, but in the hands of a steady marksman it could chill people at surprising range. But the young former bayou-guerrilla, who'd earned the nickname White Wolf while barely into his teens, wasn't exactly that. He was a knife man by nature, as befit a stealth hunter.

The slavers had reckoned that the ambush was all wrapped up with a pretty red bow from the get-go, and that made the shock of the sudden turnaround hit hard.

It didn't matter that Jak only hit one coldheart by luck—ace for him, less so for the slaver. Nor that Jak was only one lone shooter. As far as they—or their bladders and bowels, suddenly letting go in sheer fear—knew, a whole nuke-sucking army was about to land on them like an avalanche.

Ryan raced into the trees without breaking stride. The risk of running into another ambush weighed less in his judgment than the certainty that their pursuers would chill them unless they got clear fast. Same in J.B.'s reckoning—although, as always, he'd follow where his best friend led. As skillful and many-skilled, and as smart, seasoned and steady in a fight as J. B. Dix was, he wasn't the leader type.

Ryan Cawdor was, so J.B. followed his old friend—and tried to keep him from getting too deep in hot rad waste.

The rest of the companions joined him. J.B. got in between two firs and turned to cover their backtrail. No more shots came from that direction. He reckoned the slavers were holding a hasty palaver, the subject of which would most likely be Plan B.

Jak raced toward the trees, seeming to fly across the snow, his elbows pumping. The vented rib down the barrel of his chromed handblaster managed to cast a few dull glints in the semidarkness. His white hair snapped behind him like a pennant. His ruby eyes were wide and glaring.

"Run!" he yelled when he saw J.B. standing to cover him. "More come!"

A sledgehammer hit J.B. in the chest. The impact whirled him helplessly clockwise.

And down into blackness.

Chapter Two

"J.B.'s down!"

Mildred's racing heart stumbled in her chest at Jak's cry.

She was already a good forty yards up the road between close-crowding, snow-clad trees. She might have been short and stocky, but her powerful legs could carry her at a brisk clip when the situation demanded.

Without waiting for orders from Ryan, she wheeled around and raced back to where Jak knelt protectively over his friend's body. J.B. lay slantwise off the north verge of the road, his face buried in the deeper snow. His Uzi lay near his outflung hand. Red stained the snow around his upper chest.

Not the heart, she prayed silently. Dear God, please don't let it be the heart! Jak's big handgun spat bright yellow fire, followed immediately by a thunderclap report that seemed to slap Mildred in the face. One of the shadow-figures moving through the thickening snow and gloom flopped forward to the ground. Others shot back with winking muzzle-flares.

Mildred snapped out her right arm in full-extension. In violation of all her training and instincts as an Olympic-qualified target-pistol shooter, she got a flash picture of a pale oval blur of face over the square-topped front sight post and squeezed the trigger. The revolver roared and kicked her hand.

She'd aimed for the center of the nearest slaver's face. She missed. Instead, she saw his right eye explode out of his head in a black spray. His head snapped back in his fur-lined parka and he folded.

Jak's Magnum blaster ran dry. He had speedloaders for the Python, but the coldhearts were closing fast. Instead, as bullets kicked up tiny fountains of snow around him, he dived for the fallen Uzi. Somehow the young albino managed to free the strap from J.B.'s prone form as he rolled into the snowbank, which was so deep he disappeared almost completely.

As Mildred sprinted forward, dropped to her knees and skidded the last ten feet to J.B.'s side on the snow-covered road, Jak reared up, shedding snow chunks and powder like some vengeful spirit of ice, and blazed away vigorously with the blaster.

She fired again, across J.B.'s body. This time she had a more stable platform, but all the pursuers in sight were already throwing themselves down in the face of the impressive amount of fire and noise the Uzi was producing. Bullets continued to crack overhead as Mildred jammed her ZKR into her belt and rolled J.B. onto his back.

If the bullet clipped his vertebrae I could be paralyzing him, she thought. But if he suffocates, that doesn't mean much, does it?

Apparently the slavers' blind shots were going wide in another direction, too. She heard a voice, oddly muffled by the snow, shout, "Hey, you triple-stupe assholes, cease fire! You're hitting us."

From the corner of her eye she was vaguely aware that the Uzi's slide had locked the back, meaning Jak had fired it dry. He tossed the blaster into the snow next to J.B.

John's breathing, Mildred thought. It was shallow and labored. But happening.

And from the pink froth bubbling from his nostrils and a corner of his mouth, she knew just why his breathing came so hard. He had a sucking chest wound!

J.B. WAS COLD, colder than he remembered being in his whole life, and he hurt bad.

He was short of breath, and when he breathed in, it felt like somebody was stabbing him in the chest with a big Bowie knife.

"His eyelids are moving!" he heard Mildred say. She had to have shouted it, he reckoned, but the words sounded as if she was speaking down a well.

He began to remember where they were, what they were doing: they were being ambushed, shooting their way clear.

The Armorer managed to crank his eyelids open. At that point, the knife-pain in the right side of his chest actually helped. Once he started coming to, it all but kicked him back to full awareness.

His vision took a moment to sharpen vague moving blurs and a whole lot of white to clarity. The first thing he saw was Mildred's face, turned down, chin to chest, knotted in frustration as she tore at some kind of cracked plastic packaging. He realized in a vague sort of way she'd opened the front of his scuffed leather jacket and torn open his shirt beneath. The cold wind and snow felt like fire and embers on his exposed skin.

He tried to sit up.

"Lie down!" he heard Ryan's voice rap from somewhere hard to the left. "Are you trying to get hit again?"

He heard the bang of Ryan's longblaster. The Scout carbine was chambered in 7.62 mm, a serious round, but the length of its barrel made it even louder. He felt the sting of the vibrations more than he actually heard them, though.

"You—" He stopped, literally choking on the words. Fluid clogged his throat.

He coughed, turned his head and spit in the snow. What came out was a pink spray. He knew what it was: lung blood.

"You got to leave me," he said as clearly as he could. It came out in a thin gurgling wheeze. He couldn't seem to get enough air. "I can—still trigger a blaster. I can rig a booby-trap on me triple-fast, fight till I can't, then let the bastards send me and themselves off in style."

Mildred's strong blunt fingers finally tore the wrapping apart. Letting the dressing spill down on her thighs, she pressed the blue plastic onto J.B.'s chest and leaned on it.

The Armorer set his jaw. The pressure made him feel like he was being shot all over again.

"Here." It was Krysty, kneeling by his other side. Her red hair had tightened into a cap against her skull. If she hadn't been Ryan's life-mate, body and soul, he might have been more than a little impressed by her bust hanging right over his face—not that his own partner, Mildred, was any slouch in that department. He wasn't a man much given to matters of the flesh. But he was still a man.

Get your mind back on business, he told himself as Krysty unreeled a long gray strip from a roll of duct tape.

With Mildred's help, Krysty lifted his upper torso and started taking long, tight turns around his chest, clothes and all, to hold the patch over the hole.

For a fact, he did feel better. Less like he was leaking.

"Where are they all coming from?" he heard Ricky

Morales ask. His English was as good as anybody's—
he'd grown up speaking the lingo, after all—but heavily flavored with what sounded like a Spanish accent.
It was, in fact, from his Caribbean home—a place that
he knew as Puerto Rico and everybody else knew as
Monster Island.

J.B. heard the metal clacking that told him the youth
had opened the top-breaking British handblaster to shuck
the empties and slam in a fresh moon-clip loaded with
.45 ACP cartridges.

"There're too many to be trying to take a group as
small as we are."

The shattering blast of Jak's Colt Python made J.B.'s
eyes water.

"Must be near their base," the Armorer said.

"Don't talk," Mildred gritted.

"Better than having nothing to do but think about
how triple-good I don't feel," he said.

"Got it," Krysty stated. "What are they doing?"

She had to have meant the coldhearts.

"The blackguards have stopped shooting for the moment," J.B. heard Doc say. He had only a vague sense of
where people were. There was no cover to speak of anywhere near—nothing that would stop a bullet. He just
hoped his friends had found some concealment.

At least nobody else seemed to have gotten winged
yet.

"Perhaps we have discouraged them at last?" Doc
suggested.

"Not a chance," Ryan said. "If we're near their camp,
they're likely just waiting on reinforcements."

"But that means this road—" Ricky began.

"Is still the only one we got," Ryan said. "So are we
good to go?"

Mildred winced as if she'd taken a round. "No," she gritted. "But we *can*."

"Then let's get rolling."

Krysty looked across J.B. at Mildred. "Ready?"

Mildred nodded. J.B. felt himself gripped by both upper arms. The two women got their boot soles beneath them, then stood up as one—deadlifting him to his feet. They were both strong women. He came right up.

He knew right away he wasn't going to remain standing in his condition.

He also knew better than to argue any more about what they ought to do with him. It warmed him inside, despite the cold and pain, to know that his friends refused to leave him behind. But he still felt a cold certainty they were being triple-stupe not to.

"Doc, get J.B.'s Uzi and what extra mags you can find triple-fast," Ryan ordered.

"Indeed!"

"Jak, grab the shotgun and take point."

J.B. heard the thump of Ricky's hand-modified longblaster. A scream answered it, still filtered through falling snow and J.B.'s own hazy consciousness.

"One stuck his head up just as visibility broke," the youth reported. J.B. heard him jacking the action. Good boy, he thought. Good habits. Makes a body proud.

"I'll hang here and give them something to think about other than your shapely ass, Krysty," Ryan said. "I'll give you a head start."

"Ryan—" the redhead said.

"Do you think I'm going to throw my life away when we got at least a stretch of clear road in front of us and trees we can try to get lost in if we need to?

"Now, go! Double-time!"

They started running. J.B. did his best to help, but

his boots seemed to keep getting tangled up in the snow packed over the road-ruts, harder than the new stuff, but not enough that they didn't sink in.

"Knock it off," Mildred snarled. "It's easier just to drag you."

He let them. The jarring was like sheets of glass getting busted up inside him.

The run was a nightmare. He was aware of his friends as fuzzy shapes in front and to the sides—and not just because the snow was still coming down hard and the dusk had settled in for serious now. He heard the labor of their breathing, the crunch and thud of their steps.

From behind he heard the flat crack of Ryan's Steyr longblaster: once, twice. He glanced aside at Krysty. Her face was white and perfect, and as hard as a marble statue's. But she showed no sign of extra concern.

He'd lost his time sense pretty much completely. At some point he heard Ryan's rasping cry from not far behind.

"I'm up with you, but they're coming now. I just made them cautious."

J.B. concentrated on trying to get enough air. Even though Mildred had patched the leak in his chest, however temporarily, the rad-blasted thing wasn't working well. Mebbe his lung had collapsed by now.

It sure didn't hurt any less. He concentrated on fighting through the pain to suck down as much air as he could.

Unconsciousness tried to pull him down like the soft yet strong arms of a woman—like Mildred's. He yearned for it as much as he'd ever yearned for her sweet flesh. But he didn't give in to its seduction. He fought to stay awake.

He'd been born a fighter. That was the only way a sawed-off runt like him ever survived past being a pup.

Then he heard the unmistakable voice of his own M-4000 blaster speak from up ahead. Bullets cracked overhead.

Then Jak roared, "More!"

J.B. was slammed back out of consciousness at last as Krysty and Mildred, carrying him, crashed into the snowbank beside the road.

"WHAT NOW, RYAN?" Doc asked.

Ryan knelt by the reddish bole of a spruce as he fed a fresh magazine into the well of his Scout Tactical rifle. They were getting low on ammo, but that was the least of their worries.

They had discouraged both the pursuit from behind and the blocking force ahead. For the moment. Miraculously, they still hadn't taken any more hits, though a slug had ripped through the upper left corner of Krysty's backpack—fortunately missing her shoulder.

They were saved because the snow and increasing gloom made it hard to see and shoot, and they could use the densely packed trees for cover north and south of the road. And they'd put out a brisk enough volume of fire to make the slavers uncertain just how many enemies they faced.

Occasionally shots cracked out from up ahead and behind. Ricky was pulling tail-end Charlie with his DeLisle; Ryan now had point. Their longblasters had the best range and accuracy when targets presented themselves.

The poor visibility cloaked both sides.

"The brutes are most persistent," Doc said, kneeling on the far side of the trail with J.B.'s Uzi at the ready.

He didn't look comfortable with the short, thick, heavy blaster. But it was more useful in a fight of this scale than his heavy LeMat commemorative blaster.

"They must not want us to get away," Krysty said. She and Mildred had J.B. under some kind of spiky-leafed bush by the road, and knelt protectively over him. "Not just for our sale price. I think they don't want us spreading the word where they are."

"Could be," Ryan agreed.

He drew in a deep breath and let it slide out through cold-chapped lips.

"Right. Here's how we play it. Krysty, you lead the rest and make a break south. The coast's that way. Once you get up over the ridges there you should be clear."

"What do you mean, 'the rest'?" she asked.

"Jak, Ricky, Doc, Mildred. Go fast, don't look back. J.B., you still feel up to rigging a booby? We'll take a stand."

The Armorer was propped up with his head shielded by his hat among the prickly lower branches of the bush, with his backpack keeping his upper body mostly out of the snow.

He held up a right thumb in a gesture of affirmation and even managed a feeble grimace that looked something like a grin. His thumb was more blue than pink from cold.

At least it's not white yet, Ryan thought. Not like that matters now.

"Not going leave you two," Jak said. He was hunkered with Ryan up front, on the south side of the trail to Ryan's north.

"I didn't hear that."

"Me, neither," Mildred said. "You either both come or we all stay."

"Mildred," J.B. croaked. "That doesn't make any sense—"

"Shut up," she said.

"I'm with Mildred," Krysty stated. "I won't leave you and J.B."

"I fear I am with the others," Doc said.

Ryan heard Ricky swallow loudly. "Me, too. *Lo siento*—sorry."

"Don't be triple-stupes!" Ryan snapped. "We're caught between fires here. There's no point in everybody getting chilled together!"

"Of course there is," Krysty said. "We're a team, family."

Rage rose within him—and warred with the love he felt. For a moment he couldn't speak. What he had to say got jammed tight in his throat, like a crowd trying to flee a burning building through a single doorway. I fought so long and hard to keep us together! he wanted to shout. But alive, fireblast it! Not as chills!

"It's settled, Ryan," Mildred said in as hard and flat and definite a voice as he'd ever heard the woman use.

"Shit," he said. "Then I guess we better get ready to die a lot."

From off to the north came a strange scream, like a brass-throated droid in mortal pain.

Chapter Three

The terrible blare resolved itself into a melody of sorts in Krysty's ears.

"A bugle?" Doc asked in tones of wonder.

Instantly the volume of fire coming their way slackened.

"The blackguards flee!" crowed Doc, who was looking west along their backtrail. Kneeling next to Mildred and J.B., aiming her snub-nosed handblaster down the rutted road, Krysty glanced quickly over her shoulder. Though the scene was turning to an overall gray blur shot with light patches of still-falling snow, she saw localized whirlwinds of paler gray, clearly kicked up by slavers retreating rapidly to the cover of the far trees.

Yellow muzzle flashes still flickered from up ahead. Ryan's Steyr longblaster boomed. Someone screamed. Krysty saw a violent spasm of shadow as the recipient of the heavy 7.62 mm bullet threw up his hands and fell.

From the left, more people burst onto the trail from the trees to the north, stumbling down a short steep bank like an avalanche. Krysty aimed at the nearest. It was a long shot for her short-barreled .38; she hoped someone else would take the shot if the shooter turned his longblaster toward her companions. But she was ready to try.

The figure stopped in the trail and swung his weapon back. Even though he was no more than twenty-five yards ahead, Krysty couldn't tell what it was, or anything about the wielder other than that he, or *she,* seemed to be dressed in black, as many of the slavers were.

"No shoot!" Jak yelled.

Krysty froze. The fact that the hot-blooded Jak was crying out a warning against violence was fully as shocking as the ambush.

The others held their fire, too. She sensed Doc and Ricky, who had been covering their backtrail, wheeling to look east.

A giant shadow burst from the bank in an explosion of snow-dust like smoke. It had four legs and a strange protrusion from its back. Then, as the shape descended to the road, it resolved in Krysty's astonished eyes as a horse with a man on its back.

The man had a long, curved sword, and he slashed down at the kneeling slaver with a brutal stroke across the face before the other could shoot.

As the slaver fell, the horseman was silhouetted in a sudden dancing flare of orange light. Sound hammered Krysty's ears. He was shooting some kind of longblaster full-auto down the trail with his left hand.

He turned and charged away from the companions. Another pair of riders erupted from the left to follow. Already a tumult of shots and shrieks was blowing out of the enemy blocking force eastward.

"Did I just see some cavalry guy kill another guy with a sword?" Ricky asked. The youth's normally olive face seemed to have turned a shade not much darker than the snow around them, which now seemed to glow with its own light in the last vestiges of dying day. His dark eyes were huge.

"It would certainly appear so," Doc agreed, straightening and dusting off the sleeves of his long-tailed frock coat.

"Get down, stupe!" Ryan hissed.

Doc did. But he turned a mild, complaining, deceptively old-looking countenance to Ryan.

"But you saw them dispatch those slaver devils smartly!" he protested. "Surely the enemy of our enemy is—"

"Our enemy's enemy, and not one other thing," Ryan finished sharply. "You ought to know that by now. Mebbe things were different back in the Middle Ages where you come from, but these days, it's pretty much bastard versus bastard, wherever you go."

"Ryan! You know perfectly well I was born during the reign of Victoria Regina—"

"Yeah, he does," Mildred said. "Step back off the trigger there, you old coot. Ryan's yanking your chain."

With the men still on their feet aiming along the trail where the trio of horsemen had vanished in the gloom— except for Jak, who cautiously and characteristically was covering behind them with his Magnum handblaster— she turned her attention to Mildred and her wounded lover.

"How is he?" she asked.

"Bad." Mildred's face was set like a statue's in a grim look. A tear rolled down her right cheek but she was clearly holding her emotions in check. "I got the holes blocked—the bullet blew through but didn't leave a huge exit wound. That's a blessing, anyway. But—"

She shook her head. More tears drew tracks down her ashen cheeks to join the first in turning into icicles.

"I'm afraid if he doesn't get some kind of medical attention fast, he's a goner. I've done all I can."

"Someone's coming out of the trees to the north," Ricky reported tersely.

"Good eye," said Ryan, who knelt behind a tree peer-

ing over the top of the long-eye relief scope set atop his
Scout rifle. "Now, you keep your finger easy on the trigger until we know whose side they're really on."

"Other than their own, of course," said a voice that
was cracked like a heavy clay pot that had fallen off the
shelf onto stone. It broke into coughing.

"J.B.!" Mildred shrilled. "Don't try to talk!"

The Armorer had regained consciousness. Of a sort.
He patted Mildred's hand and offered her a smile, which
might have been reassuring, a little, anyway, if there
wasn't still blood leaking out both ends of it down his
chin. Then his eyelids fluttered and closed.

Krysty caught herself before she gasped aloud. She
realized he was still alive; his chest was heaving seriously in the unconscious battle for breath.

"Easy," Ryan repeated.

Krysty looked up. People had walked onto the road
seventy or eighty feet ahead. They were dressed in white
parkas with the hoods up, and mostly white pants. Some
turned and knelt facing Ryan's group, holding longblasters—pointing their way, but with muzzles down. Not
quite aiming at the strangers, but making it clear they
could, triple-quick. Behind them she saw other people
carrying what could hardly be anything but spears, about
eight feet long.

The firing had died down to nothing. The stillness
seemed as sudden as a gunshot, and so deceptively complete it was almost hard to believe what a horrific tumult
had been raging a few breaths before.

Tall dark shapes resolved through the falling snow,
which had begun coming down faster but in smaller
flakes. Krysty heard a horse snort. The white-hooded
men blocking the road pulled away to either side without
taking their eyes off Krysty and the rest of the compan-

ions. A tall man on a black horse rode into clear view. He had a long face made longer by a black Astrakhan wool hat, broad cheekbones, dark beard and pale eyes that pierced even through distance and gloom. He carried his saber in his right hand and a bugle in his left. A short but obviously two-handed weapon was slung across a chest that looked massive from the bearskin coat that covered it. The blaster was a Krinkov submachine gun.

Behind him, winged out slightly to one side, rode a slimmer man with brown bangs hanging out from beneath an old Red Army-style winter cap. Krysty felt a bit of a shock as she saw the red star burning from the middle of it. To the other side rode a young woman holding a lever-action longblaster in one hand. She wore the same type of cap. Her hair looked little, if any, darker than Jak's; the white locks streamed down over the shoulders of her parka.

"Who are you?" Ryan called out.

The big man in the Astrakhan laughed. "I am Baron Ivan Frost," he called in a cheerful boom. "And inasmuch as this is my domain, I believe that question rightly belongs to me!"

"Fair enough," Ryan said. He stood, lowering his rifle, and stepped out into the path.

Krysty let go a long breath. She felt tension slide out of her shoulders. Her own intuition matched Ryan's warrior instinct: these people weren't hostile.

If they were, her mind reminded her, they'd have stood off and let the slavers take us down before they made their move.

"I'm Ryan Cawdor," he said.

"What is your business in Stormbreak?"

"Surviving. Trying to keep out of the hands of these nuke-sucking slavers."

The baron nodded. "And the rest?"

"My companions," Ryan said. "And begging your pardon, we'll be short one triple-fast if my wounded man doesn't get help soon!"

The baron gestured with his saber. The sec men on foot started moving forward, lowering their weapons.

Krysty heard Mildred growl, "Ricky! Can it."

Looking sheepish, the youth let his own longblaster slump back again to point at the ground.

A young woman followed the sec men. She dismounted a few feet away and went swiftly to J.B.'s side. She nodded to Mildred, then leaned in to look at him.

"Make a travois, fast," she directed the sec men. "The outlanders tell the truth."

"You have done us a service, Ryan Cawdor and friends," the baron announced, still sitting astride his big black horse. "You helped guide us to these wretches— and thinned their ranks for us. I thank you and extend the hospitality of my home. Can the man be moved?"

"I believe so, Baron," the woman called.

"If he doesn't, at the least, get inside quickly," Mildred said, "he'll die. So he *needs* to be moved."

"Then we shall go. I fear that, with the travois, you have an hour's journey to my home. I will ride ahead to tell my healer to prepare for your wounded friend."

J.B. stirred and murmured something inaudible. Mildred patted his hand.

"Hang in there, baby," she whispered. "We're among friends now, anyway."

Krysty saw her glance quickly at Ryan, who stood by holding his longblaster in patrol position. He had a neutral look on his face.

"Or at least, not enemies."

Chapter Four

J.B. floated in a strange pale fog shot through with bright red flashes of pain.

When they hit, the first thing he was aware of was the endless struggle to breathe. And cold. And jostling.

And the smell of...horses?

His eyes tried to open, but couldn't. Dark night! he thought. I can't breathe, and now I can't see?

He set his jaw. At least that didn't hurt. Any extra. He willed his eyes to open.

The lids broke free like scabs. Instantly tiny cold needles stung through the blur in his vision.

Snow!

It came back to him then, in a sick, cold flood, what had happened. Did the slavers catch us? he wondered frantically. Did we lose? Where are my friends? Are they all still fit to fight? Or triple-screwed-up like me?

He became aware of the odd rhythm with which his whole body was bouncing, and the intricate muffled drumbeat pattern running through it like a bass-line through a melody. He wasn't the artistic type, and was even less musical, but those were the only words he found that would do the job, so he used them.

His vision sharpened and cleared as he blinked away the snowflakes falling. He saw the tail of a horse between the familiar scuffed toes of his boots—he was lying on his back, it turned out. Rolling his eyes left and right, then craning his head back on the sling he seemed to be lying on, he realized two more horses were tight behind to either side, both with riders, both looking like shadows in a white swirl in the dark.

The slavers hadn't had any horses. They didn't seem the type. He caught a vague memory bubbling to the surface of his foggy brain—sense impressions of a bugle calling, and the slavers falling back in panic.

So, he reckoned, these people beat the slavers. Did they rescue us—or capture us?

It was all too much. Though they moved at a brisk walk, like a trot but smoother, seemingly to combine speed with gentleness, the fact was that every little impact sent a fresh stab of pain like a knife blade through his chest. As did every attempt to breathe.

Consciousness started to fade. That was probably best, he knew. But he still fought to hold on to it as long as he could. He never was a man who knew when to quit. Nor a boy—that was the only way he'd survived in a brutal land where the weak got no breaks except for their bones: he just plain hung on and didn't quit—

But the blackness won again.

JUST WHEN MILDRED thought she couldn't stagger another step, they saw a yellow glow through trees made ghostly by snow loading down their boughs and falling lightly now. The pain in her legs from trudging through deep snow and sheer fatigue was so all-encompassing and yet so sharp it sometimes overwhelmed her grief and fear for J.B.

"We're almost there," Lucas said. He was a young man with a clean-shaven face who seemed to be in charge of the ten-man sec crew that was escorting Ryan and his party through the woods in the wake of the horses carrying J.B.'s improvised travois. Between the darkness and the fur lining of his parka that completely rimmed his features, that was as much as Mildred could tell. He seemed uncommonly cheerful for a sec man, although that might have been elation at seeing off the slavers so readily.

She huddled under the weight of two packs, hers and J.B.'s. His weapons were being toted by others—Krysty had his shotgun, Jak his Uzi. Ryan had looked a question at her when she hoisted the second pack but said nothing.

My legs are strong and my back is sturdy, she thought. It's the least I can do at this point.

"It's right up ahead," sang out another young sec man.

They came to a wide road that led through the tall conifers. Immediately they turned right. You'd have to have a better direction-sense than Mildred did to have any clue which actual way that was. She guessed even Jak might find it a challenge. At least a bit—even though he was about as far out of his element as she was, here in the snowy dark Northeast. Bayou-born-and-bred as he was, he seemed to have little difficulty coping with any environment in which he found himself.

They turned to walk in single file down the road, with sec men in front and bringing up the rear. Whatever Ryan thought of that arrangement he kept to himself; he was a man who lived by the principle of picking his fights, and this was a poor one however you looked at it. Anyway, so far as Mildred could tell, the arrangement was as advantageous from the viewpoint of her party's survival as any other. Despite her years awake and abroad in this harsh new world, she was no tactician yet. Ryan was. So she was content to follow his lead in such matters.

It had kept them alive, time and again, under the most impossible circumstances.

To keep her mind from straying back to J.B.'s open wound and the prospect that he might have reached the end of his road, she studied Ryan. Or, rather, his back. He walked at the front of his companions, barely bowed by the weight of his backpack and Scout longblaster at all. She knew that, as much as she loved J.B., his state had to be hitting Ryan harder. They had been best friends for years, since they met while J.B. rode with the enigmatic Trader. They had known each other, saved each other countless times, long before they ever met any of the others. In some ways, the Armorer was closer to Ryan even than his soul mate, Krysty.

Whatever came, Ryan preferred to meet it with head high and eyes—eye—ever-moving.

Krysty walked close behind Ryan. Her hood was down, allowing Mildred to see that her prehensile hair was curled into a tight cap on her head. Krysty wondered what their friendly sec men escorts would say when they noticed that little phenomenon; right now, they seemed too stoked to spot the fact they had a mutie in their midst.

Then came Ricky, J.B.'s apprentice, the group's newest member. Of all of the companions, he felt closest to J.B.; the Armorer and he were kindred spirits, born tinkerers and gun nuts. He was trying hard not to cry. And not succeeding very well, to judge by the sheen of frozen tears on his pale olive cheeks, even in the faintest of light, every time he turned his head left or right.

Mildred had a few of those caked on her own cheeks, as well. More than a few.

After her came Doc, twirling his stick with the concealed sword and humming an absentminded little tune to himself. She was too spent and miserable to snap at him to knock it off.

Last walked Jak, sharp features grim, his eyes alert and ever-active. He didn't like being chained to the group, any more than a guard dog liked being chained in a yard. It wasn't his role; it didn't accord with his restless spirit. His style was to be a ghost, escorting the others unseen, always patrolling for enemies—something for which his albino pallor ironically suited him in this snowscape.

But Ryan had told him to fall in, so he had.

The wind picked up. Mildred heard a strange rushing roar.

"There it is," Lucas called. "The castle."

Mildred looked up. Her first thought was that the place sure wasn't making any effort to hide—perched, as it was, forty or fifty yards ahead on a glistening dark crag of rock, swept bare of snow by the wind that had commenced to howl and cut. It had plenty of windows, and yellow light seemed to glare out of each and every one of them, like a dozen lighthouse beacons calling out, *Here we are!* to the ill-intentioned.

Beyond it was a darkness only relatively lighter than the damp black rock and the structure itself between the golden-gleaming windows. Mildred could only tell it was a sky full of clouds by the fact she saw no stars.

She smelled saltwater.

Her second thought was that it didn't *have* to hide. It wasn't hard at all to see why they called it the castle.

She could see little detail in the darkness. The glare from the windows made it harder, not easier, to make out detail. She had a sense of looming walls, a steep pitched roof and great solidity.

As they approached up a path that crunched with

gravel beneath her boots, the front double doors swung wide. An almost intolerable blaze of light poured out onto the broad front steps.

Silhouetted against that light was the tall figure of Baron Frost.

"Welcome to Castle Stormbreak, my friends," he said. "Come in."

Chapter Five

"He seems pretty sure we're friends," Mildred muttered darkly behind Ryan as the friends followed the tall, black-clad form of Baron Frost down a wide corridor lit by kerosene lanterns.

"Are you complaining?" asked Krysty, walking beside her.

"They have permitted us into their stronghold," Doc stated, "and not relieved us of our weapons. So, apparently so."

"Don't check a gift blaster's bore till you get out of sight," Ryan said. "Stow it."

Mildred emitted what sounded like a low growl. Ryan ignored it. J.B. was dangerously wounded and she was upset. Well, so was he.

He was glad Doc seemed to have pulled his focus together again. Yes, the Stormbreak locals, from their black-mustached baron on down, seemed well-disposed toward them. And had they harbored bad intentions it would have been easy to take down Ryan and his companions a dozen times over, starting with allowing the slavers to take them down before mopping up the slavers.

But as a baron's dispossessed son himself, Ryan knew that if there was any bigger mistake than relying on a baron's gratitude, it was relying on his consistency. Or anybody's in the Deathlands. He'd learned that lesson the hard way, growing up alone as a young teen.

"Not cold now," Jak said with satisfaction, bringing up the rear with his new best pal Ricky.

That summed it up as far as Ryan was concerned. For Jak, who almost always far preferred being outside of walls to being inside them, to be pleased at being indoors, for once, told the tale.

Baron Frost led them between framed portraits of thin, austere women and burly, grim, bearded men to a right turn, which took them into a large room. After the crushing gloom and marrow-biting cold outside, its shining chandelier, white walls and roaring fire both dazzled Ryan's eye and seemed to scorch his face.

A woman stood before the giant hearth, which looked big enough to roast a bull moose whole without sawing off the antlers.

"Katerina, my dear," the baron said in his deep voice, "I want you to meet our new friends."

The woman turned. She was tall, with black hair veined by silver. Startling blue eyes looked out of a finely chiseled face. The black fur-collared dressing gown she wore wasn't so loosely tailored as to conceal the fact that she had kept her figure despite the onset of middle age. Or that it was a pleasing one. She was strikingly beautiful.

She seemed well matched to her husband the baron. Ivan Frost's black beard had his namesake in it, and he had a white blaze in the close-cropped raven hair above his rugged face. His eyes were a paler blue than his wife's.

She smiled.

Ryan glanced back at Krysty, who stood by his right shoulder, half a step behind. She wasn't touching him, but he felt her warmth and knew her presence.

She gave him a tiny wink.

Baron Frost was already introducing Ryan and his companions in a resonant baritone. His manner was certainly that of a baron, though Ryan couldn't forget watching him lead his two fellow riders into the thick of battle.

Nor could he see any reason for the baron to take part in a battle. At the very least, Baron Frost would be a bad man to underestimate.

Katerina Frost shook Ryan's hand and gave him a warm smile. She did the same with Krysty and Doc.

When she got to Mildred, the physician said, "Listen, my lady, I'm pleased to meet you and all. But your husband decided that my man should be brought here. I want to see him now."

Ryan gave her a look. Belatedly she accepted the baroness's hand and shook it.

"The wounded man is your husband?"

"Close enough," Mildred said. "Right now, the important thing is, he's my patient. And I need to see to him. He needs immediate treatment or he'll die."

"He is being tended to right now," the baron said.

"I'll be the judge of that," she said harshly.

"No, Mildred," Ryan said. "*I* will."

She shot Ryan a glare. He met her look calmly.

She was an intelligent woman and a well-educated one. And sooner or later the former would get the better of the latter, he knew.

Mildred dropped her gaze and her shoulders slumped. She had remembered either that Ryan was their nominal leader, or which of the two of them had ridden with J.B. longer.

Still smiling, Lady Katerina patted Mildred gently on the shoulder. Then she moved on to be introduced to Jak and a blushing, stammering Ricky.

Krysty moved up and took Ryan's arm. He knew she was trying to reassure him about his best friend. He didn't brush her off.

"On my word as a baron," Frost said, "your friend is receiving care as good as any which is likely to be available in our blighted world."

Ryan met his eye. "I'm a baron's son myself," he said. "I know what the word of most barons is worth."

Frost laughed. "Fair enough, Ryan Cawdor. Then, on my word as someone who has fought by your side."

Ryan shrugged. "You seem a straight shooter. I'll take your word because of that. But we want to see him."

"Soon," Frost said as his wife came back to his side. "But first, we must discuss a proposition."

"It figures," Mildred said. "You're going to bargain for John Barrymore's life."

"And it's lucky for us that they are," Ryan rasped. "They could've let him die in the snow. All of us. Fireblast, Mildred, have some nuking sense. Haven't you learned yet that the usual bargain you get offered in this world is 'we kill you and take everything'?"

He felt Krysty squeeze his strong arm. Loving, gentle—and hard enough to send a message.

"Easy now, lover," she said. "She's worried."

"So am I, rad-blast it," he muttered back.

He looked at the baronial pair and rubbed his jaw. Stubble grated his palm.

"I'm listening," he said. "Name your bargain."

Katerina smiled; Baron Frost nodded.

"You're clearly warriors," he said. "Not just brave, but resourceful. We need your help."

"We want our daughter back, Mr. Cawdor," Katerina said. "We want your help."

"Where is she?" Mildred asked. "If it takes more than a few hours, J.B.'ll be dead!"

"Our healers are confident they can keep him alive longer than that," Frost said.

Krysty had moved to Mildred's side and put an arm around her. Glancing back, Ryan saw her give the stocky healer a hug—that clearly carried the same import her hand-squeeze had to Ryan. Mildred glared and rolled eyes as bloodshot as those of a buffalo bull pissed off hotter than nuke red, but she held her peace.

"We will operate on your friend," Katerina said. "And save his life—if that is possible. When you bring us back our daughter, we'll let you have him back. And an appropriate amount of jack. All accounts squared."

Mildred uttered a strangled noise. Ryan waved a hand as if batting back a mosquito.

"Why so generous?"

"Generous?" Mildred squawked. "What the hell are you—"

"Stow it."

She shut up. Ryan hadn't raised his voice. He only made it crack like a blaster.

"Generous, I said. Because it is. Barons don't commonly put themselves out for the sake of random strangers who happen to wander into their land."

"We try to hold ourselves to a high standard, Mr. Cawdor," Frost said. "But the fact is, you've done us a powerful service already."

"Chilling slavers?" Ricky piped up. Ryan scowled but didn't turn it on the boy. The fact was, the kid was one of them now. So, like any of them, he got his say in council. Within reason.

The baron nodded. "Yes. And helping us locate their base."

"So you can wipe it out?" Ricky asked.

Ryan did shoot him a glare this time. The youth's dark eyes got wide and he drew his neck in between his shoulders like a frightened turtle.

"Sadly, that lies beyond our capabilities. Although, given time, we could get help from some of our neighbors. They've been hitting us all hard for months—not just stealing our people, but chilling, raping, looting. And destroying what they can't carry off.

"But what we can do is harry them. Make it hard for them to do any more raiding. They do what they do to turn a profit, after all. We can, and will, increase their costs until they find some grounds that are easier to hunt."

"So, make them somebody else's problem, huh?"

"Exactly, Mildred. If you have a better solution, I implore you to share it."

"She doesn't," Ryan said. "I wouldn't mind hearing it, either, truth to tell. So this is the bastards' main base?"

"By no means, Mr. Cawdor. It's merely a forward base for a segment of the sizable network of slavers that has plagued this coast for years. They invade a territory in force, plant themselves and send out smaller raiding parties. Then withdraw."

Ryan heard a rustling that he knew meant Ricky Morales was shuffling his booted feet as if he needed to take a piss. His adored older sister, Yamile, had been kidnapped by the slavers who trashed his home ville and murdered his mother and father before his eyes. He traveled with the companions, searching for her, convinced she was still alive. And despite the fact she had been taken on the distant island of Puerto Rico, they'd learned enough in recent months to know that the slaver network extended from the islands of the Carib to the Cific Ocean.

Ricky also knew what thin ice he was walking on—alien as that was to his tropical homeland. Also, he probably knew that the baron and his wife were unlikely to know anything about his sister's fate. No matter how much they knew about the slavers.

"Right," Ryan said. "We'll do it."

"Ryan!" Mildred couldn't hold back anymore. She even tore free of Krysty's arm—and Krysty was as strong as most men her size. "We don't know what they're doing for him! We don't know what they *can* do!"

"It wouldn't matter a bent empty cartridge case if all they could do was sacrifice a bastard goat, Mildred," Ryan said. "We already know *we* can't save him. We're empty."

"Ryan," Krysty said urgently. "She does need to see him now. We all do."

"Me, too." Ryan turned back to the baron. "Take us to see him. Show us what you can do."

"With pleasure," Frost said.

The baron gestured. A slender young man in linsey-woolsey tailored to look like a uniform came to his side. The baron murmured a brief command. The aide nodded and took off.

Ryan's brows rose.

"Your pardon, Baron," Doc said, "but if I may be so bold—was that language you were just speaking Russian?"

Ryan already knew that answer.

"Yes," Frost said.

"Will you kindly tell us why you speak it here?"

Katerina smiled again.

"Why, because we—our family in particular, but

pretty much everybody hereabouts, these days—are descended in part from the crew of a Soviet submarine that foundered off this very shore as the skydark began."

Chapter Six

"The B-276 *Kostroma* was her name," Baron Frost stated as he led the companions briskly down a corridor into the depths of the fortress. "She was a cruise-missile-armed Sierra-class nuclear boat. As the war began she was cruising at shallow depth near the coast of what was then the state of Maine, when she was hit by an Mk-48 torpedo launched by an American attack sub. Tradition says she was SSN-706, the USS *Albuquerque*. How the crew could have known any such thing is debatable, but this is what we are taught."

He led them down a stairway to a basement with damp concrete walls, faintly lit by a single kerosene lantern hanging halfway down its short length. At the far end of the basement was a double swing door.

"For reasons unknown, the American boat broke off the attack. *Kostroma* did not sink—at least, not right away. But with her titanium pressure hull breached, Captain Andreyev managed to ground her in shallow water not far from this very cliff, at a place where the land descends to the sea. Most of the crew got ashore alive. They even managed to offload most of her supplies, including her surgery and medical gear. And, speaking of which—" he pushed open the double doors "—we are here."

Katerina stepped into the glare of light, then to one

side. Ryan strode into a basement room with walls painted glaring white and a drain in the brown tile floor.

But unlike most such rooms in baronial basements, this was not a torture chamber. Or, if it was, it was a sophisticated one.

The walls were lined with cabinets and sinks, like a predark infirmary. Ryan had seen plenty in his time, buried deep in the lost redoubts, that contained valuable salvage—and the secret mat-trans network.

In the center of the room stood a table, gleaming chrome like the vanadium-steel doors of a redoubt. J.B. lay prone on a pallet atop the table. His head was back, with a roll of cloth to support his neck, and a mask covered his mouth. An olive-drab Army blanket, evidently American, covered his body to the rib cage. The top of a bandage was visible above it.

Mildred uttered a little gasp. But when she walked by Ryan she was upright and in full command of herself. She was a professional, in a way almost no one was in this desperate and decaying age.

She bent to examine J.B. His color didn't look promising to Ryan: his skin looked as if it was dusted in double-fine wood ash. But Mildred did some gingerly probing, then nodded.

"He seems stable," she said, looking up. "For the moment. He's feverish, just by touch."

"Because we have been unable to fully clean out the foreign material, including cloth, injected by the bullet," a crisp female voice said, "we expect that infection has set in. I have given him antibiotics, and I believe we can contain the infection."

Everyone had turned to face the speaker. A door stood open to a side room. Ryan, who was in the habit of taking in every detail of his surroundings at a glance, had noticed it the instant he walked through the doorway. He frowned; he hadn't taken adequate account of the fact that someone might be in that other room.

He frowned at his lapse.

The person in question wasn't threatening at first glance. She was a tiny woman, shorter even than Jak. Ryan would be amazed if she was a hair over five-nothing, and she might not be that tall. Her skin was darker than Mildred's, though of a different color-blend. Her eyes were big and black in a squarish yet undeniably pretty face. She wore a pale green lab coat over a dark T-shirt and jeans, and she carried a clipboard.

Mildred stepped back and glared at her. The other woman put her head to one side and peered at her like a large, quizzical bird.

"This is Lindy Rao, our healer," Katerina said. "She has earned our complete trust with her skill and knowledge."

"Is that oxygen?" Mildred demanded, gesturing at the mask.

The Stormbreak healer shook her head. "We generate and store emergency electricity by various means, largely windmills and batteries. It is insufficient to separate water into hydrogen and oxygen electrically. But enough to allow us to run a low-power air pump. That is merely air under moderate pressure to help him breathe."

"Is that a good idea? He has a pneumothorax." Mildred glanced at Ryan and her friends. "That's, uh, a collapsed lung. Sucking chest wounds usually cause that."

Ryan gestured for her to continue her discussion with the local healer.

"I'm aware of that," Lindy said simply, with neither

defensiveness nor apology. "We have a chest tube to release the air that has escaped into his pleural space."

They started discussing which antibiotic J.B. had been dosed with. Since they knew about that, and Ryan didn't have to, he turned to their hosts as Krysty went to stand by Mildred's side.

Partly, he judged, to check on their wounded friend herself. Partly to lend emotional support to Mildred. And partly, he was sure, to serve as control rod should Mildred show signs of becoming critical.

"Lindy comes from a family of healers famous in this part of New England," the baroness explained. "They have preserved much medical knowledge from predark. The healers they train are as good as any we have heard of in our modern world."

"Fair enough," Ryan said. "So tell us more about this deal we're getting into."

Baron Frost gestured at the door through which they'd entered. "If you will accompany us, we can discuss the matter in more comfortable surroundings. In which we are less likely to disturb your friend."

"Fine with me. Mildred?" Ryan turned to look at the woman.

"I want to talk with Healer Rao more," Mildred said. "About J.B."

"It's ace, lover," Krysty said. "I'll stay here for a bit and keep her company."

Ryan scowled. "You're in this, too, Krysty. And I don't have J.B. to talk sense into me when I need it."

"I'm fine," Mildred said in a subdued voice. "Really. I just—I just need to talk it out."

Krysty hugged her. Then she turned to Ryan. "She'll be fine," she echoed. "Really."

"Then catch up with us when you're done here," Ryan told Mildred. He followed the Frosts out.

"OUR DAUGHTER, LYUDMILA, is a free-spirited young lady," Katerina said.

Krysty sipped green tea. They were all, except for Mildred and J.B., seated in the sitting room where the baron and his lady had first received them. She felt oddly comforted by the pale, elegant surroundings. It was a room where Doc, a man of the nineteenth century, might feel at home.

Doc had been trawled out of his time and family by the whitecoats of Operation Chronos, to be ruthlessly used, prematurely aged, driven the better part of mad and abandoned in the middle of Deathlands when he had proved too difficult a subject for their experiments.

And clearly Doc did feel at home, sitting with one storklike leg crossed over the other in a floral-embroidered chair, smiling pleasantly and nodding his white-haired head into the steam rising from his teacup.

The stout walls of granite reinforced by concrete muffled the brutal buffeting of the wind, and left its angry howl an impotent whisper. The fire crackling with lunatic cheerfulness in the hearth made the life-sucking cold outside a mere memory. But Krysty could feel the Earth itself, through its very bones in which the roots of the castle were sunk, despite the fact that the rock below was honeycombed with basements and bunkers— mentioned by their hosts in passing as they returned from the infirmary.

Gaia, the Earth Mother, was strong here. Krysty felt it in the sense of well-being and invigoration she felt, despite exertion and exhaustion, post-adrenaline letdown and worry for her friend.

"She's fourteen now, and showing streaks of rebellion. As both her parents did at her age—hard as that might be to imagine from our absurd appearance of respectability now."

She cast a smiling look at her husband, who smiled back and nodded. His strong, bearded face was harshly shadowed in its hollows and crannies despite the cozy light. The lines of tension were deeply etched around mouth and eyes. He was a man much worn by care—much more so than most barons Krysty had known.

"In order to teach her more fully and properly than we can here," Katerina said, "we sent her south to Miss McBurnie's Finishing School and Commando Academy for Girls, in the barony of Candlewick. It's down the coast a hundred miles. They're all a bit more...Draconian there. We were hoping she might be tamed a bit by the experience, at least."

She stopped, smiling. Krysty saw tears glimmer in her pale blue eyes.

"Ah, thank you, Caine," she added hastily, as the gaunt, silent butler with the lank fringe of mouse-gray hair poured fresh tea into her upraised cup.

"They took her," Baron Frost said. He rose and went to stand by his wife, taking her free hand in his. "Slavers did. Charlie, a member of her sec man escort, came back within hours of their setting out. Despite being terribly wounded, he gasped out a tale of ambush and slaughter just a few miles south of here, along the coast road. The slavers had attacked."

"They took her," Katerina said, with a combination of stark despair and ferocity. "They took our baby."

"There, there, Katya," the baron murmured, patting her shoulder. She laid her head briefly against his forearm. A single tear escaped the gleaming pools of her eyes and ran down one cheek.

Then she patted his arm and nodded to him. He nodded back, walking with grace remarkable in such a powerfully built man, and resumed his own seat a few feet away.

"Poor Charlie died before he could finish the story," the baron said. "Lindy said it was a miracle he'd survived as long as he had. He did tell us they had taken her south."

"Not to that base we almost blundered into?" Ryan asked.

"No. As I mentioned before, it's only a forward operating base. There is a vast and powerful network of slavers at work here on the Northeast coast. Indeed, what we learn from other baronies and from travelers suggests that either it stretches clear across the continent, or is tied into other such networks clear across the Deathlands. To whatever extent that distinction matters, I suppose."

"Don't the barons have enough peasants to suppress?" Krysty asked. Her own vehemence surprised her.

Ryan shot her a warning look. As action-centered as he was—as impulsive as he could be—he was still a baron's son. He feared no man, but he respected power that could snuff out his life and the lives of his lover and his friends like the flame of a candle.

Such as the power of their host and hostess.

She shook her head. Her sentient hair was curled close to her head in reflection of her dismay. She hoped they'd think it was just a 'do.

"I mean, other baronies—"

"Don't worry, Ms. Wroth," Katerina said. "We are not easy to offend. There are surely those among our subjects who find us unreasonable. Sometimes even harsh. Though we try to rule as...decently as we can."

Ryan's look was a combination of surprise and skepticism that mirrored what Krysty felt inside.

"Our relationship to our people is close, my friends," the baron said. "Though, like any family, we have our disagreements. Some more heated than others. But we—the family now called Frost, who have ruled Stormbreak for generations—have always managed to remember that we spring from the people, are of the people. And that we are for them as much as they are for us. It seems that, contrary to what one might expect, our...peculiar origins as a barony knit us closer together, rather than the opposite."

He had leaned forward intently as he spoke. Now he sat back and waved an almost airy hand.

"But that's a matter for another time. And now—would you care for more refreshments, my friends?"

Ryan sipped and made a face. "Tea's fine and all," he said. "But it could use something with a little kick."

"Ryan!" Krysty admonished.

Baron Frost chuckled. "A man after my own heart," he declared, with more heartiness than he'd shown in a while. "High time to add a shot of vodka to our cups! Caine, if you please. You're sure you're not part Russian yourself, Mr. Cawdor?"

He shrugged and laughed. "Sure as I can be of anything happened long before I was born."

"I thought Russians preferred to take their vodka neat, Baron," Doc said.

Frost laughed. "No doubt they do. In that I suppose I'm showing my *Amerikantsy* side. I can't actually abide the stuff straight. It smells like kerosene and tastes about the way it smells. Still, it adds a punch to tea. And some warmth. Much needed on a night like this one, yes?"

"So," RYAN SAID, sipping at his newly fortified cup of tea. "Why haven't you gone after your daughter? Or at least overrun the slaver camp and gotten some answers?"

Krysty waved away the impassive Caine and his bottle of clear fluid. She agreed with the baron as to how vodka tasted. The thought of blending it with her green tea—which was delicious—turned her stomach.

The baron sighed. "We lack the strength, Mr. Cawdor. My sec men—and women—are brave and capable. We maintain both the skills and standards of certain of our ancestors. They are also few. And while our people tend to possess arms and know how to use them, they do so to protect their homes and one another. They lack the temperament to sally forth to attack others. That is not our way and never has been. Leave us in peace, and we leave you in peace. Bring war and suffering to our land, and we shall crush you.

"As we shall these slavers. Indirectly, I fear, unless my overtures to some of our neighboring villes bring fruit in the form of a military alliance. But our neighbors have their hands full with this latest slaver incursion, as we do."

"How do you mean, indirectly, Baron?"

Everyone turned to look at Ricky. He sat in a chair behind the adults, who occupied chairs set in a semicircle facing their host and hostess. His eyes were wide and his cheeks first dead-pale beneath their natural olive, then bright pink.

"Oh—sorry—I didn't—"

"Yeah, you did. But that's okay. Look, kid," Ryan said, "we let you in, so you can speak your piece. Long as you squeak sense, squeak what you like."

Baron Frost nodded. "A perceptive question, young man," he said. "We lack the strength to dislodge the sla-

vers by force. But we can do what you encountered us
doing today—harrying their raiding parties. They have
taken some of my people. And we have taken them as
casualties. None alive yet, sadly—so we can get no further information as to where they might have sent our
daughter.

"They do what they do, of course, not merely out of
the darkness of their souls, but for gain. We are at least
ensuring they reap more cost than profit, which will in
due time force them to withdraw."

Krysty and Ryan exchanged glances. *Mebbe,* she
could feel him thinking. *And mebbe they'll reinforce
to teach you and your people a lesson that the surviving baronies'll never forget.*

But it wasn't their place to say such a thing, here and
now. Looking from bearded face to drawn and icy near-
perfection, Krysty suspected the baron and baroness
knew the risks as well as they did.

They played the hands fate dealt them, like everybody else in the Deathlands. And barons didn't always
get the best cards.

"So you want us to take off south in pursuit of your
daughter," Ryan said. "Beyond that—flying blind."

"Substantially so," Frost said. "Though not entirely
blind. We'll provide you with a guide. A reliable person
who knows this coast well. And who knows combat—
you've seen her in action already."

Her? Krysty thought. She recalled the young horse-
woman who had ridden with Frost, with her hair almost
as pale as Jak's flying out behind her from beneath her
fur cap.

"You will help us, won't you, Mr. Cawdor?" the baroness asked.

In the look the woman shot Ryan, Krysty saw *hun-*

ger. Yet it didn't strike her as a sexual thing. At least, not primarily.

She never worried about competition for Ryan's love. Any more than Ryan felt challenged by Ricky's obvious infatuation with Krysty. As if any man worthy of the title, much less a man worthy of being the life-mate of Krysty Wroth, could feel threatened by a horny sixteen-year-old.

Ryan showed no sign of sexual interest in the baroness. Krysty could hardly have blamed him if he had. Though she was clearly into middle age, probably early fifties—which for many in the Deathlands, of course, was wretched and ragged old age—she showed a striking beauty, with just a hint of pink flush in her cheeks rescuing her from ice-sculpture frigidity.

Still, there was something…not right about Baroness Frost. Krysty's intuition told her that the baroness harbored no ill intentions toward Ryan and the companions. All Krysty could sense in her was the overwhelming desire for them to save her daughter and return her safely home.

But something about her appearance and her manner—perhaps just a hint of greenish pallor in the shadows of her fine face—rang a discordant note in Krysty's mind.

Ryan sat back in his chair, chin sunk to clavicle, thinking. Krysty's heart went out to him, seeing how tired he was.

He polled the others with his eyes. Krysty nodded once, trying not to be too emphatic.

She glanced around. Doc shrugged and smiled vaguely, as if concurring; Krysty hoped he was still focused enough to realize what he was agreeing to. Jak looked skeptical. *That* wasn't anything unusual for

the albino youth. Had he felt any serious misgivings—
beyond the ones he knew the others shared—he would
have spoken up pretty briskly, as little as he liked to talk.

Ricky nodded so vigorously Krysty was half-surprised
he didn't sprain his neck.

"Fine," Ryan said. "We're in." He rubbed his jaw.
"Reckon it's a better deal than we usually get."

Chapter Seven

"This is the coast road, clearly."

Ricky watched keenly as Baron Frost tracked the blunt tip of a finger from northeast to southwest down an old USGS contour map by the light of a combustion lamp. By smell Ricky could tell it was fueled by some oil other than kerosene. Nonetheless, it burned brightly. Or enough to do the job.

The room seemed to be a study of some sort. The walls were lined with shelves crowded with books, folios and rolled papers, some of which were maps, judging by the one the baron had unrolled on a drafting table. Ricky found the whole scene, made more mysterious by pervasive shadow, fascinating, though not as interesting as if it had been a workshop where things were actually *made*.

Ryan and Krysty stood across the table from the baron. Doc sat beside them. Ryan leaned on the table on the knuckles of one hand. Ricky, who sat in another chair a few feet away while Jak lounged against some shelves looking bored, tried not to stare at the redheaded woman's rear end. It was hard.

He knew it was unwise. If Ryan ever bothered to notice the attention Ricky paid to Krysty, the one-eyed man might cut him loose from the group. For her part, Krysty treated his admiration with amused indulgence. Which, in a way, was worse.

Not that he would do anything to impede or disturb

the lives of the two. And certainly those who *did* tended to wind up with dirt hitting them in the eyes in short order.

Ryan and Krysty formed a pantheon of living, walking gods for him—along with J.B., of course. The rest were important to him, too—the often vague yet often incisive Doc Tanner; the brusque yet deeply compassionate Mildred; his new best friend, Jak. But they couldn't compare to the Big Three.

And now J.B. was hurt and fighting for his life. And they were finding out how they could buy it back—if that was even possible.

"The coast road's pretty decent," the baron was saying. "The baronies along the way tend to maintain it, and it's mostly far enough inland that the eroding shoreline hasn't encroached on it. But it's not used as much as it might be. Travelers frequently prefer to make their ways along back trails farther inland, even though they're not as good and it takes longer."

"Weather?" Krysty asked.

"Storms," Frost stated. "And raiders from the sea. Not just the slavers, of course, though they're our biggest menace now."

Doc, who had been sitting with head back and eyes half-closed, as if wandering through the often-tangled pathways inside his head, shook himself, drew his brows together and leaned forward with his sky-blue eyes no longer unfocused.

"It is curious to me, Baron," he said, "how the economics of the slaver raids work. They themselves appear to be many. By the very nature of predation in all its forms, they need to acquire far more numerous victims than their own host in order to thrive. How is it possible that they do so?"

"Good question," Ryan said, straightening.

Baron Frost frowned and nodded ponderously, as if feeling the weight of the situation on the back of his neck. "Their numbers have grown markedly in the last ten years or so, all up and down the coast.

"As for how they make profit enough to sustain their growing operations, Dr. Tanner, I can't really say. They haven't exactly opened their books to me. I can say that, despite the fact that the enormous population concentrations along the Eastern Seaboard were hardest hit of anywhere in North America, and the plagues and starvation reduced the population to lesser numbers than in many areas originally far more sparsely settled, some of the same factors that led to the area being so thickly settled in the first place have led to a substantial rebound in the population, especially over the last fifty years or so. Not to anywhere near former levels, of course. And while trade across the Lantic's no real factor—it's far too rare and sporadic—the relative fertility of the environment here, along with the enormous amount of scavvy available in the ruined cities, has more than sufficed."

He shook his head. "Not that life here is easy, by any means. Though we are far from the most desolate of areas, they still call these the Deathlands, and for good reason."

The door opened. Caine looked a question to Frost, who nodded. The white-haired butler bowed Mildred into the room.

The stocky woman seemed shrunken and subdued.

"How is he?" Krysty asked.

Mildred lowered her head further for a moment. Then she drew a deep breath, squared her shoulders and raised her head.

Ricky clutched the silver crucifix he wore inside

his shirt. He tried to feel guilty about avidly watching the rise and rebound of her enormous breasts as she breathed. He didn't.

"Better than I expected," the healer said in a voice frayed around the edges. "Their facilities here are surprisingly good. Better than I'd expect outside—outside some predark hospital.

"And while I almost hate to admit it," Mildred went on, "this healer knows her stuff. She's...well-schooled for the time. Remarkably so."

"We have found her so," Frost said, nodding.

Mildred stepped forward to the map table. "What's going on here?"

"The baron's giving us the rundown on the tactical situation," Ryan said.

For a moment, the woman frowned down at the map, then she looked up at Frost.

"Okay, now, this is too good to be true!" she blurted. "Ryan, you always say we can't rely on the gratitude of barons. What's the deal here, really?"

"Mildred—" Krysty began.

Ryan cut her off by raising a hand.

"Might as well let her say her piece," he said. "If what she says is going do damage, it's done now already."

"No damage," Frost said. "You are prudent to want to understand the terms of our agreement fully."

"I like to know where everybody stands," Mildred said, not at all mollified. "In particular, I like to know for sure what the other side looks to get out of a deal. Isn't this the Deathlands, where everybody's always out for himself and eats the weak?"

"In the...circumstances in which you and I lived our early lives," Doc said, "people were also out primarily for themselves, dear lady. They could simply afford to act more genteelly, owing to generally less brutal circumstances."

"But what are you getting out of this?" Mildred asked the baron. "You're already spending lots of resources on J.B. Your healer is prepping for surgery—that's why I left, to get out of her hair. Why are you trusting us? What's the catch?"

For a moment, no one spoke. Ricky waited for the baron to assure them there was no catch. Instead, he continued to look at Ryan with calm, somber eyes.

Ryan vented a gusty sigh. "You're right, Mildred. I do know better than to rely on a baron's gratitude. But a baron's vengeance—that's like sunrise."

"But they don't have any guarantees we can get this girl back from the slavers! Or even that we'll try."

"As for what can be done," Frost said, still in a perfectly calm and even voice, "whether she…can be rescued depends largely on fate. This my wife and I know. As for your capabilities, we know them, for we have seen them in action. And as for your exerting all your formidable abilities to return Milya safely to us, I believe we have all the guarantees we need."

"Are you going to walk away and leave J.B. here?" Ryan asked Mildred. Her eyes went wide. Her face went pale. "Or do you reckon I am?"

She turned away, tight-lipped.

"Come," the baron called.

The door opened. A woman stood there. Or maybe a girl. On the tall side for a female, an inch or so taller than Ricky, an inch or two shorter than Krysty. She stood as straight and slim as a bayonet, and wore a drab uniform tunic and trousers closely cut to her frame. She wore a handblaster in a flap-covered holster in front of her left hip, with butt reversed for a right-hand cross-draw.

Ricky thought it was a CZ-75 semiauto, which would have made it a 9 mm weapon.

He felt his own brows rise as he recognized her as the girl who'd ridden to their rescue, knee to knee with the baron himself, shooting and sabering slavers with cold ferocity.

She didn't show much of a figure, but he liked her already.

"Ah, Alysa," the baron said, brightening.

"Baron," she replied, stepping into the room.

Ricky caught himself staring. He blushed and moved his eyes back to the lamp-lit contour lines of the map.

Then they strayed back to her as if magnetized.

When the baron's men had rescued the party from the slaver ambush, the girl had slaughtered with a fierce and fearsome joy. Now her posture and face were stiff, as if she was not just uncomfortable but trying to keep some powerful emotion in check. Fear? He wasn't sure.

"My friends, permit me to introduce Lieutenant Alysa Korn. Despite her age, or lack of it, she's earned the rank among our baronial defenders."

Frost didn't seem to care for the universal Deathlands term "sec men." Not that Ricky saw how that made much difference.

Frost finished introducing Ryan's group with Ricky. He stammered some nonsense he hoped sounded polite. She barely flicked him a glance with her pale green eyes. She might as well have been a lizard on a rock. Or *he* might.

"Alysa will be your guide on your journey," the baron stated.

Ricky looked at Ryan. The one-eyed man frowned.

"You know the area we'll be searching in?"

"I have some familiarity with it," she said.

Her already hard face hardened another degree. Oddly it made her look younger and more vulnerable to Ricky, somehow.

"At least," she said, as if the words were being pulled from her mouth like teeth, "I know whom to ask for information."

Ryan stared at her a moment more. She didn't wither under the blue flame of his glare. Ricky sure would have.

He nodded. "More than we'd know," he said.

He looked back at Baron Frost. "What else can you give us?"

Chapter Eight

Through half-open lids J.B. saw a dark, concerned face hovering over his. It was mostly covered by a surgical mask, but what he could see of it seemed nicely engineered. Good eyes, big and dark.

He wished it were Mildred, all the same.

The face frowned. "He's still not all the way under," she said. "We need more chloroform."

"That's all right, Miss—" he started to say. But he realized he didn't have the breath to spare to make words.

And then he was swirling down, down into the dark depths.

Of remembering…

"So, TRADER, YOU signed on a new guy?" a woman called out from the doorway of a spectacular vehicle. A pristine fedora was cocked to one side of her head, and she smoked a long black cheroot.

"That I did."

"Welcome aboard War Wag One, sonny," the woman said. She was a rangy-looking specimen, with baggy olive-drab pants covered in pockets bulging with gear and a rust-colored tank top hugging a none-too-generous chest.

"Go easy on him, Rance," said the bearded man who followed a step or two behind J.B., prodding him along by sheer force of personality.

The woman blew blue-gray smoke out of her up-turned nose.

"Skinny little guy," she said. "Why'd you bother, Trader?"

"Because he has skills we need and shows promise."

The woman nodded. "Shows promise."

"I just said that."

The woman left the vehicle and walked up to J.B., stopping several feet away. She looked him up and down with hands on narrow hips. Her boobs weren't anything to write home about, J.B. thought. Neither was her face, long, a bit mannish and sporting a couple of pale scars beneath a shock of straw-colored hair held up by a grimy yellow bandanna. She had an M1911 handblaster holstered at her right hip.

Normally, J.B. would only have noticed the blaster—which, from what little he could see, was well-worn but well-kept. But she was a woman, after all. One who was actually pretty presentable, having all her teeth, eyes and limbs.

And as much as young J.B. may have preferred tinkering with gadgets—especially the chilling kind—to dealing with people, he was still male.

"So what good are you, kid?" the woman demanded.

"J.B., this is my chief wrench, Rance Weeden," Trader said.

"Short for 'Rancid,'" said a skinny man with a luxuriant mustache and long dark hair tied up into a horse-tail at the crown of his head. He strode past them and headed for the vehicle.

Rance shot the man the bird. "It's Ransom. As well you know, Abe, you skinny dog turd."

"Known far and wide for her tact," the Trader said,

deadpan. "And her skill. So feel free to speak right up and answer her, J.B."

"I know my way around blasters, some machines," J.B. told her. "Locks, too."

She grunted. "Well, it happens that I can use another mech."

He frowned. "I'm better with blasters," he said pointedly, looking at Trader.

"We've got a weapons master," Trader said. "Ace DeGuello. And he doesn't need a helper right now."

"Helper? I know I'm better."

"You might be," the Trader said.

"You've seen my work!"

"You roll with me," Trader said, "you do what I need you to do. Right now I need you to help Rance. You'll work with Ace when there's an opening."

Rance walked closer to him.

"Listen, kid," she said, not unkindly. "You work with me, odds are double-good you'll get a chance to show your chops with blasters. We keep this snorting warthog rolling, after all. And, anyway—if you're really mechanical, then a machine's a machine."

She stuck out her hand. It was grease-stained and visibly strong, but somehow feminine.

After a moment he grinned and took it. Her grip was as strong as it looked like it'd be.

"You're on," he said. "I'm J. B. Dix. And I'm gonna show you how good I am!"

"You better," she said, and walked away.

Chapter Nine

"Lyagushki," the ice-blonde woman said beneath her breath.

"What was that, Alysa?" Krysty asked.

The sea-scented wind whined and slunk around Krysty's jeans-clad legs like a mutie dog begging for a handout. Their guide squatted on winter-dry grass next to a patch of bare soil brushed over rocks, inshore of a clump of scrub oak. Krysty and her companions stood around Alysa surveying the crossroads clearing. Though the forest wore its dense white coat of snow, both fresh and old, that starveling ocean wind had licked the open area clean down to dirt and stone.

To their surprise the Stormbreak sec woman had led them to a low point near the coast—the coastline here running mostly east to west.

"Frogs?" Ryan muttered. "Did she say frogs?" He stood with his longblaster at relaxed ready before his groin, scanning the dark gnarled granite boulders and the surrounding scrub and trees, here mostly firs, for signs of trouble. Doc and Mildred stood nearby, frowning—the stocky black woman clearly worrying about J.B. and impatient at any delay, no matter how warranted.

As usual, Jak prowled the snowy woods nearby, patrolling for enemies. It amused Krysty to think how well Jak's coloration suited him for an environment in which he felt out of place. He still managed to slip through the underbrush without so much as the snap of a snow-coated twig.

As she had when the friends first saw her, bursting out of the white forest to their rescue the day before, Alysa wore a heavy coat with a wolf-fur collar. She'd worked her hair into a long braid that fell out behind her red-star cap across the saber-scabbard slung across her back. She had her Marlin lever-action longblaster in her hand.

Alysa continued to scowl at what looked to Krysty like plain granite, mostly bare but for the wind-blown dirt and rust-colored lichen. She didn't respond to the implicit question for Ryan, who had understood the Russian word.

"The ambush for Milya was here," the young woman said. Though she rose, she never took her eyes off the ground. "The slavers took them by surprise. Our men never had a chance."

"Why the nuke did they come this way?" Ryan asked. "Baron Frost told us everybody stuck to the inland roads because of danger from the coast."

She sighed. "West of here the way inland becomes uncertain for a few miles. A coldheart chieftain named Goat has set himself up as baron of a ville called Windy. It's a tiny place, but his small gang of coldhearts makes the inner road even more dangerous than the coast."

"The baron indicated the inland road had been preferred for years," Doc said. "Perhaps generations. Why, exactly, inasmuch as he also told us the intense slaver activity was a recent development?"

"There are other problems," Alysa said curtly. "Right now I'm trying to see if there's anything we might have missed when we first rode to Milya's rescue."

"Jak can pick up a trail on a stretch of predark sidewalk after two days of rain," Ricky called from where he stood, mostly supervising their horses as the animals browsed the dry grass. "Why not call him in to help look? Oh, sorry."

Krysty smiled. The young Latino showed a number of contrasts. Prominent among them was how his natural reticence failed to prevent him from sometimes blurting whatever popped into his mind. Whether at an opportune moment or not.

Ryan shook off the apology with a toss of his shaggy-curled head. "Good suggestion. Korn."

Alysa brought her head up sharply, a startled look in her pale green eyes.

"If you're going to guide us, you need to talk to us. You need to tell us what we need to know."

For a moment she glared at him with a naked fury that set Krysty on her heels. Then she dropped her head and her shoulders slumped. She nodded, once.

"I'm sorry," she said. "I haven't done my duty."

"So what have you learned here?"

Krysty feared Ryan's peremptory tone would spark the girl's rage again. Instead she all but snapped to attention.

"They laid in wait at the crossroads," she said in clipped tones. "Clearly they knew to expect our party. They opened fire and cut down Milya's escort before they had a chance to respond." She shook her head, looking worried, frustrated—and also somehow sad. "Nothing we didn't know before."

"You say they knew your group was coming," Mildred said. "Maybe they have a spy back in the ville?"

Alysa's eyes went wide. "That's impossible! We are loyal. To our baron—to one another. We are tightly knit."

Mildred sighed. "Sounds like you people could use a bigger dose of good old-fashioned Russian paranoia."

"I hate to come in second to anybody in paranoia," Ryan said, "but it's just as likely they had scouts out on the road. I'm guessing the girl and her escorts were well-dressed and looked prosperous?"

The Stormbreaker woman nodded. "She is the baron's daughter."

"Yeah. So they didn't have to know who she was to know she was a real ace strike."

"Would they make that much effort just to capture a single girl?" Mildred asked.

"She was a looker, right?"

"She is a beautiful young woman, yes. Although she takes some pains to hide the fact, in her rebelliousness."

"So there's a market for pretty high-born girls out there," Ryan said. "The younger the better. She'd fetch a primo price from the right buyer."

"One more thing, Ryan," Krysty said. "If they actually knew she was the baron's daughter, wouldn't they make a ransom demand? Or anyway offer the baron the chance to outbid other offers to buy her back?"

Ryan glared off into the snowy forest.

Krysty could feel Gaia's heart practically pulsing here, up through the stone beneath her feet. The Earth Mother seemed to be trying to tell her something.

"Too many variables," Ryan growled. "Too much we can't know. Though who knows? Mebbe they sent a demand or sale-offer and it crossed us by a different road. The key here is we can't assume there's a spy back at the ville."

"And if your surmise is correct, Ryan," Doc said, "we can assume hostile eyes are watching us."

Ryan grunted a laugh. "And that's different from the

usual situation how? Still, ace on the line you reminded us to keep our eyes skinned triple-hard, Doc."

He looked at Alysa, who had fallen into a sort of parade-rest position with her longblaster's steel-shod butt grounded in the earth at her feet. She seemed most comfortable when a strong man gave her orders. Happy, almost.

"Yes, sir," she said crisply.

It hurts to be this one, Krysty realized. She hoped that inner pain would not lead to rashness that would get them all chilled. Alysa seemed dedicated to her job and good at it. But the very ferocious, heedless courage she'd shown against the slavers the previous day might possibly get them all killed.

"All right," Ryan called. "Let's mount up and ride, people. The one thing we know for sure is the rad-blasted girl isn't *here*."

"You know," Doc said from the back of his white-stocking black gelding, "these Maine woods used to be largely if not exclusively deciduous, back in my— Back a long time ago."

The horses' hooves crunched on the hard snow-pack of a forest road. Ryan rode his notch-eared black-and-white pinto gelding knee to knee with Alysa Korn on her blood bay mare at the little column's head. Krysty and Mildred rode right behind them. Krysty was aboard a strawberry roan mare, Mildred a grumpy dun mule with a roached mane.

Doc rode next, then Ricky with his short legs sticking out from the flanks of a chubby palomino pony, and beside him Jak was astride a small, scrubby, copper-colored mare.

The sun was sliding down a mostly clear sky toward

the trees ahead, which looked like white cones in the fading light. The air was crisp and cold and still. The snow deep on the ground and heavy in the trees around seemed to make hearing double-acute, as if they were in some kind of room with acoustic walls. Ryan could hear Doc fine over the crunch of the horses' hooves through the thin crust of ice overlying the previous night's snowfall, the swish of their tails, their frequent blatting farts.

"Mebbe so," Ryan said without looking back. "No way to tell."

He had little use for knowledge for its own sake, but as a baron's son, he'd been well-educated by the standards of the time. Extremely well, given that in most places "well-educated" meant "able to read."

"But there is," Alysa said.

Ryan raised a brow in surprise. Their guide didn't speak much. As he'd pointed out that morning at the ambush site, she didn't speak *enough,* sometimes. She'd spent their brief acquaintance mostly white-lipped, as if holding in anger just short of nuke red.

"We had among us people very wise in the ways of nature, and green growing things," she said. Her stilted manner of speech—almost suggesting she spoke English as a second language, although her accent was as American as Ryan's—made him think she felt uncomfortable talking. Except in clipped, informative phrases.

"Throughout skydark, our ancestors regularly emerged into the world to forage and hunt. After all, the conditions weren't terribly different from what we experienced during our long winters. As we do now. Much vegetation died back, starved of sunlight. Foraging was hard, and became harder until the sky cleared.

"Once it did, various conifers had moved in to replace dead deciduous trees. Where before the war had stood great hardwood forests, they grew back mixed. As they are today."

Doc nodded sagely. "Indeed," he said. "Not an uncommon situation."

"Usually the fruits of skydark were more bitter," Krysty said.

The young woman shrugged. "What we endured, and what we inherited, is bitter enough."

"How do you know so much about growing food in winter?" Mildred demanded. "I mean, yeah, your people were used to long, cold winters. From both sides, mostly. But most places I know, it gets cold, growing season crashes to a screeching halt."

She actually turned a smile over her shoulder. A brief, tight-lipped one. But a smile.

"Before the war some people in Maine began experimenting with various forms of greenhouses for cold-weather growing," she said. "Also, some of the *Kostroma*'s complement of Spetsnaz troops had returned to service after a spell at the Valaam Monastery near Leningrad."

"Spetsnaz?" Mildred asked. "Soviet Special Forces?"

"Special Purpose Forces," Alysa said, translating *spetsialnogo naznacheniya* literally. "Yes. The monastery was a popular shelter among those who served there, especially on active combat duty in Afghanistan and elsewhere."

"And what were these Spetsnaz commandos supposed to do aboard a nuclear-missile submarine, exactly?" Mildred asked darkly.

"They were meant to be landed to perform acts of sabotage and assassination in the wake of the thermonuclear exchange," the blonde woman said matter-of-factly.

"Those sons-of-bitches!" Mildred said. "They were

coming here to commit acts of full-on terrorism against my people and my country?"

"Back away from the trigger, Mildred," Ryan said. "Those bullets left the blaster more than a century ago. Everybody concerned's dead. Except, well, you."

Alysa glanced at him with a V of puzzled frown creasing the pale skin between even paler brows. Ryan ignored her. He was a bit angry at himself for mentioning Mildred's past as a freezie.

"Obviously," Alysa said, "they decided to change their objectives when the submarine was forced aground. Their original mission seemed to them as futile as their allegiance."

"I thought Spetsnaz types were all supposed to be super-fanatical Party members," Mildred said.

Alysa actually uttered a sort of faint coyote-yip of a laugh. "The stories say that some were," she said. "Some were very good at fooling the *zampolit,* the military commissars. We tell stories of how they did so."

"What sort of methods did your ancestors employ to grow food in the depths of the savage northern winter?" Doc asked. Ryan didn't know whether he was impelled to switch the subject back by his keen scientific curiosity, or to deflect Mildred from worrying that particular loose tooth any more.

He and their guide began a detailed discussion involving greenhouses and soil preparations. Ryan didn't care about that worth a bent shell-case, so he looked back to take stock of his companions.

Krysty immediately caught his eye and flashed him a big smile. As always, it hit him right in the chest. But he just let his pressed-together lips stretch out a little wider to the sides and—reluctantly—let his eye slide past her beautiful face.

Mildred had her head down. He couldn't see her expression, but he guessed it was either grim or worried. She hadn't shown too many other expressions since J.B. went down. Ryan couldn't much blame her.

Doc looked chipper: head up, blue eyes bright, pink spots glowing in the cold on his sagging cheeks.

Ricky was doing his blatant best to look eagerly attentive. Ryan suspected he was actually working on the skill of sleeping with his eyes open. Next to him Jak's face was as hard as ice and his ruby eyes glared.

They came to a creek or small river. They had long since headed back inland but were no more than a mile or two from the coast. Though ice lined the water beside both banks, a clear channel ran lead-colored between them.

Alysa had slowed her mare to a deliberate walk. Ahead on the road, which wasn't much more than a wide flat stretch in the snow here, a timber bridge crossed the forty feet or so of water. The banks were fairly steep, perhaps six feet high, and broken up here and there by piles of granite boulders that were dark and evil-looking through their coverings of snow.

The Stormbreaker sec woman looked keenly everywhere: at the bridge, the rocks, the scrub and trees on the far side, even the heights of the trees around them. The shadows had grown deep and were beginning to darken. She had her Marlin longblaster in her gloved right hand.

"What?" Ryan demanded. "I thought we'd passed the coldheart ville. And we're away from the coast. What's got you fretting here?"

She stopped her horse and her scanning and looked at him. Though she had been nothing but crisply professional and respectful, if perhaps a bit tightly wrapped, since they'd met her the night before, the expression she showed him now suggested she was wondering whether he was a feeb.

"Have you found anywhere in the Deathlands that's safe, Ryan Cawdor?" she challenged. Then, in a softer voice, "And if you did—why leave?"

"All right," he said, "fair enough. But it's an honest question. Something's got you bothered way more than you were just a minute ago. You don't think pirates rowed all this way upstream to lie in wait for us?"

"Not pirates, no." She was searching again. "This is just—a logical ambush point."

"True." Ryan turned in his saddle. "When our guide gives us the go-ahead, Jak and Ricky, you hang back and cover while we cross."

Jak gave a microscopic nod. Ricky said, "Yes, sir!" and bobbed his head so hard he almost fell out of the saddle of his stout, pony-size Palomino. He started fumbling with the sling that held his DeLisle carbine across his back. A child of the Tropics, he still hadn't gotten the hang of cold.

After another moment swiveling her head side to side, up and down, Alysa nodded. "I see no threat," she said. "We can proceed."

"I'm right here with you," Ryan said.

The weathered timbers made muffled booms beneath their horses' unshod hooves as they rode forward at a walk.

Alysa still swiveled her head restlessly. "We must find a strong place for the night. Soon."

Ryan nodded. "With you there. How much far—"

Behind him, Ryan heard Jak yell, "Frogs!"

Chapter Ten

The planet hit J. B. Dix in the ass with authority. It whacked his shoulders a moment later. And last the back of his head cracked against dirt as hard as the fist that had put him on it.

"Your asses are mine," he croaked through puffy lips. He tasted blood, which pretty well had to be his own. Since he hadn't managed to bite anybody, or hit them hard enough to splatter. Leastways, not on him.

His answer was a boot in the short ribs. Steel-toed, by the feel.

At least nothing was broken. Yet.

But the day was young.

Actually, the day was dying in an explosion of clouds in the sky over the parched, cracked, table-flat land to the west, whose reds and hellish oranges and general clotted-mustard undertones suggested the possibility they presaged acid rain, rather than just sunset. Spring crickets were creaking like unlubricated joints. It was the *fight* that was relatively new.

There were maybe six of them, five men and a fireplug-shaped woman with one ear named Betty Lou. J.B. judged she was the one who had put the boot in.

J.B. was the type who tended not to count the odds when he started something, which meant that he was experienced in fighting when badly outnumbered.

"Think you're good enough to jump us and push out

Ace, do you, punk?" a man asked in a voice that made the question itself sound friendly.

A shape loomed over J.B. His glasses had fallen off, and he was too nearsighted to make out much more detail than that. But his experience on the losing end of past gang stomps served him well: he recognized a boot being raised to, yes, stomp him good.

If people were just looking to rowdy a body up some, the best response was to curl up in a tight ball and try to take most of the punishment in parts that could absorb it best as a general rule. But these rowdies weren't well-known to J.B., to the extent anybody was after several days on the road, even his boss, Rance Weeden. They *seemed* triple-serious in their intent to do grievous bodily harm. So J.B. rolled to the side. The boot came down onto the hard, cracked, dried yellow mud. He promptly rolled back, grabbed the boot toe and heel in his strong hands and twisted.

The boot, which had a cracked and worn waffle sole separating from stiff and grimy uppers, ended a long, lean leg cased in jeans that seemed to consist mostly of the grease and road dust that imbued them. So it came as no surprise that instead of a hoarse but female shout, the counterattack drew a masculine bellow of pain and fury.

The guy was agile. He twisted with J.B.'s hands, so that the sudden torsion didn't snap his ankle. It did mean the man planted his face on the ground with an ax-hitting-wood sound.

A kick hit J.B. right by the kidneys—close enough to sting. He rolled with that, up onto all fours, then bounced up. He was resilient, anyway, and all wire-wound armature and spring steel.

He put up his fists in boxing stance. "I warned you," he said, spitting out a mouthful of bloody saliva.

A blow clipped him on the back of his head. The world whirled. Then the bastard hit him again, this time in the shoulder and the side of his face.

Okay, he thought. Now I'm fucked.

The real stomping commenced. The unfriendly parties were enthusiastically putting the boot in. This time J.B. would've been glad to curl up in a ball, which he couldn't, by way of the savage bootstorm.

He felt ribs crack. A toe to the jaw loosened teeth. At least he had sense to keep his hands balled into loose half-fists. They were his livelihood. If they got broken, Trader would have no reason in hell to keep him on his crew.

"So, what's the story?"

As if from a great distance J.B. heard the words. They barely penetrated the roaring in his ears.

He heard a meaty thunk that wasn't associated with any impact to his person he could identify. Have I lost feeling someplace? he wondered in near-panic. Is my spine busted?

He realized light was falling on his upturned face. It was an orange and sour light that warmed his skin slightly. He saw it through eyelids puffed next thing to closed.

"Here, now, Rance, you got no call to do that," a nasal man's voice whined.

"Yeah, I do," she said. "I told you pricks to back off. You don't listen, I'll make you."

"Listen, bitch," another male voice said. This one came from J.B.'s left side. "Where do you get off—"

J.B. felt as much as heard the man to his left fall beside him. The man rocked side to side, bumping into him. It sounded as if the guy was moaning through his fingers.

The others had stopped thundering on J.B., and he had gotten some of his composure back. Drawing a deep breath, he snapped to his feet. He flicked open a Spyderco lockback folder from his pocket with his right thumb.

"All right, you coldheart rad-suckers!" he yelled. He couldn't see much for the sweat and blood that promptly streamed into his eyes when he got upright. He waved the four-inch blade before him in what he hoped what a threatening manner. "I got you now. Who wants some?"

"Shut the fuck up, Dix," Rance said. "Fold your manhood back up and stuff it back in your pants, before I gave you a dose of my pacifier, here."

Blinking at her, he could make out the blurred, sort-of-feminine figure he'd come to recognize in the past few days. She was holding a long metal barlike thing in one hand and beating its shank against her open palm. Because he knew tools, he recognized the "pacifier" as one of the big open-end wrenches used to fasten external stores and armor plate on War Wag One and War Wag Two. It had to be two and a half, three feet long.

"You chilled Earl!" the nasal voice said. It whined even more now.

"Bullshit," Rance said. "Just busted his jaw. He won't die of that unless he's triple-weak and not much good to begin with. That's my assessment of him, anyway. As for Leon, he probably got off with a concussion. He doesn't think double-good on his best of days, so after he stops wobbling and running into things he should be about as much use to you as he was before, Tully."

Grumbling, the members of the gang still on their feet hauled up the still-motionless Leon and Earl, who was sobbing through his hands now, having found it hurt too much to try to complain in words, and dragged or steered them away, as the case may be.

"Thanks," J.B. said.

Having obeyed her order about the knife, he looked around for the glasses. Spotting them, he stooped by them. He grinned when he found out the lenses were intact, though the wire wings were twisted a bit out of true.

"What in the name of glowing nuke shit made you get into it with that bunch?"

"They started it!"

"Don't lie to me, Dix. I'll make you regret it."

"Well—" He was fingering his own jaw gingerly. His probing tongue confirmed at least one tooth loosened in its socket, as he thought. But he reckoned it'd firm up in a couple days and he wouldn't lose it, barring further misadventure. He had a certain amount of experience with that sort of thing, too.

The ribs were going to make it feel as if somebody was stabbing him every time he breathed for a week or so. But he could live with that. He may've always been a runt, but he was tough.

"I had to do it, Rance," he blurted, his mind coming back to her question—and to the way her hazel eyes were fixed on him. "They said the 1911 sucked! Claimed the Glock was more reliable!"

"I'm guessing you ain't had experience with a wide variety of handblasters, Dix."

"I know all there is to know about the Colt 1911!"

"In my experience, Glocks *are* more reliable than 1911s. And don't go getting fresh with me or I'll bust *your* jaw so I don't have to put up with your bullshit for a spell."

"Yes, ma'am!" He had already learned his new boss didn't bluff.

He had also learned that if you did what she told you, and listened when she instructed you, and tried your best, she was a pretty ace boss. It was belatedly occurring to him that she had stepped up to save his bacon when she didn't have to.

"Thanks," he said again.

"Heard you the first time. What the nuke were you even arguing with them about that for? They're the armorer's crew."

"But I'm an armorer, dammit! I'm good, Rance! You know it!"

As if reluctantly, she nodded. "You're good with your hands and you got a touch with mechanicals. I'll give you that. You're even a halfway-decent kid, if you can learn to use a little judgment before your attitude gets you chilled—and mebbe people around you. Which would not please Trader at all. Reckon you might get your shot at showing your stuff as a weaponsmith."

He stood up straighter despite the aches.

"But not for a spell. And not until you show you can keep your shit together. Before you go and do anything else, you gotta show you can ace the job you got. So shake the dust off your rad-blasted heels, youngster. We got a tore-down engine waitin' on us, and those parts ain't gonna wash themselves!"

Chapter Eleven

A gnarled misshapen blob of shadow lurched up and over the wood rail at Ryan.

He met it with a left boot to the face. Or, at least, the head. It toppled backward to crash through the thin scrim of ice with a big splash.

A gunshot shattered the crisp evening air from close by. Ryan was already hauling out his big-bladed panga. Flash decision, it seemed a lot more useful in the present circumstances than his 9 mm SIG-Sauer handblaster.

Apparently their guide thought so, too. She dropped the lever-action carbine to hang on its short sling across her saddle pommel and whipped out her saber as she spurred her mount forward.

As she charged forward, Ryan's blade hissed free as another shape lurched onto the bridge from beneath the rail to his right. He caught the forward-thrust muzzle with an upward swing. He felt a slightly rubbery impact. Then the head snapped back, flinging a long trail of blood, black in the gathering gloom.

It confirmed his initial impression of a mouth full of huge curved teeth like a great white shark's.

The bulky, hunched shapes surged up on both sides, along with an evil croaking mutter of malice. A pair blocked the exit from the bridge to the wagon-rutted road, shadowy shapes, at least man-size in heft, but seeming short because of the hunched-over way in which they carried their big heads in front of their barrel chests. They raised wicked-taloned hands to rake the approaching horse and rider.

The bay mare squealed in what Ryan took for terror. Instead of shying back from the terrible living mutie blockade, though, she sprang forward. Her hooves struck the stooped shoulders of both crouching shadows and knocked them spinning.

Ryan shouted, "Krysty! Mildred! Follow me!" and charged after their guide.

There were more of the humanoid frog muties waiting on the far side. Ryan slashed wildly with his panga, left and right, just trying to carve a path for his companions.

He scored no solid hits. The hopping, shambling monsters' rubbery skin wasn't easy to cut. And their sloped skulls were apparently thick and tended to send the broad blade glancing away. But the creatures gave way before him and the solid mass of his panicking, eye-rolling mount.

In a moment he was on the open snow-covered ground on the far bank. About fifty yards farther on the road went into a tunnel of mostly deciduous trees, bare but for snow. The mixed woods closed into the riverbank about the same distance away upstream and down.

While Ryan, though a seasoned horseman, wasn't experienced at mounted combat, clearly Alysa was. She had cleared a space of frogs in the middle of the clearing. Her horse was spinning in place, biting and lashing out with its rear heels, while its rider laid about not just with her sword—its curved blade flinging plumes of blood, inky in the twilight—but the barrel of her Marlin longblaster.

He winced as she slammed the black barrel across the froglike muzzle of a mutie. And not just because he heard the snout bones crunch and the monster squeal in horribly human-sounding pain. Usually using a blaster as a club was a sure, fast road to having a blaster that was only good *as* a club. But Ryan knew as well as any, even in this brutal world, how little use a working blaster was to a chill.

But in that instant of capturing the scene in his one good eye, as he had learned to do by hard practice over harder years, he also noted the distressing fact that only a couple of the weird misshapen forms lay on the ground.

These bastards take a lot of killing, he thought.

As he booted the pinto toward Alysa's circle of destruction, her bay mare caught a frog full in the side with both hind hooves in a brutal kick. It flung the massive monster a good five feet through the air, with a loud snap of ribs breaking. But Ryan saw that the creature never even went fully down—from a hurt that would've at least temporarily incapacitated any human, if not chilled him or her outright.

He kept the panga going, still not trying hard to bite the blade deep. Just enough to clear his way until he could help the girl, whose pale blond hair was whipping like a pennon out from behind her cap. And to help cover his friends…

Reassuringly he heard the sledgehammering of hooves on weathered, sturdy planks as the two women, presumably followed hard by Doc, crossed the bridge.

Then, as he rode up to Alysa, a scream pealed from behind him. He heard a giant, cracking, splintering sound.

He spun to see Krysty's little red roan mare falling on its side just at the bridge's end, saliva flying from its face. The horse's thrashing body smashed free a whole section of the heavy timber top rail on her right.

Blood hosed in a ruby arc from a throat torn open by black frog-mutie talons.

"USE MORE FORCE, LUKE."

The chunk of concrete, twice as big as J.B.'s head and with nasty jabs and hooks of rust-reddened rebar sticking out of it, clanged against the long steel handle of the wrench. The hard sharp-edged concrete bit at his palms. He wished he'd thought to wear gloves.

"What's that, Trader?" he asked.

Standing in the shade of War Wag Two, Trader chuckled. "Bad joke. And an old one, a reference to an old-days vid."

J.B. blinked owlishly at him, in part because his exertions had worked his glasses down his nose and he couldn't rightly see the man as anything but a long, narrow, shadowy blur. But also because he never reckoned a man as triple-hard and bottom-line as the Trader to go in for such foolishness.

As if reading his thoughts, the man said, "I deal in scavvy, son. I like to know the quality of my own merch. What exactly do you think you're *doing* there, anyway, abusing my tools like that?"

That stung J.B. as deeply, but he had the sense to throttle down the sudden racing of his temper.

"I'm trying to get this cable loose so we can haul that cargo wag out the ditch," he said, speaking slowly and tautly so as not to lose control of his words. It wasn't so much that Trader was his boss—he had no reflex fear or deference to authority. To say the least. But the man was *Trader,* as formidable a figure as the Deathlands knew.

"Son, I know that," Trader said, and now his gravelly voice had a touch of steel in it, like the broke-off chunk of roadway foolishly clutched in J.B.'s chafed hands. "I know what goes on in my convoy. What I want to know is why you are pounding on the handle of my four-foot open-end wrench with a nuking rock?"

J.B. frowned. Sweat ran into his eyes, stinging like anything and blurring out his vision worse than before. He fought the impulse to blink it furiously away. He was afraid that would make him look as nervous as he was.

"Well, I'm trying to get at this steel tow-cable," he said, struggling a bit as he tried to keep the words from tumbling over each other, without making it sound like he was lecturing a feeb. "The bolt's froze."

He could make out Trader's head turning. His heart sank. The shape approaching through the hot sun was little more detailed to his weak eyes than Trader's. But he'd learned to recognize his immediate boss and mentor in pretty much any visibility.

"Hear that, Rance?" Trader asked.

She spit in the dust between her and J.B. "What you're doing would be ace on the line if it was frozen, boy. But it ain't."

He shook his head in total bewilderment. "But—but—it won't turn. I tried and tried. Even tried hanging on the handle. My ass ain't that skinny!"

Rance sighed in audible disgust. "This is outside stowage, Dix."

He hated when she called him Dix.

"Do you think Trader wants his shit walking away every time we stop for a piss-break? We can't have eyes on every square inch of every wag every minute of the day. So the bolts securing outside stores are reverse-threaded."

Trader was lighting a cigar. J.B. could tell by the smell it wasn't one of the cheroots Rance favored. Trader liked the big hand-rolled ones.

"Be surprised how well that works," Trader said, whipping the match until it went out and then holding it to let it cool off. "Most thieves who make a go at helping themselves to my stuff like that react the same way you do."

The spent match cooled, Trader stuck it in a pocket of his worn jeans, faded near-white by countless suns. He didn't believe in leaving any more signs of his passage than dead necessary. He insisted his people do the same.

J.B. stared at him as if struck in the head with that damn traitor wrench. He looked at Rance. He still couldn't make out her features, but the hands on the hips spoke clearly.

"So, what do you think about your new acquisition now?" Rance asked Trader.

The man hunched a shoulder. "I take it this isn't the best performance he got in him?"

Rance laughed. "No. He's good with machines—most of the time. But his problem is he has no conception of how good he ain't yet."

"So he thinks he knows more than he does?"

She gestured at the wrench and the rock J.B. had forgotten he was holding at crotch level. Sheepishly he let it go, and remembered just in time to hop back to keep it from smashing his own feet.

Trader grunted, then he grinned.

"Your problem mainly is that you're young, boy," he said, not harshly. "That's a problem most of us get over. The question is whether we do it walking or lying down. With dirt hitting us in the eyes."

He walked off in that purposeful manner of his, not hurrying but going somewhere fast.

Staring after him, J.B. blew out a long breath.

"That could have gone better," he said.

Chapter Twelve

Mildred wasn't a woman accustomed to screaming.

But the cry of helpless fear was torn from her throat when she saw Krysty's horse go down with its throat torn out.

Mildred's mule shied, braying. In the dash through the monstrous, hunched forms that suddenly crowded the bridge, the two women had gotten separated. Krysty had made it all the way across, only to be brought down.

Mildred's way was blocked. Not only by the mortally wounded animal, but a ten-foot length of top-rail timber as big around as her thigh.

Uttering a sharp croak, a huge shape hopped off the intact rail on the west and landed in front of Mildred's mount. It raised a hand that had five fingers, webbed and tipped with long, curving claws.

Her mule slammed the mutie down with both hooves on its chest. Mildred heard a crunch and a gasping wheeze.

Another frog swiped at the mule. It laid its long ears back against its neck and bit a big chunk out of the mutie's face. Screaming like a human woman, the creature fell back against the rail. Blood spurted past the webbing of the claws that covered its snout.

Mildred tried to shoot another that lunged at her with her ZKR 551 target pistol. The frog slapped the sturdy revolver between its palms, trapping it, thrusting the muzzle skyward—and clamping the cylinder so that it wouldn't turn.

Meaning it also wouldn't shoot.

That angered Mildred. Screaming was an uncommon reaction to fear in her. Her usual mode was rage, which hit a beat later.

She began to kick the creature furiously in the side with boots that had reinforced steel toes. The frog grunted dismally but held on.

Its eyes were large and bulbous, like frog eyes, but the irises were a bright shocking blue, like a human's. Mildred tried not to think about that.

From the corner of her eye Mildred saw a mutie loom over Krysty, whose thigh was trapped beneath the still-thrashing body of her mare. Ryan had turned his black-and-white mount back and had fisted his SIG-Sauer handblaster. But there were too many stooped-over mutie bodies in the way to reach her in time.

Mildred roared now in sheer rage. She felt her opponent's ribs break under a savage kick. But still the mutie held her blaster.

Over the ruckus she heard a distinct, heavy thump. The mutie standing over Krysty froze a moment with claws upraised. Its weird froglike face looked puzzled somehow.

Then it turned its snout back down to its prey, as the mare uttered a final strangled gasp and went still atop the struggling redhead.

"Dark night! Where do these little bastards come from?"

No sooner had he shouted the words than the .50-caliber blaster mounted in the rear casemate of War Wag One cut loose with a wag-size flame and a world-size noise right over his head. Cursing in a voice not even he could hear for the catastrophic sound, J.B. flattened himself in the sandbag emplacement atop the Mercedes-Benz panel van running right behind the war wag.

The convoy rolled down a sandy, dry stream bottom between steep walls of red Oklahoma clay with bits and pieces of acid-rain-scorched vegetation clinging to them. The tops of both sides seemed to be lined with muties, small, toothy and scaly. They rained down rocks, crude spears, and not infrequently themselves on the vehicles of Trader's vehicles.

"All over," said the man hunkered beside J.B. He was another wrench from Rance's crew, a compact balding black man named Marcus. "I hate coming this way. Little fuckers always swarm us like anything."

The air was full of pink dust and the smell of hot diesel oil and lubricants—and a triple-heavy stink of burned propellant from the Ma Deuce blast. J.B.'s ears rang so badly he could barely hear the man a foot and a half from his head.

Marcus whipped up his massive SPAS scattergun and triggered a blast to the rear of the box. A mutie, a little over three feet high, like a tailless reptilian humanoid—or humanoid reptile—emitted a squeal as the charge of Number 4 buck hit it, exploding the yellow-pink finely scaled skin of its chest and belly above the filthy rag loincloth it wore. It flipped over the back end of the box.

On the vehicle behind, a former rental truck now painted in an absurd camo of streaked gray and green, a woman in a leather cap and goggles raised a fist and hollered curses at the Mercedes from her own sandbag emplacement. Apparently a few stray pellets from Marcus's shot had sung past her ears.

J.B. was sitting facing forward. He had the steel butt-plate of the SKS he'd been issued for this day's run pressed to his shoulder and was swinging the heavy longblaster left and right, searching for targets. So far, no muties had come down on the front end of the box or the cab. And the ones along the gully's walls popped up and down too fast to waste a cartridge on.

"Dark night!" he shouted, as the M-60 mounted in a hardpoint atop War Wag One's middle segment ripped a burst along the cliff-top to their left. "Why are we driving this way? We're triple-fat targets down in this nuking ditch!"

Marcus shrugged. "Business," he said. "That's what makes Trader Trader. He's willin' to take risks others ain't."

He chuckled. Owing to a vagary in the incredible ruckus of gunfire, shouts, screams and the weird squalling of the blunt-snouted muties, J.B. actually heard him.

"O' course, he's got the *firepower* others ain't," he said. "Not to mention the armor."

"Which we aren't inside of," J.B. said sourly.

The convoy had two of the monstrous war wags: three-sectioned vehicles capable of running on both tracks and big knobby wheels, plus every known kind of fuel that could burn. They were a combination of salvaged predark military tech and the wizardry of Trader's crew—not least J.B.'s boss, Rance Weeden, and the man he secretly longed to work for, Weapons Master Ace DeGuello. Trader's personal ride, War Wag One, rolled point this day, as it generally did. War Wag Two brought up the rear.

The M-60 snarled. J.B. approved of the way the gunner was firing in measured bursts—three shots, four, then five, and three again. It was a way to minimize overheating in the big weapon and to maximize the shots between barrel changes, which were double-hard to do in action—a major design flaw of the machine gun.

And then the big blaster fell silent.

J.B. frowned. He could see muties popping up on the gully walls ahead. It should be a target rich environment. Mebbe the barrel melted, he thought. Sooner or later heat caught up with a machine gun.

Marcus clapped his hand to the side of his head as if he'd been stung. Johnny knew he had to be listening to the earpiece stuck in his ear from the compact walkie-talkie stuck in his shirt pocket.

"Fuck!" the assistant wrench exclaimed. "Sixty's jammed. And it's the only top-mounted blaster on War Wag One!"

"¡MADRE DE DIOS!" Ricky yelped in frustrated fury as he threw the bolt of his DeLisle carbine. The copper-jacketed 230-grain .45 ACP slug had hit the monster square in the side of its inhumanly deep chest.

And it had barely distracted the humanoid frog. It was either extraordinarily durable, like a stickie, or simply too bulky and well-protected by thick hide and heavy bones for what was still a handblaster bullet to stop it with a single solid torso shot.

When the muties had suddenly boiled up over both sides of the wood bridge to assail his friend, he had swung off his stubby yellow pony and onto the ground. His reflex was to provide covering fire.

The pony had panicked and reared, neighing shrilly. He had lost valuable seconds trying to fight to keep control of it. Then he realized that, small as the beast was, it was stronger than he was, and that his job now was shooting, not minding his ride.

By that time, Krysty's horse was already falling, fatally wounded.

He heard a strange, heavy crunching in the snow from right behind. He set his jaw. I have to take the shot, he told himself. Mother Mary, give me strength.

He got the picture above the iron sights of the suppressed longblaster just as the beast leaned forward into a downward blow aimed at the helpless woman. Ricky had accounted for a slight forward motion.

Just enough. The huge head jerked visibly. Black blood sprayed away from its head. It crumpled.

Ricky spun, frantically working the bolt action of the weapon, which promptly jammed. In his own haste he had short-shucked it, managing not to yank the bolt far enough to properly feed even the short .45 cartridge.

The monster was right behind him, staring at him with gigantic hazel eyes. It had a claw upraised to slice open his face.

The right eye exploded in black. Dragon's breath washed, scalding, across the left side of Ricky's face. Terrible noise threatened to implode his eardrum as fast tiny particles stung his cheek and temple.

The mutie dropped. A cloud of its brain and gore hung in the chill evening air for what seemed an eternity before falling like clotted rain on the snow.

Jak was at Ricky's side. His face was set in a predator's grin, the ruby eyes slits of fierce joy. Blue smoke wisped thin from the ribbed barrel of his huge .357 Magnum Colt Python handblaster.

Again operating on reflex, Ricky hauled the bolt open in an effort to clear the cartridge, which had stuck upright in the breach. His second furious attempt worked. The round spun free.

But by then a heavy inhuman hand, black-green, both

webbed and cruelly clawed, had come down on Jak's right shoulder, too late for Ricky to intervene.

MILDRED SAW THE frog mutie's head explode.

Then the one she was fighting with squealed. She looked back at it to see a slim length of steel withdrawing from the blood and the aqueous, fluid-spurting ruin of its left eye.

Mildred shoved her now-freed revolver's muzzle into the other eye and fired. She saw the rubbery face inflate like a giant balloon from the sudden gas overpressure of the muzzle-blast.

For a horrifying instant, it looked almost like a mottled green mask of a human face.

Then the creature slumped back against the rail. Its arms twitched and big hind legs kicked. But it was clearly dead.

A huge boom on Mildred's other side told her that Doc, having stabbed her attacker with his swordstick, had unleashed the shotgun tube slung under the barrel of his LeMat revolver on another mutie.

Ryan was closing in on the fallen Krysty, shooting and stabbing. Behind him, Mildred saw Alysa and her horse fighting like demons to keep their way clear. But the monsters were plentiful.

They had closed in a circle around the trapped Krysty. Mildred tried to charge them, but her mule refused to get too near. She started blasting humped backs. Her bullets seemed to have no effect.

Krysty screamed.

A HEAVY, COOL calm settled on J.B. In the heat of the firefight, the dust and noise and danger, his heart and been racing so hard it threatened to pulverize his rib cage from the inside.

Now he felt it slow as he drew in a deep breath. There was just one thing to do.

So, naturally, he did it.

Slinging his longblaster, he stood up out of the sandbag nest. "Have you gone crazy?" Marcus yelped. "Get down, you feeb!"

A spear from above flashed by in front of J.B.'s face. He didn't flinch. His mind had already calculated it wouldn't hit him.

He took a couple of halting steps to the front of the cargo box, leaped the palm-size gap to the roof of the cab. Fortunately the Mercedes had a flat snout, van-size, instead of a coffin hood like the truck following.

Hunkering down on the cab, dropping one palm to the sun-hot metal of the roof as the other secured the downward-slung muzzle of his SKS, J.B. hung his face down beside the driver's window.

Unexpected motion in her peripheral vision made the driver glance over. Her brown eyes widened.

"Close up!" J.B. shouted.

The driver was conscious of her craft—Trader's people were good at their jobs, or they didn't have them. She kept glancing at the armor-clad mass of the vehicle just ahead, then back at the unexpected apparition of an upside-down head in her window.

J.B. let go of the SKS to make a rolling gesture at the driver with his finger extended. "Close up!" he yelled again. He made sure to mouth the words exaggeratedly.

The driver's eyes actually got wider. Then, apparently deciding if this crazy new kid wanted a novel way to wind up with dirt hitting him in the eyes, that was his lookout, she put the pedal down. The heavy-loaded truck shuddered, then lurched so that its flat nose almost slammed the rear weapon mount of War Wag One.

The perforated barrel of the .50-caliber Browning M2 machine gun mounted there was already turning and rising slightly as its gunner found a new target. He probably didn't even see J.B.

Marcus cried out a warning. J.B. judged the distance and leaped.

There were two possible handholds. The fifty's barrel would be so hot from firing that it would melt the skin of J.B.'s palms.

That left the projecting top of the casemate, a sort of armor box fixed to the back of the war wag, with the machine gun mounted on a pintle inside and sticking out through a narrow slot. The gunner had a little polycarbonate window right above to sight out of. It really was a wizard design, J.B. noticed, as he caught the top edge with both hands. And the workmanship was just what you'd expect from Trader's techs: exquisite.

Fortunately he had a fast eye. He didn't have time to hang around. He scrambled up onto the casemate like a monkey.

The roof of War Wag One's three sections was armored like the rest. It wasn't as heavily armored as the sides, front and rear; not even the specially rebuilt, massive engines that drove the vehicle had infinite capacity to haul mass. But in an age when functioning aircraft were rarer than good mouthfuls of teeth, and the most common danger from above came from the carnivorous mutie fliers called screamwings and much smaller chillers called stingwings, there was no need to armor the top heavily. The relatively thin plating was plenty sturdy enough to resist the spears and even the biggest rocks the muties were chucking at it.

That was also why Trader only bothered mounting the one machine gun in a hardpoint welded to the top of the wag. He didn't usually need much top cover for his rolling HQ.

But unlike screamwings and stingwings, scalies had hands with opposable thumbs. They could drop down to the roofs of the three segments and find their devilish ways inside to work havoc among the crew.

And there were a dozen or so between J.B. and the quiescent blaster mount.

He ran forward. One mutie turned and opened its mouth to screech a warning to its fellows as it raised a spear. Its tongue was long, shockingly red and forked like a sidewinder's. The creature carried a weapon that was a tree branch with a head that looked as if it was made out of a hammered tin can.

J.B. blasted the monster from the hip. The steel-jacketed 7.62 mm Russian bullet didn't have the raw smashing power that Marcus's Italian-made 12-gauge did, but it punched a big hole through the mutie's sunken sternum and blasted through its skinny body to smash the forearm of the mutie standing behind it.

The shot mutie toppled off the armored roof. The huge war wag's three joined segments had heavy suspensions and its sheer mass absorbed a certain amount of road impact. And the relatively soft sand of the dry river bottom didn't give a rough ride. But the big machine was hauling mass, and the ride wasn't silky-smooth, either.

The mutie who'd been hit by the blow-through round had its left hand flopping loose on the end of its arm. It was a human-looking hand, except for the fact that it had but three fingers, instead of four, along with a thumb. And the black, curving, needle-tipped talons, of course.

But the mutie had a projecting lizardlike muzzle filled

with double rows of razor teeth. It showed them to J.B., opening its jaws to snap his face off.

Instead, he smashed it across the open jaws with the buttplate of his SKS. The blow knocked the mutie off the war wag, trailing blood and a couple of teeth as it turned over and over in the air.

J.B. was halfway down the rear segment. The machine-gun nest was in the middle of the central one. He heard single shots from that way—handblaster shots. Its crew was apparently fending off the muties with side-arms. And that was a problem. If he shot straight ahead he might hit one of his own guys.

But J.B. was still in machine mode; it was the way he got when he had a problem to solve, something to fix.

The reptilian muties were merely preliminary problems to his smoothly clicking mind. As for the blaster crew, they weren't his pals. He wasn't concerned if he blasted one by accident. It was easier to get forgiveness, he reckoned, than permission. And he reckoned that for Trader to get pissed at him for incidentally blasting one of his personnel, J.B. would have to survive this goat-screw.

Trader, too, for that matter.

But J.B. was going to need to spend some quality time head-down in the guts of the broken M-60 to get it churning and burning again. That meant he couldn't constantly be swatting off the muties. That meant he needed the blaster crew to clear his back while he worked the magic that he knew in his bones he could do.

Problem defined. Problem solved. He just waded into the muties, jabbing with the muzzle and bashing with the butt, as if the longblaster was a truncheon. The semiautomatic SKS wasn't really a close relative of its better-known successor, the famous AK-47 assault rifle. But it was designed and built to the same philosophy: to be maintainable and operable by conscript troops who were shit-scared, half-trained and less literate, and to fire every time the trigger was pulled with a round chambered, in the absolute worst conditions available anywhere on planet Earth.

Which, not altogether incidentally, meant that unlike most blasters you could just bash the hell out of people, or muties, all day without it malfunctioning on you.

The muties were fast little bastards, but then, so was J.B. They weren't strong, either in muscle or frame. For his size, J.B. was.

And he was on a mission, which meant he was a machine.

A killing machine. Even though a few more muties dropped down from above, and he had to dodge the odd rock or spear hurled down at him, he waded through them at scarcely less speed than if he'd been running unimpeded on flat ground.

He reached the gap between segments, then leaped. A mutie barred his way with upraised spear and bared fangs. He knocked the spear aside with his blaster butt and put a shoulder into the mutie as he landed. Fangs tore his shirt and the skin beneath, but the mutie went down caterwauling on its back with its spear haft broken in two.

J.B. pointed the longblaster and fired a shot, aiming to the side to minimize danger to the gunners just ahead. The bullet drilled through the creature's belly and bounced off the armor-plated roof, ricocheting to punch a couple of bloody yellow ribs out of its sternum, tear off its lower jaw and go whining away. J.B. vaulted the body and kept going.

He found a woman, squatting in the blaster pit alone,

hefting two handblasters. She had pushed her goggles up onto her brush of short brown hair. The lack of road grit around her hazel eyes gave her a photonegative raccoon-mask appearance that accented their near-panicky wideness.

"Who the fuck are you?" she demanded, as J.B., with a buttstroke from behind, stove in the skull of a mutie that had hopped up on the rearward armor shield.

Since that wasn't essential information, he didn't bother to answer. "What's wrong?" he asked, dropping into the emplacement beside her.

The M-60's feed-tray cover was open. It and the weapon's receiver were mint-shiny black, meaning Ace DeGuello or his armorers had re-blued it relatively recently. J.B. had to admit the Trader's weapons master was triple-ace at his job,

Which didn't mean J.B. wasn't going to replace the man.

But that concern was as distant from his mind as the back side of the moon right now. His mind narrowed to laser focus on the machine gun's open receiver.

"Bastard's jammed up jelly-tight," the gunner said. "Tore the head right off a spent casing. We're fucked."

A shadow fell across the receiver. The sun was an hour or so past the zenith.

The gunner stuck the short-barreled revolver in her left hand—a Colt Trooper .38, J.B. reckoned—into the mutie's midsection and blasted it as it raised a steel tomahawk over its head.

"Where's your partner?" J.B. asked, reminded of the question's relevance.

"Chilled. Poor bastard panicked and ran when the blaster jammed and the muties started droppin' down.

He didn't make it fifteen feet before they swarmed him. All biting like piranhas and shit. Never stood a chance."

"Got a mitt?" he asked.

She blinked at him a moment. Had he not been so razor-sharp in focus he would've flashed into anger at her useless delay. But in this mode he didn't have any feelings at all. Except utter certainty that he would finish the task at hand.

And more importantly, could.

She nodded. He slung the SKS. "Asbestos?" he asked. "Yeah."

Though it had been about two minutes since the M-60 had fired, he could feel the heat beating off the receiver and barrel assembly. M-60s had originally been issued with asbestos mitts so that barrels could be swapped out when they overheated in combat. As expected, what he pulled out of a little niche under the ring mount was an improvised article. But it would keep the skin on his palm.

"Keep the fuckers off my back," he said. He pulled the spare barrel assembly from its clamps inside the emplacement.

"But it's fucked, plain as day," she said. "You—you can fix it? Here? Now?"

He flicked a look at her over the tops of his glasses, then he bent to work.

Chapter Thirteen

The mutie who had grabbed him from behind squalled shrilly.

Jak's grin widened.

The hand came off Jak's shoulder as if it was red hot. The creature had discovered the razor-sharp bits of metal sewn into the collar of camo-colored vest.

Jak spun. The monster had reared up on its short, bowed rear legs, standing taller than the albino youth did. Not that that was hard; you could call Jak Lauren many things, and many had, but none of them was *tall*.

He plunged the two-edged blade into the belly of the beast, which was pale and thin. The knife sank in all the way to the knuckle-duster grip. Jak yanked up and twisted.

The frog shrieked in intolerable agony as the knife shredded its guts.

Jak pulled the knife free. Another frog was attacking him from the left, more hopping than running on its strong, bowed back legs. He shot it in the face. The bullet smashed its toothy lantern jaw and drove like an out-of-control semi into the chest cavity behind.

He heard the hefty *thump* of his friend's suppressed weapon. His fighting smile widened for a brief instant.

Ricky would cover their friends, and Jak would cover *him*. It was how things should be.

Another frog mutie sprang at him. He met it with spikes of brass.

RYAN GROUND HIS teeth in fury and frustration. Krysty was trapped, and the horde of hopping, slithering muties had surrounded her, blocking rescue by him, and by Mildred and Doc from the other direction.

He quickly found out that even though the frogs had their humped backs to him, his horse wouldn't charge in among them, no matter how hard he slammed his heels into its flanks and cursed. He fired his magazine dry to little visible effect. The 9 mm hardball bullets did nothing when fired into the creatures' thick torsos. And the thrust-forward skulls were hard to hit—and just plain hard. He shot one in the back of the head only to see a bloodred groove appear on the bare scalp where the slug had simply skipped off the bone.

He heard a roar and glanced back. Alysa and her horse had pulled to a few feet behind them. The blonde girl was keeping the monsters off Ryan's back while he tried to rescue Krysty.

But he couldn't. He roared in frustrated fury and prepared to throw himself out of the saddle right onto those broad, bent, spine-knobbed mutie backs.

And then great, kicking frog mutie bodies erupted in front of him like a fountain of twisted evil.

MILDRED YELPED IN startled pain as a frog-mutant dug black talons through the faded but still-tough denim of her right pants leg.

Out of ammo, she slammed the butt of her ZKR target pistol into the monster's snout. Bone crunched, then the mutie squealed and let go.

She grabbed a speed-loader from a pocket of her parka and fervently wished she had some kind of melee weapon. Preferably an oversize knife like Ryan's panga—or better yet, the Stormbreak girl's full-on cavalry saber. But she'd settle for an ax handle, a ball bat, or even a stout tree branch right now.

What she had was her heavy boots, with which she kicked furiously in both directions, and her chunky, cranky mule, whose ill nature was helping keep her alive. It was kicking muties and biting chunks from them.

But they were tough and took a packet of chilling, and they kept coming.

With the heavy timber snapped off the bridge rail blocking her way, she couldn't get to her helpless friend Krysty as the hopping, croaking monsters swarmed her.

Mildred heard a furious chanting, then moments later frogs were flung away from the fallen mare and trapped redhead like abandoned baby dolls. Krysty stood. Her sentient hair waved around her head in angry scarlet tentacles. She had yanked her leg out from under her mount and engaged in a counterattack.

The broken beam had to weigh a good two hundred pounds or more. A tall woman, and strong, Krysty still should have been able to do no more than deadlift it, using both hands and driving with her long, powerful legs.

Instead she picked it up in the middle and started spinning with it.

Mildred actually winced when she saw the raw broken beam-end crunch into a mutie's face sideways. The creature dropped as if its skeleton had dissolved, its skull crushed and neck fractured.

The timber hardly slowed. It caught another frog full in the chest and bent it double. Black blood geysered out of its mouth.

Krysty stood over the body of her mare and whipped the beam the other way. Frog muties were knocked in all directions like bottles off a gaudy's bar by an unruly drunk.

No normal woman could have swung the bar like that. Or any normal man. But Krysty was no longer normal. The red-haired woman had the ability to channel her tutelary spirit, Gaia the Earth Mother, deriving incredible strength. Calling on Gaia for strength took a terrible toll on Krysty.

Whirling the massive beam like a broomstick, Krysty cleared muties off the north end of the bridge. She flung the timber away from her, spinning like a propeller, to take down a quartet of frogs between her and Ryan. Then, stooping, she grabbed her dead mare by a foreleg and dragged the inert 750-pound horse from where it blocked the exit from the bridge.

The corpse slid down the bank toward the ice that edged the river. Krysty's emerald eyes rolled up in her head. With a groan she sank to her knees.

Ryan was beside her. He bent from the saddle, caught her under the arms and, with a near-superhuman heave of his own, flung her up to a sideways position behind his saddle.

"Come on!" he bellowed. "Power over here!"

Mildred needed no second urging. She booted the mule hard. It bunched its haunches and lit out like a jackrabbit, almost losing her over the cantle of the Western-style saddle.

STILL HALF-TURNED in his saddle, holding Krysty behind him with his blaster hand, Ryan rode hell for leather off the bridge and past him into the clearing, followed closely by Mildred and Doc. Jak and Ricky had already remounted and were riding toward the bridge.

Nothing barred their way. The frog muties, it seemed, had had enough.

Ryan felt Krysty's arms go around his waist. Although she was spent and half-conscious, she locked hand on wrist, securing herself.

He glanced back. She rallied, raised her beautiful but more-than-usually pale face and kissed him on the lips.

"I knew you'd get me, lover," she murmured. Then her head fell against his back.

He released her and turned in his saddle. The muties had melted back from the clearing on the north side of the bridge. Alysa headed her horse toward where the road ran in among the tunnel of snowy tree branches.

Almost instantly she wheeled back. "Frogs!" she cried. "They're blocking the way!"

Ryan turned his pinto west, the way the nameless stream ran as it wound its way to the sea.

"Follow me!" he shouted.

"But I'll get lost!" Alysa complained. "These are bad woods, and I only know the roads!"

"I'd rather be lost and alive than knowing where I am when I'm staring up at the stars," Ryan shouted back. "Wouldn't you?"

She shook her head, making her long blond hair fly out to one side and then the other. But apparently it was a gesture of despair, not negation. She joined the others lining out after Ryan as he booted his gelding into a gallop.

Branches splintered and sprayed his face with powdery snow. He blinked his eye clear. With the light nearly gone it hardly mattered. He couldn't see where they were going anyway.

The only thing that mattered this instant was that they were racing away from the frog-mutants.

TWENTY MINUTES LATER, long slowed to a walk, Ryan admitted to himself they were well and truly lost. In his desire to avoid plunging accidentally into icy water he had quickly led his little party away from the stream. Now they followed a narrow game trail—with utterly no idea where it led.

The sky was overcast. Inside the dense forest it was next to coal-mine-shaft black. It was all Ryan could do to fend off the occasional branch hanging at head-level, to avoid having it slap him in the face. Or Krysty, now sitting astride behind him with arms draped over his shoulders, snoring softly into the back of his neck.

Because of the game trail's narrowness, they had to go single file. Ryan's pinto had its pink-and-white nose almost pressed to the black tail of Alysa's horse. Ryan was a skilled enough horseman to know it was an ace on the line the two were herd mates that got along. Otherwise, that sort of poky intimacy would have been an open invitation to a faceful of hooves.

The blood bay stopped abruptly as its rider, slim despite her bulky coat, raised a hand. Ryan raised his own hand to pass the signal back along the line.

His gelding squealed, flattened his ears, and cocked a hindleg for a kick as Mildred's mule walked right into the horse's butt. She had probably been dozing in the saddle. Ryan couldn't rightly blame her.

The mule backed off on its own initiative, with a snort that let the world know it wasn't giving in to a mere *horse*.

Alysa pointed a gloved finger ahead, once, twice.

Ryan saw it now; a warm yellow gleam from ahead. Just enough to reveal, as he looked closer, the outline of a not very regular but sturdy-looking pitched-roof house of stone and timber, with smoke trailing out a stone chimney, darker gray against the low overcast sky. He smelled the smoke now, a piney tang that made him suddenly feel the chill he'd been ignoring all the way down through his marrow, and his stomach rumbled with suppressed, unacknowledged hunger.

Alysa turned back. Her pale, strained young face looked a question.

He nodded. She straightened in her saddle and nudged her bay toward the light.

"Are you sure this is a good idea?" Mildred, clearly wide-awake now, asked from behind.

Ryan actually chuckled.

"You rather sleep out here in a snowbank, Mildred?" he asked softly. "And take your chances with what we know is wandering around out here? I'll roll the dice on whoever's inside, myself."

With gentle but firm pressure of his knees, he urged his horse to a walk in the wake of their guide.

"HEY, YOU THERE!" A VOICE called through the dusk.

The convoy was laagered-up in a circle in a clearing on mostly level ground to recover from the attack. The surroundings here were fairly green, indicating that this microclimate got more water rain than acid rain. The sun was already sinking behind some jagged trees on a ridgeline to the west.

J.B. sat on a patch of bare red dirt with his knees up and a canteen in his hand. Around him, people went about their business in a sort of controlled frenzy. Rance hadn't come looking for him to lend a hand.

He was glad. The only hand he could've offered shook like a leaf in a stiff wind. His skinny body was wrung out like a gaudy-bar rag from exertion in the heat—and complete concentration.

But his mind was racing. Despite the exhaustion that weighed down his slight frame like an anvil strapped to his back, he felt elation, the satisfaction of a tough job well done.

"Hey, you there," the voice called again, closer this time. "You the kid who messed with my 60-blaster?"

J.B. reckoned that meant him. He looked around.

A man was striding toward him across the circle walled in by Trader's wags. He was medium height, meaning a few inches taller than J.B., wider across chest and shoulders and double-wider across the gut. He had a mop of black hair, a mustache and beard stubble sprouting on round jowls and chins that was almost as dark. His face showed an olive strip across the eyes and monobrow. The rest was darker brown and looked a bit sunburned beneath. It wasn't road-grime, but residue from being hunkered down over the receiver of a machine gun at close quarters, firing flat-out for an extended stay. J.B. knew that sort of thing.

He jumped to his feet. The man was Ace DeGuello, Trader's personal weapons master and chief armorer.

"Yeah," he said. He felt a roil of conflicting emotions in his belly that overrode the hunger that was starting to creep into the place where post-adrenaline-rush nausea had been for half an hour after they'd parked. There was his natural defiance, warring mano-a-mano with his desire to please the man he most wanted to work for.

Well, and replace. But first things first.

The boss armorer stuck out a hand. Though the belly straining the grease-and-sweat-mottled front of his generically dark T-shirt was soft, the hand was rock-hard from working on blasters and ineradicably stained with the grease and powder residue such work ground in over time.

Numbly, Johnny took it. He managed to meet firm grasp with firm grasp. He was happy the Latino didn't play the hand-crushing game. J.B.'s hands were big for his size, and strong. But DeGuello's mitt was like a bear's paw.

"You worked a wonder out there, boy," he said. "I don't mind saying we'da all had our asses stuck in a crack if you hadn't got that wep firing again when you did. We had a pair of the little fucks get into War Wag One as it was."

J.B. could only shake his head. He couldn't put the words in order to explain that it hadn't been that big a deal. The book remedy for a shell jammed in the chamber was a simple barrel change. The gunners just hadn't known that. Or, more likely, forgotten under the mind-blanking stress of their powerful blaster's sudden slam into uselessness and the sudden swarm of muties falling like razor-fanged rain on their heads. J.B.'s gyros were so tumbled by recent and current events, he couldn't even muster a twitch of contempt at them for losing their heads.

In fact, there was nothing wrong with the locked-up barrel. It'd take about ten minutes to chuck it up in a vice in one of Ace's shops and work the headless case free. But that was nothing anybody could do in a firefight. Not Ace—and not J. B. Dix.

"You're one of Rance's wrenches, right?" Ace asked, letting go of J.B.'s hand.

"Uh. Yeah."

"Man. Your skinny gringo ass is wasted working on engines. You need to come work for me, my friend."

J.B. opened his mouth to say, "Dark night, yes!"

A hand like a steel clamp locked down in his shoulder from behind. It seemed to trap the words right in his throat.

"I'm not done with him yet, Ace," Rance said.

Ace frowned. "Listen, Rance, cut me some slack, here—"

"Not this time."

J.B. turned to look at her. His heart had been soaring like a dove. Now it plummeted like that same dove after sucking in a charge of birdshot.

The chief wrench wasn't a bad boss, as bosses went. She as was hard as 304 stainless steel, but she was also straight-edge fair. That, he wasn't used to.

And she was…not hard on the eyes. Not a beauty by any means, with her long, worn, somewhat square-jawed face, the small breasts whose shape his mind had worked out with some precision despite the loose work shirts she always wore, and the fact that her waist wasn't that much narrower than her shoulders or skinny hips. Still, Rance Weeden was a handsome woman.

But he *had* to be an armorer. He had to show his real stuff to Trader.

"Please" spilled out his mouth without his even meaning it to. Not that he could've stopped it, likely.

A small frown furrowed her brow between her hazel eyes, which even in the sun's last light showed a touch of green. His shot-down heart sank further. He was afraid she was about to rank him out in epic style, which he knew well she could do.

She pushed her fedora up her brow. Her face had the odd raccoon-mask effect, too. Like him, she'd been sitting on top of a cargo wag fighting off muties until they won clear.

Which hadn't cost them that much, surprisingly. Just three chills, including Jody Marks, the 60-gunner on War Wag One who'd panicked and gotten pulled down. Five wounded, three walking, all expected to make full recovery. Trader had good healers—though he himself would never see one, famously mistrusting them all as quacks and witch-doctors.

Even more surprisingly, they hadn't lost a wag or a load. The last cargo wag in line had broken a front axle on a big rock thrown down by the muties. The convoy had halted for no more than two minutes while a tow cable was rigged to the wag ahead. Those were a hot two minutes, at least for J.B. and the female gunner whom he'd served as loader—especially since they didn't dare shoot any more or more often than absolutely necessary, as they were already using the lone spare barrel. In the end, between the next-to-last wag pulling and the occasional push from the blunt snout of War Wag Two, they'd gotten the disabled vehicle moving again at little less speed than they'd managed before. And within half a mile they were clear of the canyon and the persistent and apparently limitless tribe of muties that had bushwhacked them.

Now J.B. mostly wished he could die. He was stuck as a wrench. And he'd pissed off the boss.

Rance sucked down a long breath, then let it out slowly.

"I reckon I can lend him to you, Ace," she said. "When I can spare him."

"Thanks, Rance," DeGuello said. "I appreciate it."

J.B. stared at her with saucer eyes. "Really?"

"Did I stutter?"

She cuffed him on the side of the head, but lightly. Kind of.

"But I can't spare your lazy ass now, J. B. Dix. We got us an axle to fix by morning. So march!"

"Yes, ma'am!"

Chapter Fourteen

"Here, Ryan," said the plump, cheerful woman in the heavy maroon shawl and dark brown dress. Her face was red from working the hot stove in the kitchen in the back. Her bun of hair was as white as bleached bone. "Have some more spuds. Plenty more where those came from!"

"Don't mind if I do."

Ryan and his group were gathered around a big, crude but sturdy plank table loaded with food and drink. The inside of the house in the dark woods was cramped yet cozy, and warm from a giant fireplace roaring at one end of the main room. By the watery yellowish light of lanterns obviously fueled by fish oil, the walls seemed to be a semi-random mix of rough, dark-stained planks and granite chunks. But it wasn't easy to tell from the jars and random bric-a-brac that crowded the many shelves on every wall. These held everything from crude ceramic vases and pots containing dried flowers, or what struck him as random sprays of weeds, to a few coverless books, to faded and cracked predark toys, to sealed glass jars containing vague hints of objects indiscernible for the murky fluid that filled them. Most were coated thickly with dust.

He found it mildly disquieting, like the odd smell that pervaded the house. Even beneath the fishy smell.

The visible patches of the wall, few and small as they were, were often marked by tufts of gray-green moss or seemingly random clumps of weeds stuffed in to stuff the chinks in the walls. It didn't keep the occasional chill breath from wafting through the room and down his neck, but it was still better than being out in the frigid night.

He accepted the heavy, cracked ceramic bowl from the woman's hands, which were reddened and chapped from housework, much of which was no doubt conducted out in the cold. The bowl, like the plates and utensils he and his friends had loaded up with rabbit stew and boiled greens and beans, at least seemed clean. Mostly. Which was more than you could say for the floor.

But squeamish folks tended to starve in the world they lived in. This was better than he generally got. He doled out a second helping, with bits of cut-up potato skins mashed in with them, onto his plate.

"Eat up, everybody," boomed the man at the head of the table. He had bushy brown hair streaked with gray and an enormous beard. It spread out over an even more enormous belly; the man had to be four hundred pounds easy, maybe five, stuffed into a red-and-black-plaid flannel shirt and canvas coveralls that his wife had to have cobbled together for him. Possibly out of predark tents. Ryan, who sat at his right hand, had mostly gotten used to the smell of sweat and grease wafting from him. "Plenty where that came from. Mama Bear hates to send anybody away hungry."

The woman bustled back in through the door from the kitchen in a wash of fragrant steam. She carried another bowl full of green peas in her hands. The dish was painted with a dull green stripe and a misshapen-looking yellow-gray pear, and it had a big crack running down the side.

Seated toward the foot of the table with Ricky between him and Krysty, Jak was sniffing the air in the room. His nose wrinkled. *He* wasn't fastidious, either— to say the least.

"Smells like death," he announced.

"Jak!" Krysty exclaimed. "That's rude." She had sprung back remarkably fast from the usual exhaustion brought on by channeling Gaia into a burst of superhuman strength. Her eyes were a bit sunken, her cheeks more hollow than usual. But her eyes still sparkled like emeralds, and the smile she flashed Ryan when she glanced his way and caught his eye was like fingers tickling the underside of his cock.

But Ryan frowned. Yeah. That's it, he thought.

"Oh, dear," said Mama Bear. She pottered around the table to stand next to her husband.

But Papa Bear chuckled indulgently and scratched his colossal belly.

"Aw, it's nothin' but honesty, Mama Bear," he said in a thunder-rumble voice. "Boy speaks his mind. Fact is, it's a thing we're well aware of and find highly regrettable. Seems like a rat musta crawled in the walls and died where we can't find it, or such."

Unlike most of the people they'd encountered in Stormbreak—and Alysa—the pair spoke in a broad down-east Maine accent. With Mama Bear standing by her husband, Ryan was struck by the fact that, as hefty as she was, she seemed almost willow-slim by comparison. Ryan was also struck by how similar they looked other than bulk: pink cheeks, small, watery-blue eyes, noses that kind of splayed out at the nostrils and ends. Both exhibited the swollen forehead he associated with inbreeding. Mama Bear had the retreating lower jaw, too. Papa Bear's imposing beard concealed what chin he had. Or didn't have.

"They call these the Deathlands for a reason," Ryan said. He was inclined to accept the explanation of the smell. And also the fact that their host and hostess might've been related before they got married. Inbreds weren't in any way uncommon in smaller villes.

The big thing that concerned Ryan was that the food was hot and plentiful and kept coming. And that being inside these four walls, as grimy as they were, was better than being out in the wind and cold. He offered up a taut smile to Mama Bear as she spooned peas onto his plate.

"How do you get all these greens here in the dead of winter?" Mildred asked. She sat at Ryan's right. "Seem pretty fresh."

Ryan frowned slightly. The question sounded almost challenging, and there was no profit to be had in pissing off their hosts. He made himself take into account that she was on edge over J.B.'s state.

Mama Bear dished out the peas and then perched on the end of her chair. She seemed to spend most of her time shuttling in and out of the kitchen. Ryan wondered when she'd eat. Obviously she did a fair amount of it.

"Oh, a goodly number of folk hereabouts have learned how to grow food through the winter," she said. "We trade. We get a fair number of visitors, despite being out here in the woods."

The house was an inn of sorts. For a reasonable amount of jack, Ryan's group had secured lodging for the night in a mostly log annex heated by its own wood-stove, as well as meals.

"What brings you folks this way?" Papa Bear asked.

He picked up his bowl of stew and tipped it toward his mouth. A fair amount ended up on his beard. As much food as he had to take in, the beard had to be well nourished, too, Ryan reckoned.

Krysty looked at the one-eyed man. He shrugged. No point in not telling the truth. Or at least some of it.

"Slavers kidnapped some people out east along the coast, in Stormbreak," she said. "We're looking to find them and rescue them."

Ryan glanced past Mildred and Doc, who was mumbling with his chin on his breastbone, to Alysa. The young woman had been eating dutifully with her eyes fixed on the table. Now she looked up sharply.

"Slavers," Papa Bear repeated. "Rad blast 'em. They've been a burden to us all the last few years. They been bringing their prisoners along the coast from the north and east. Seem to be taking them somewhere down past Tavern Bay."

"Tavern Bay?" Ryan asked.

"A small port ville south of here, at the mouth of a river called the Tavern," Mama Bear said. "They do lots of fishing, some trading. Even a little bit of manufacture."

"We know of it in Stormbreak," Alysa said. "We trade with the people there. But do not trust them. Even though the baroness came from among them."

"Why not?" Mildred asked sharply.

"Baroness Katerina is warm and kind. Not all the people there are so," Alysa said.

Papa Bear shrugged. "They've got a reputation for driving a hard bargain, that's for sure."

"You have a good idea about the slavers' movements in these parts?" Ryan asked, as Mama Bear got up to vanish into the kitchen again.

"Middlin'," Papa Bear said. "Like I said, we get a fair number of visitors. We get a pretty good idea of who goes where and does what around here."

Ryan saw Alysa giving him a pointed look. He wasn't

sure if she wanted—or wanted him—to ask if they knew anything specifically about Milya or not.

He just nodded. Their hosts didn't need to know the specific import of their mission. The slavers might well reckon on the baron sending somebody to try to fetch his girl back. It wouldn't help to have them make Ryan's bunch as the people who were doing that.

He heard Doc muttering over the brief lull as everybody gave their attention back to eating. He couldn't quite make out the words, though the man sat just three feet away from him. He knew what he was saying, though: Emily, Rachel, Jolyon. The names of his wife, their daughter and their infant son, from whom he'd been snatched toward the end of the nineteenth century.

A brilliant man, well-educated by the standards of an earlier time, vastly more learned than people today, what Theophilus Algernon Tanner was not, was old. In absolute terms, of course, he was beyond ancient—well upward of two centuries. In terms of the time he'd actually lived, he was, at most, middle-aged. Yet his experiences had aged him beyond his lived-in years, body and mind. And though he could well be the smartest of all of them, with quick wits and vast knowledge that had saved everybody's lives a dozen times over, in times of stress or fatigue he could lapse into mental vagueness as his mind slipped its tether and wandered down the pathways of his long-lost past.

This night, with a double burden of fatigue and the post-adrenaline letdown that followed deadly combat, was clearly one of those times.

Well, Ryan thought, mebbe he won't need to be sharp. Mebbe we'll get the good and safe night's sleep we paid for.

Mama Bear emerged from the kitchen on a wave of

steamy air that this time smelled of cinnamon. She carried a big green glass bowl filled with some lumpy pale substance triumphantly held up before her.

"And now, for our special visitors, a special treat!" she exclaimed.

Ryan noticed that despite her ceaseless smiling and giddy magpie chatter, she never showed her teeth. Nor had he seen her husband's. That fact passed quickly from his awareness, leaving small impression; most people had bad teeth. Some were shy about the fact, for whatever reason.

The stout woman plunked the bowl on the table between Jak and Doc. Jak's head jerked up from where he was assiduously trying to clean the last possible dribs and morsels of food from his plate without licking it—something Krysty had sternly warned him not to do in public. He frowned, his ruby eyes looking momentarily distant.

"My special bread pudding for dessert!" Mama Bear warbled.

As she began to ladle out portions, Doc's head snapped up. He looked wildly around, blinking his pale blue eyes. Past him, Ryan saw Alysa go stiff, as if in outrage. Then she looked at Jak, who nodded once, crisply.

A few heartbeats later, Ryan felt Mildred squeeze his hand.

He nodded. Message received.

RICKY MORALES'S SKULL felt as if its insides were anvils, and half a dozen 'smiths were pounding out glowing-hot iron ingots on it. He realized he was awake by the gurgling of nausea in his belly and the peculiar taste like copper in his mouth.

His eyes seemed gummed shut.

Just before he forced them wide open, he heard a strange voice say, "Can we eat this one, Pa?"

Ricky froze. The voice was strange, so slurred he could barely understand it.

I'm dreaming, he told himself without much conviction.

"Nope." His hope that it was a dream died. *That* voice he knew: there was no mistaking Papa Bear's subterranean growl.

"But he's plump and juicy!"

"He's young and strong. He can work. Plus he's got a purty mouth and kind of an apple butt. That might bring double jack when One-Eyed Willy and his bunch come by this morning."

The answer was an inarticulate growl. It came with a gust of breath that almost made Ricky betray the fact he was awake by gagging. It was like the stink of a big predator's mouth, full of teeth with shreds of rotting meat stuck between.

Santa María, Madre de Dios, he thought, what is happening to us?

Chapter Fifteen

J.B. stood in the middle of the road located between the steep banks of a natural cut that led down the gray karst cliffs of the Cumberland Plateau to the Nashville Basin of what had been Tennessee. A cheroot like the ones Rance Weeden smoked was stuck in his mouth, and a smile spread out to either side of it.

Down that narrow gulch, straight toward J.B., came a pair of Trader's wags, throwing up bow waves of dust, rolling as if seven devils were on their trail.

As indeed they were. The Seven Devils Motorcycle Club was a long-established coldheart gang originally operating out of the ruins of Nashville. The Seven Devils, so J.B. had heard tell, were nominally ethnic Chinese. Like most such groups they had been diluted considerably since the Megacull. Now they were made up of all kinds of people, largely of Asian descent but some of everybody. The bosses, though, tended to be the ones with the most claims on Chinese heritage.

This was information J.B. remembered only because he'd heard it recently, as part of his mission briefing. It wasn't the sort of stuff he cared about enough to retain.

Trader had sent a fast cargo and a blaster wag Toyota Tacoma to snatch some prize item of scavvy. It was a raid, pure and simple: high-reward, high-risk. Because the important fact about the Seven Devils club was that it was extremely proprietary about its turf, and everything above, on, or beneath it. The odds were good, or bad, that they'd be spotted and perhaps be zeroed out.

That was why only volunteers went along, led by one of Trader's most able, and daring, lieutenants.

The cargo wag, a Dodge panel truck, slewed and skidded to a halt with its front bumper less than a yard from the slight, skinny kid standing in the middle of the road. The driver, a dark-skinned woman named Joanie, gaped at him as if he'd landed from a flying saucer right before her wide eyes.

An instant later the blaster wag crunched and squealed to a stop next to it, its right side scraping bushes. A head with a long topknot sprouting from it like a horse's tail appeared over the roll bar at the back of the cab.

"What the nuking fuck?" Abe demanded. "Why are you standing in our way, you feeb? You could of got run over."

"But I didn't," J.B. said, not trying not to smirk.

Joanie stuck her head out the window. "Move!" she shouted. "We gotta go! They're right on our asses!"

"I reckoned."

"Where's the rest of your bunch?" Abe demanded. His eyes practically popped from his weather-beaten, lushly mustached face as he scanned the weeds to either side for signs of the promised blocking force.

"Sent 'em home."

"You did *what?*"

"You dark-dusted spawn of a gutter slut and a stickie, what in the name of glowing nuke shit made you do a triple-stupe thing like that? You're gonna get us all chilled."

"Nope."

"Here they come, boss," shouted the gunner from behind Abe, facing backward over the tailgate with the butt of an M-240 machine gun mounted on a pedestal bolted to the bed of the truck. It was a 7.62 mm general-purpose machine gun like the M-60, made by FN in old Belgium. To J.B.'s critical mind it was a much superior weapon to the M-60 made in America back in the day.

"Fuck!" Abe shouted. "We gotta roll. Move out the way. Better yet—Joanie, run this feeb the fuck over!"

"Got it boss," the short-haired woman said.

Even as she ducked her kerchief-wrapped head back inside the cab and reached for the steering-column-mounted shifter to run over J.B., a similar blaster wag came rolling out of the cut not fifty yards behind. It was full of men and women dressed in black, most sporting topknots like Abe's, yelling like mating cats and brandishing an assortment of blasters and cutting weapons.

And right behind them, dust suddenly boiled from both sides of the cut, like curtains drawn across the road.

Everybody turned to look—and turned to stone. Seeing something odd in her wing mirror, Joanie stuck her head out the window. Abe's topknot whipped out to the side. The Devils' wag actually panic-braked to a dead halt, slewing fifteen degrees to its left.

A rippling crackle split the afternoon air. A blast wave rolling out of the gully rocked the Seven Devils wag forward on its suspension, then washed forward to whip Abe's topknot from his shoulder where it had only just settled. The rolling overpressure hit J.B.'s face like a giant blowing on him.

All hell broke loose behind the coldheart vehicle. Boiling clouds of gray dust completely obscured the passage from the height. Chunks of limestone started to fall back into the cloud from high above.

"Sent my bunch home," J.B. called, taking the cheroot from his mouth, "because I reckoned I didn't need 'em. If your gunner knows his job, that is."

"Light 'em up!" Abe yelled.

The Tacoma rocked forward again as the M-240 cut loose. The 7.62 mm weapon was a powerful beast, though nothing to compare with the lordly .50-caliber Browning M-2. Ma Deuce was J.B.'s personal favorite, and along with everything else he was eternally grateful to Trader—and Rance and Ace—for allowing him the opportunity to get hands-on and work with some for the first time in his young life.

But it was enough to do the job on a target as soft-skinned as a mere pick-'em-up truck. To say nothing of the occupants. The horizontal sleet of 150-grain full-metal-jacketed slugs poked right through the grille and the radiator, sending up a cloud of white steam, and were still moving plenty fast enough to bust the engine block to shit.

They ripped through the faded blue cab of the Dodge Ram, taking no more notice of the bodies of the driver and the Devil riding shotgun than they had of the steam they had passed through to get them. The eight or ten coldhearts packed improbably tight in the truck bed around their own pintle-mounted M-60 danced as if somebody'd tossed a hornet's nest in with them.

Briefly. Gas from a ruptured fuel line, or the tank itself, blossomed into yellow flame that enveloped the whole wag.

A few bailed out. Only one got caught in the fire-flare, and that one had sense enough to roll in the dirt and douse the flames on his black shirt and loose trousers.

Meaning that that coldheart lived a heartbeat or maybe two longer than his or her companions who'd jumped, because Abe's machine gunner enthusiastically pumped bullet sprays left and right of the blazing wag.

Joanie turned back to look at J.B. from her window. If her dark eyes had been wide before, when they saw J.B. standing right in the way of a few tons of hurtling metal death, now they were like saucers.

"Booby?" she asked.

"You got it," he said, stuffing his smoke back between his lips.

Abe's head snapped back and forth several times between the burning wreck and the now-blocked road down from the Cumberland Plateau becoming visible behind it as some of the dust settled. J.B. laughed. It was funny to watch.

"Trader let you walk away with enough plas-ex to blow up the whole nuking patrol?" Abe demanded. "We must've had, like, twenty bikes behind us."

"Oh, dark night, no," J.B. said around the cigar. He didn't like the taste of the long, skinny black smokes, truth to tell. But they looked cool when Rance smoked them. He did like *that*.

"But I did sweet-talk Ace into letting me have a few blocks of C-4 plus detonaters."

He could see Abe's shoulders rise as he sucked in a deep breath.

His lips pooched out under his mustache as he let loose a long, gusty sigh. "You're *that* crazy, kid," he said, "but you're really that good."

J.B. laughed. "Yeah. Get the goods?"

"Yeah." Abe's gyros were still so tumbled by the unexpected break of recent events he didn't even take offense at being grilled by the youth.

"Then what're we waiting for? Give me a lift and let's roll."

"Now, YOU GET away from there, Bunky Boy," Ricky heard Mama Bear said in tones of stern reproof. "You done heard your papa."

"Yessum, Aunt Mama."

The hot, wet, stench-laden breath went away. With all his might Ricky willed one eye to open just a crack, the one away from the voices of Mama and Papa Bear.

He saw a room, dark but for starlight pouring in a window half-covered by frost, and a spill of mustard-colored gleam from a fish-oil lantern burning through the open door that led to the kitchen. That was enough for him to make out several beds with still, blanket-covered forms in them. He recognized the room as the large dorm-style one in its own annex that they'd been shown before dinner. He had no memory of getting there.

Shapes moved between the beds. Still mentally fogged for some reason, Ricky couldn't quite make out how many there were in the darkness. *Several*. There seemed something…not right about them.

"We save the women, too. Got that, you little simps?"

"Now, Papa Bear," Mama Bear said. "You got no call being mean to our young'uns."

"The blonde and redhead are beautiful. They'll fetch double-high prices for that. The black one's pretty enough, sturdy and can work."

A short, stooped shape moved in between Ricky and the next bed. From the long white hair on the rolled-up frock coat that served as a pillow, Ricky saw that its occupant was Doc. Bracing overlong arms on the plank floor, the figure leaned a muzzlelike face in close and sniffed at the upturned right ear.

Then it swiveled its head to stare back at Ricky with a horrible parody of a human face, one drawn out into something more like a dog's snout that grinned at him with horrible sharpened teeth.

Ricky steeled himself not to move or cry out. This can't be happening! he thought.

The air in the room was almost unbearably thick with the stench of filth, stale piss, sweat and decay.

"Well, who can we eat, Pa?" asked another horribly slurred voice from Ricky's left.

He opened that eye by less than the length of the lashes. Another figure stood there, this one tall and gangly, a skeletal figure loosely hung with tattered, partially patched overalls with one shoulder-strap dangling before a sunken, flannel-clad chest. The face seemed oddly asymmetrical, one eye markedly lower than the other, and smaller, as well. The mouth was a loose-lipped, lopsided gape—also full of pointy teeth.

Ricky realized what had happened. They'd all been drugged, and now they were helpless in the hands of a clan of inbreds. Cannie inbreds.

"Eat the albino and the oldie," Papa Bear directed.

"Aww, Pa," said a third misshapen son from the far side of the bed to Ricky's left. Where, he now saw from another head of white hair, Jak lay with red eyes closed and mouth hanging open. A trickle of drool ran down onto the stained covering of his straw-tick mattress.

The inbred next to Jak's bed was like a shorter version of his father—almost as wide as he was tall, with a hugely oversize forehead and almost invisible lower jaw. His upper jaw showed plenty of filed teeth, though.

"Don't wanna eat no taint meat," the fat inbred whined.

"And the oldie's stringy," complained the doglike son on Ricky's other side.

"Don't whine, now, boys," Mama Bear said from the

foot of Ricky's bed. "Slavers'll bring some nice tasty culls for us. You'll see."

"Whabbout the one-eye?" asked the gaunt one.

"He's a nice, strong one," Mama Bear said. "And so handsome. Got a lot of work in him, I bet."

Standing by the door to the main house, Papa Bear scratched his chin through his beard. "But a fighter. You can tell just to look at him. Mebbe more trouble than he's worth. Lemme calculate."

He emitted a gravelly chuckle. "Funny how they all fell for the doped dessert trick. Even the tough ones allus go for that."

Just in time Ricky stopped himself from groaning aloud. He could hardly believe that he and his companions would be brought to an end by this tribe of inbred half-wits.

He steeled himself for what he knew now he would have to do. There was no hope he could save himself, much less his drugged-out friends. But dying fighting was preferable to whatever they wound up doing to him.

"You're a genius, Pa," a fourth son said, reaching an inhumanly long hand down to stroke the unconscious Krysty's hair almost shyly. Like the first inbred Ricky had seen, this one was small, scarcely larger than a ten-year-old norm, and with long arms and semi-quadrupedal posture, seemingly more animal than man.

He looked over at his father. His face showed a less pronounced snout than his brother's.

"Can we play with the women first, Pa? Please?"

Papa Bear frowned. "Slavers don't like paying for spoiled merch, Leon."

"Aww, come on," Lee whined. "We never have any fun."

"Let the boys enjoy themselves, Papa Bear," Mama

Bear said. "What the slavers don't know won't hurt them."

"Well," Papa Bear growled. "Not the blonde. She's prolly a virgin. They'll pay triple for that."

"Yay!" the fat son flapped blubbery hands together and teetered in a circle in place for joy. "Dibs on the redhead bitch!"

"Your fat ass, Chad," Lee hissed.

"Don't fight, now, boys," Mama Bear said with an indulgent chuckle. "Plenty to go around—and meat, too. You'll see. As for me—"

Ricky's belly turned over and his scrotum shrank as she looked down at him. He reflected briefly just how little he'd gotten to *use* that latter assembly in his too-brief life.

"—I reckon your pa won't mind too much if I play some with this chubby little one."

She leaned down toward him, her massive breasts making oceanic movements beneath her heavy sweater.

"He's so sweet," she said as her horrible round face came close to his. "I could just take a big ol' bite out of him. In fact—"

Just inches from his cheek, she opened her mouth wide. Her teeth, too, were filed wicked-sharp.

Ricky couldn't hold his terror in any more. He opened his mouth to scream.

A strange, wet, ripping sound stopped him.

Mama Bear's pig eyes had gone circular. Her mouth opened farther, but it did so obviously out of shocked surprise.

Ricky turned his face up, opened his eyes wide and saw six inches of narrow red steel sticking at an angle out of the right side of Mama Bear's thick neck. On the other side, his own right, he saw a slim glinting blade going in.

Astonished as he was, he knew weapons, and that was Doc's sword, which meant—

Mama Bear screamed. Blood sprayed Ricky's face. As the blade slid back out of her neck with a squelching sound, she threw her fat hands to her throat and tottered backward, blood spurting from both sides and from her wide-open fanged mouth.

"You old bastard!" shrieked the inbred to Ricky's right. "You chilled my ma!"

He reared back to lunge at Doc, who had leaned out of bed to stab Mama Bear with his left hand and was still in a vulnerable position.

Ricky launched himself onto the stooped back. Squealing with rage, the inbred tried to turn his muzzle to snap at Ricky's face. To save himself, Ricky, his arms around the narrow chest, had to press his face into the back on the creature's neck.

This close, the smell of corruption acted almost like a mix of tear gas and nausea gas.

Ricky puked down the inbred's right arm as the kid clawed and waled on him with his overlong hands. He got his legs locked around the inbred's waist and stuck his right arm, clotted and sopping with his own vomit, around the horror's throat. Fortunately the attenuation of the face made it fairly easy to do so without getting bitten.

Ricky reached out his left hand to grab his right wrist and squeezed, hoping to choke the raging inbred to unconsciousness before talons or fists did serious damage to his shoulders and back.

Around him the dark room erupted into furious action.

The cannie threw himself on his back on top of Ricky. Though he didn't weigh much, his unexpected maneuver knocked the air out of Ricky.

He felt his grip slacken. The inbred squealed in vindictive glee. It began to twist around to bite a chunk from Ricky's unguarded face.

Chapter Sixteen

Ryan's last instructions to his friends before they lay down and feigned unconsciousness—alongside Ricky and their guide, Alysa, who hadn't understood the warning passed from Jak not to trust the pudding—had been to wait for his word or move before flashing to action.

Now he was glad Doc had disobeyed and kicked off the party on his own.

By covert sight, sound and, regrettably, smell, Ryan had worked out there were at least eight of the cannies in the room, as the clan worked its way around scoping out what was apparently the latest in a long line of intended victims. With Papa and Mama Bear came three of the weird doglike figures; one short, fat one; a tall, gawky one; a more or less middle-size one. It was clear to Ryan that along with long-term inbreeding the Bear clan carried some kind of bizarre mutie taint.

They all seemed to like to smell their victims. Ryan had been forced to grit his teeth and endure the crawling of his skin as one of the near-quadrupedal cannies bent a distorted, drawn-out face down to sniff the side of Krysty's seemingly sleeping face.

Ryan had taken the bed at the room's far end. He had Doc by his side, then the somnolent Ricky, and Jak. Then came Krysty and Mildred, who had taken those beds to buffer Alysa from the menfolk. She had mentioned her discomfort in close proximity to males in situations like this.

When Doc had stabbed Mama Bear through the neck, the normal-size cannie had been bending over Ryan. Up close, he didn't look like a norm. His jaws were a fairly standard size and shape, although his teeth were filed pointy, too. But he had barely any visible chin, and a giant bulge of forehead made him look as if he had a double-size brain, which Ryan doubted he had.

As the cannie turned his face away to see his mother staggering, spurting blood and screeching, screaming, Ryan came to life. He whipped out the panga he had under the scratchy wool blanket pile behind his back and with a long over-body stroke planted the wide, heavy blade in the side of the inbred's neck, right along the line of such lower jaw as the inbred could boast.

For all the full-body strength of the blow, the panga didn't sever the neck. It may have broken the bone. It certainly cut the carotid artery. Part of the black arterial fan that jetted out caught Ryan's cheek.

The cannie fell.

At the next bed Ricky fell off the back of the inbred he'd been wrestling and landed heavily on the floor. The creature spun to bite him. Unfolding off his own bed, Doc whipped out a long leg to catch the creature in the ribs with the toe of one of his cracked knee boots and send it sprawling and mewling against Ricky's bed.

Slow in reacting to the sudden ambush, Papa Bear lumbered from the doorway to Alysa's bed, bellowing, "I'll save the virgin! Chill the rest!"

"Oh, no you don't!" Mildred yelled. She bolted from her bed. With an agility that belied her stocky build, she did a somersault over the sleeping girl, barely brushing her. She came down on the far side of the bed. With

that to brace her muscular buttocks, she fired both
booted feet into the onrushing fat man's belly with all
the strength of her thigh muscles.

Caught by complete surprise again, the immense cannie chieftain fell back against the wall with a crash. His
head hit the logs behind him with a sound like an ax
splitting wood.

As Doc loomed over the cannie he'd kicked off Ricky,
Mama Bear staggered toward him. One plump hand
clutched her spurting throat. The other, dripping her
own gore, reached out toward Doc.

"I won't let you hurt my baby, you oldie bastard!"

His response was to haul up his burly LeMat revolver
with his left hand. With the muzzle of the long .44 barrel pressed almost to the spot between her mad, close-
set eyes, he touched off the shorter, wider shotgun tube
fixed beneath.

Ryan actually saw the charge of Number 4 buckshot
begin to implode her fat face like a screaming moon.
Then the muzzle-flame washed over it in a sizzle of
crisped fat and burned hair, and she collapsed.

Ryan had also told his party to hold off using blasters
unless absolutely necessary, to avoid hitting each other if
it came to a fight in close quarters. He reckoned Doc had.

The one-eyed man stood alone by the stove at the end
of the long room, which was still radiating heat despite
showing only a red glow of embers through the grate.
He saw Ricky dive under his own bed. The skinny cannie Doc had given the boot to stirred and swiped at him
with long arms.

Ricky came up on his knees, whirling his upper body
with crazy ferocity. The buttplate of his DeLisle longblaster cracked under the cannie's canine jaw in an up-

ward stroke. The creature's head snapped around. A long thread of bloody saliva streamed away from it.

In the gloom all was chaos. Ryan moved forward to join the fight. As he did, he saw the cannie Ricky had knocked down jump up again to all fours with considerable energy. Ricky, for his part, was vulnerable; he'd overbalanced and fallen against his bed. He was visibly still somewhat under the effects of the knockout drops Mama Bear had dosed their desserts with.

Before Ryan could arrive, Doc stepped into a fencer's lunge and thrust the tip of his swordstick right behind the crouching cannie's left forearm. The creature shuddered and went down as if its bones had dissolved.

Across the room the third doglike inbred had leaped up on the bed behind Mildred, straddling the still-thoroughly knocked-out Alysa. Ryan shouted a warning.

Apparently sensing her danger, Mildred spun clockwise. She led with her right elbow, which caught the cannie in the face and knocked him off the bed.

With a roar, Papa Bear launched himself off the floor toward Mildred with his great arms outspread and his mouth wide open to display his own shocking shark teeth. Like his namesake, he showed agility that belied his bulk.

Krysty, standing between her bed and the one Mildred had feigned sleep in, pushed out her snubby Smith & Wesson 640 with both hands and squeezed three quick shots into the charging behemoth's belly. His bellowing went up an octave as he clutched his violated paunch and fell down, rolling side to side and drumming the floorboards with the heels of his taped-together boots.

Mildred kicked him in the head to keep him down.

The fat inbred son grabbed Krysty from behind in

a bear hug. He lifted her off the floor with her arms trapped at her sides.

"Got you!" he screeched in a high voice. "Fuck you! Chill you, bitch!"

Ryan didn't even try to draw his SIG-Sauer. He had Jak fighting the tall gawky cannie in the way, as well as Doc. Plus, there was no way of knowing whether Ricky might pop into his line of fire—or if the inbred might push Krysty in front of a bullet. He vaulted Doc's bed.

Krysty's hair suddenly swung back to clutch the cannie's face like an octopus with a thousand scarlet tentacles.

The inbred screamed in a voice gone eunuchoidally shrill. "Mutie, mutie monster!"

As Ryan came down, Krysty smashed the back of her head into the inbred's face. His grip slackened. She flung her arms up, breaking his grip, and whirled away from him.

Ricky laid his carbine across his bed and fired. With its built-in suppressor and firing a subsonic round from a sealed breech, the DeLisle made no sound Ryan could hear in the tumult. But the huge fat cannie stiffened and grabbed over his shoulders with his hands as the .45-caliber slug took him right between the blades.

From between him and Krysty came a flash. The noise her snub-nosed .38 made was definitely audible.

The cannie fell.

Jak was slashing at the beanpole cannie with both a trench knife and a butterfly knife. Ryan vaulted Ricky's bed, right past the kid. He hoped the youth had more sense than he was showing, and wouldn't shoot again with Ryan in the way. But the need to help Krysty filled Ryan with irresistible fury.

The last dog-cannie sprang for Ryan's face. He met it

with a savage overhand sweep of his panga. The blade crunched into the juncture of the inbred's neck and left shoulder.

The cannie fell, squealing and snapping his jaws. Ryan kicked the lower jaw, then crushed the cannie's throat with a vindictive twist of his boot heel.

The last inbred was thrashing around on the floor squalling like an angry catamount and trying to stuff his guts back into his narrow belly. The entrails glistened greasily in the faint light.

With a shock, Ryan realized he couldn't see Krysty. "Krysty!" he shouted.

She popped up from behind her own bed as briskly as a prairie dog, as if the heavy pack now strapped on her back weighed nothing.

"I'm fine, lover!" she called back. "Grab your stuff and let's power out of here!"

"Ace on the line," he said. "Jak, chill that cannie bastard so he doesn't trip anybody on his fireblasted intestines. Anyway his screeching is getting on my nerves!"

The group recovered the gear they had stashed beneath their beds and started out of the annex, through the kitchen and out through the main room where they'd eaten dinner. Jak led off, followed closely by Doc, with both LeMat and swordstick at the ready. Next, Ricky helped Krysty mostly carry Alysa. The ice-blonde Stormbreak sec woman was showing signs of returning to life, rolling her head and moaning, but her legs still had the consistency of boiled noodles and she wasn't actually responsive. After them came Mildred, looking more pissed off at the world than usual. Ryan brought up the rear.

He'd barely gone through the door into the kitchen, which was still hot and steamy from Mama Bear's cooking dinner and washing the dishes after, when he was tackled from behind.

He slammed into a pushcart of some sort that held a stand with an ominous assortment of big knives. It also held the fish-oil lantern.

It promptly fell on the floor, which was either ceramic tile or stone, and shattered. Blue and orange flames raced across the floor and enveloped Ryan's right arm.

They spared his hand for the moment, and that still held his panga.

He looked back. Papa Bear had seized his lower legs from behind. Now he glared nuke-hot hatred from eyes that seemed to burn bluer than the oil spill from a mask-of-gore face.

"Fucker!" he slurred. "Take you...t'hell wif me!"

Ryan noticed some gaps in his sawtooth snarl that hadn't been there before. But apparently Mildred's stomping hadn't done any more permanent damage than dental.

Feeling the hair on his hand crisp and the fire bite, Ryan swung his flaming arm frantically backward. The broad blade of the panga bit into the side of Papa Bear's great head.

The cannie collapsed to the floor with a thunk. From the door to the main room, Mildred and Krysty, still supporting Alysa's dead weight, screamed contradictory advice. Mildred called for Ryan to roll out the flames. Krysty just shouted at him to run.

The kitchen was full of heavy wood fixtures, and the place was catching fire fast. So was the right half of Papa Bear's now-limp bulk. Spurred by the pain in his burning arm, Ryan yanked his panga from the side of the cannie patriarch's skull and eeled out from under him.

"Go!" he shouted as he got both hands beneath him and launched himself into a sprint for the door.

"Not very bright, Ryan," Mildred lectured as she examined his right arm by the light of the now-blazing house.

They stood out in the yard formed by the clearing surrounding the stone-and-timber structure. By its inferno glare they could also see that a pair of ruts suggesting a road used by wheeled traffic ran past it, from dark woods to more dark woods. They had approached blind from a different angle and never spotted the road.

Mildred had cut off Ryan's right sleeve, which had mostly burned off anyway. Now she was cleaning his arm with a nominally clean cloth from her backpack that had been well rubbed in snow and clucking like a disapproving mother hen.

"When you're on fire," she said, "you put the fire out first." She scrubbed at some grit embedded in a raw patch with what Ryan was double-sure was more vigor than necessary.

"Just reckoned the giant crazed cannie looking to gnaw his way up my legs'd chill me 'fore a burning sleeve did," he said. "Anyway, it's only skin."

She actually growled. He grinned, knowing as well as she did the desirability of keeping one's hide intact and the dangers of infection.

But the fact was, he already knew the burns, while painful, weren't serious. A cleanup, some of Mildred's homemade salve and some clean bandages would keep infection at bay.

The rest of the group stood in the yard before the front door, which gaped open to shoot forth yellow flames. Shafts of fire were starting to lick up through the roof.

"Whole thing's coming down soon," Krysty observed. She sounded a trifle wistful. Ryan wasn't sure whether her essentially gentle heart felt bad for the need to chill the whole clan of awful inbred cannies—or if she was mourning the loss of a warm, soft, relatively safe place to pass the remainder of the icy Northeastern night.

Well, we knew that last was a no-go when Jak sniffed something in the pudding, Ryan thought. He grunted as Mildred dug a chunk of grit from an open burn.

Alysa had come back to her senses enough to get to her feet and even shake off a helping hand from Ricky. The youth was always eager to help out a pretty girl, Ryan noticed with amusement. Not that there was anything wrong with that. So long as he didn't let it get in the way.

Krysty moved in close to their guide, as if accidentally. Alysa didn't move away.

Ricky looked around as if just becoming aware of the general situation. His pal, Jak, was patrolling the woods around the burning house for possible dangers drawn by the blaze beacon. Doc squatted with his long, stilt-like legs to one side, propped on his swordstick, which once more had the sword concealed in it. He seemed to be staring into the fire moodily.

"So, what just happened?" Ricky demanded.

"The usual," Mildred muttered. She had finished cleaning Ryan's burns and was surveying them with frowning clinical thoroughness. "Bunch of crazy inbred cannibals tried to eat us. We escaped. They died. Just another day in the Deathlands."

"Okay," Ricky said, in a tone of voice that made it clear it wasn't. "So how did that happen? I mean, specifically, how did Alysa and I wind up sound asleep, while everybody else was apparently wide-awake?"

"Jak smelled something funny," Krysty said "That's

why he squeezed your knee when Mama Bear brought out the bread pudding."

Mildred began to daub healing salve on Ryan's arm from a clay pot with a carved-cork stopper. It was a pungent herbal mix; despite Mildred's mistrust for the general state of modern healing, it was a common enough recipe because it worked to diminish the chance of infection. It also did diminish the pain—though it hurt like hell when it was going on.

"What did you think he was doing?" Mildred asked without looking up.

Ricky's olive face flushed red to the tips of his ears.

"Good thing I nudged Krysty to make double-sure she got the message," Ryan said.

"So that was a warning?" asked Ricky, finding his voice.

"Yeah," Ryan said.

"We pass along nonverbal signals when one of us spots something we don't like," Mildred said. "Pretty much anything serves to spread the alert. Then Jak nodded a couple times toward the pudding bowl. Didn't you see? The rest of us worked it out."

"Except Alysa," Krysty said. She put an arm out to steady the ice-blonde young woman when she swayed slightly. She still didn't seem to have returned mentally to the here and now. "She had no way of knowing."

"You know who else is new and had no way of knowing about your super-secret danger signal? *Me! I'm* new. Remember?"

"You didn't figure it out on your own?" Ryan said as Mildred began to wind gauze on top of the stinging, minty-smelling ointment. "You thought mebbe Jak had gotten fonder of you than you knew? Haven't you been with us long enough to figure some things out?"

"Ryan," Krysty said sternly. Then, more gently to the outraged boy, "We're sorry. In the stress of the moment we just never stopped to think we hadn't told you about that."

"Welcome to the learning curve, kid," Mildred told him.

He pressed his lips together so hard they disappeared. His cheeks seemed to swell as with the internal pressure of his outrage. But his anger quickly passed and he folded his arms and walked a few steps off by himself.

Alysa had come awake. Now Krysty had her crimson head next to the almost-white one and was quietly and calmly filling her in.

The Stormbreak sec woman frowned at one point. Krysty touched her arm and spoke more urgently. The frown smoothed away—mostly. Ryan reckoned they'd come to the part of the story where she blamed herself for missing the signal she had no reason to expect or recognize, letting herself get knocked out and rendered unable to carry out a key part of her mission.

Alysa shook her head as if puzzled.

"We hear…stories," she said, speaking haltingly. "Tales of a cabin in the woods, where wayfarers are welcomed with open arms—and come to terrible ends."

She drew in a deep and shuddering breath.

"They say it changes locations, and is never seen in the same place twice, which is why the occupants were never stopped."

"Not likely," Mildred muttered, tying off the end of the wrap. It ran pretty much from Ryan's wrist to midbiceps. Fortunately his elbow hadn't gotten too badly scorched, so she was able to leave it clear and thus freer to move. She straightened. "More likely nobody ever got out alive once the cannies got them in their clutches."

"Until today," Krysty said.

"Yeah," Ryan said as a section of the now fully involved roof caved in with a negative shower of red sparks. "Well, it's not going much of anywhere now. Except down in a heap of ashes in another couple minutes, max."

In the bottom of the fire-belching front doorway, a shadow appeared. Like a mobile mountain of char and hard-baked core, it actually emerged into the frigid night air.

One terrible eye stared from the round black-and-red mask of Papa Bear's face. The shriveled remnants of beard and hair wreathed his partly melted face in smoke like wisps of morning fog.

"Chill you," he growled in a voice compounded of rage and agony, both intolerable, as he dragged his tremendous bulk forward on fingerless stumps of arms. "Chill...you...*all!*"

A shattering noise overwhelmed even the roar of the flames. A flash came from Ryan's left.

That single staring eye exploded. Papa Bear's head jerked back.

Krysty's .38 handblaster exploded again. The second bullet caught the cannie at the bridge of his nose.

The brain inside the brutally burned face destroyed, the head fell forward, lifeless.

"Nice group, Krysty," Mildred said, reholstering her own half-drawn revolver.

"Why waste a cartridge?" Ryan asked. "He'd never have reached us. Even if any of us was triple-stupe enough to stand here and wait for him."

Krysty smiled at him as she cracked open the cylinder of her short-barreled Smith & Wesson.

"Never hurts to make sure," she said, pulling out the

two empties, dumping them in a pocket and reloading the chambers. "You told me so yourself. If I happen to put him out of his misery in the process, is it so wrong?"

Ryan growled.

"You know what he intended to subject us to," Mildred said. "Yet you did him that favor."

Krysty shrugged. "You'd have done the same if I hadn't beaten you to it."

Mildred scowled even more thunderously. "Yeah."

"You're a better person than me, Krysty," Ryan said huskily. "Hope it doesn't get you chilled."

She went to him, slid her arm around his waist and turned her face up to kiss his stubbled cheek.

"You just summed up perfectly why we need each other, lover," she said.

The rest of the roof caved in with a crackle and a voiceless roar. She put her head on his shoulder.

"There go our nice, warm beds."

He slipped his un-seared arm around her waist.

"Well, at least we got a nice fire to keep us warm till morning," he said.

Chapter Seventeen

"J. B. Dix," a voice said from the warm darkness ahead of him. The convoy was parked among low rolling hills.

J.B. was returning to the area where the wrenches hung out, down closer to the Ohio in a stand of black walnut and river birch trees. He was bone tired and ass dragging. He'd worked doing mechanical repairs and maintenance all day, then helped Ace strip, inspect and clean the armament on War Wag Two that evening. He loved that part of it, but a double shift was a double shift. Crickets were trilling. A night bird let out weird hoots at random individuals from down by the slow-rolling water, whose smell reached back here to join that of dark rich soil and trees.

"Yeah, Rance," he said in a leaden voice. "What is it? Don't tell me that damned Chrysler's gearbox is breaking down again. I got to sleep or I won't be worth a toad run over by War Wag One."

The convoy had swung northeast. It had stopped for a couple days—at least—to do business at Dombrowski's End, the major trading post in this part of the Ohio River Valley. It lay a few miles upstream of the ruins of Evansville. The town had taken a two-megaton nuke pretty much dead center, for no reason anybody nowadays could guess at but sheer meanness, which J.B. knew was the go-to answer as to why the old-days folk did much of anything. More than likely, though, the missile had been a stray.

"I want to talk to you," Rance said.

J.B. thought it odd to hear such unaccustomed softness in her usually brash and brassy voice.

"All right," he said.

The rad levels in Evansville had only died back to even marginally survivable levels the last ten years or so, which meant it was a mother lode for scavvies willing to brave the numerous still-lethal hot pockets and deposits of heavy metals. Some of the hot heavy metals would chill you quick, like plutonium, others slow, like cesium. Neither would chill you in a way you liked worth a damn.

Dombrowski's End was where much of the plunder ended up. The Lin clan that owned it was triple-rich—barons in all but name of this stretch of fertile river valley. Who Dombrowski was J.B. didn't know or much care. He reckoned the place name was descriptive, instead of any flight of bullshit fancy.

It would have been a prime destination for Trader's unique wag train in any event. And it was, as he had learned from coworkers who had started to treat him not just with newfound respect but something tinged with awe for his skills and ice-cold resourcefulness. But it was a double-ace destination because of the Toyota plant that'd been there, leading to abundant availability of replacement parts.

"Go get yourself cleaned up," she said. He could see her now, with his glasses, as something more than a vague human-shaped blur in the early darkness. She stood with hands on hips and her short-haired head canted to one side, as if she was studying him. "Then we talk."

He nodded. He was clean by nature. Even somewhat fastidious, at least by Deathlands standards. He
wasn't afraid to get his hands dirty, and was proud as
any wrench or 'smith of the permanent grease stains on
his hands and under his kept-short nails. Neither was he
a picky eater—if he had been, he simply wouldn't have
made it as long as he had. But he had an orderly nature,
as befit the intricate nature of the work he loved most
to do. Excess dirt was disorderly. And it fucked up machines, especially blasters, which ran directly contrary
to his nature and inclination.

He went back to where he'd set out his bedroll on soil
fragrant and springy with leaf mold, and collected his
second set of underwear, a scrub brush, his towel and a
bar of harsh lye soap. Towel over his shoulder, he trooped
down to the river and bathed in a designated spot. There
was a pair of guards with longblasters nearby, keeping
watch—especially since stickies had been reported in
the area in recent weeks. The guards ignored his skinny
pale ass and he ignored them.

For most of his crew, the trading post, which was the
size of a substantial ville, provided much-needed R & R,
with some of the best gaudies in the Midwest. Meanwhile
Trader was paying primo prices for the meds that were also
in abundant supply in the fairly virgin ruin—and which
he would turn around and sell for a double-primo profit.

But there was little rest for Rance and her crew of
wrenches. Even though Trader had a whole truck con-
verted into a rolling machine shop, there was a limit to
the repairs or remanufacture or making from scrap they
could do on parts for his hard-driven wags. The ready
supply of wag parts—not just for Toyotas, though about
half Trader's cargo fleet were those—meant it was an

opportunity to turn the spit-and-baling-wire repairs into proper fixes. *Plus* the duties J.B. had taken on working as an armorer under Ace. And part of the scavvy up for sale were replacements and upgrades for weapons—even for the heavy blasters on his two big, armored war wags. So J.B. was extremely busy on the second job, as well.

He was thriving on it. He loved working with his hands—and his mind. He was having to learn all kinds of new stuff: electronics, communications, even optics. And he ate it up and hungered for more.

But it did take a toll on his slight frame, as durable as it was.

He was happy to be finally working as a weapon-smith—his destiny, as he'd always seen it from early days. J.B. knew a lot about his craft, but he was intelligent enough to know there was always more to learn. Ace was a good teacher, patient—more so than Rance, despite the fact that J.B. had announced himself as a potential rival from day one. But much as he enjoyed working with the weapons master, he hadn't asked to be transferred. He liked the wrench work too—more, now that he could scratch the itch to work with blasters pretty much every day.

But there was more to it, he realized. Rance Weeden was a hard boss but a fair one—a triple-good one, really—who, when he was honest with himself, taught him as much as Ace did. And she stood up for him. Not many had done that.

Bathed and dressed, he trudged back up to the wrenches' camp. He found Rance sitting on a rock on the outskirts, away from everybody.

She rose as he approached. "Come with me," she said.

He sighed. His body longed for sleep. He reckoned it would put him horizontal any minute now whether he wanted it to or not.

"Why?" he asked. "Because you're the boss?" That was a common answer of hers when he asked one more question than her patience abided.

But she shook her head. She wasn't wearing her customary do-rag. Her short brush of rust-colored hair looked softer somehow. As did her usually stern hazel eyes.

"No. Because I asked you to."

He caught himself before he could utter another dramatic sigh. He didn't care much for dramatics, least of all in himself. He liked to stay more in control.

Which was one reason, it struck him, he disliked dealing with other people. Because so often they put him in a position where he had to flash over into anger to survive. He never totally lost it—giving in to the fight/flight/freeze reflex was a stone guaranteed way to get chilled, as he had learned young and hard—but he still had to let the brakes go and let his rage drive him. Because berserk yet directed fury was the one way he'd found to stay alive when hard up against it.

"Sure, Rance," he said. "Anything you say."

She smiled at him. Instantly he became wary.

"Hold that thought," she said, and turned away.

She led him about fifty yards up into the hills, away from the Ohio's slow roll. A blanket lay on the ground in the middle of a little clearing among some scrub oak. Dark trees constrained the stars to a rough circle overhead.

She went to the blanket, stopped, then turned back to him.

With a shock he realized her shirt was open and that she wasn't wearing a bra beneath it.

"What…" he managed to say.

She came to him and put an arm on his shoulder.

"You got little knowledge of women," she said.

"That's not true! I—"

She kissed him. He stood there with his eyes half-closed, staring at her face in the light of stars and a crescent moon.

Then her tongue pressed between his lips and seemed to wedge his teeth apart. And was tangling his, hot and strong and urgent.

Her face seemed to soften and fill out before his amazed eyes. He grabbed her arms and kissed her back, his movements slow and languid.

He could feel the heat of her skin, smell the fragrance of her body, which she kept as clean as he did, for the same reasons.

Rance reached down and stroked him through the front of his trousers.

"Nice," she said, pulling her mouth back from his and squeezing his raging hard-on. "You're not all a runt, are you?"

His mind locked up. He couldn't find one thing to say.

Her strong, nimble fingers unfastened the buttons on his fly. She kissed him again as she reached inside the front of his boxers. Her fingers were cool on his erect manhood. Yet somehow they seemed to burn the sensitive skin.

He moaned as she ran her closed hand up and down his shaft. Then she removed her hand and stepped aside, kissing the tip of his nose. Then Rance stepped back and shed her shirt. Her nipples were pale; he could tell that even in the faint light. They were also hard and sticking out from her small breasts like the tips of little fingers.

She undid her own cargo pants and skinned them down her strong, smooth legs. He realized when she kicked out of them, held them up and folded them before setting them neatly down on the leaf mold, that she had been barefoot the whole time.

"You still have clothes on," she said reprovingly as she straightened again. She was wearing only dark panties now.

His usually reliable fingers betrayed him as he tried to fix that. He was fairly sure he popped off at least one shirt button. Then he lost his balance and fell on his rear while trying to take his pants off without taking off his boots first.

She laughed at him. It was a hearty laugh—she didn't laugh by half measures, any more than she did anything else. But he didn't feel put down by it.

Maybe it was because it was true what he'd always heard: a stiff dick had no morals. And he was hard, all right.

Rance nodded and stripped off her panties. She had a surprisingly small, soft-looking bush.

"Nice," she said. "Now shift over onto the blanket."

He did.

She stepped to stand astride him. He stared up at her in disbelief. He'd had only a couple of partners in the past, but he was always the one on top.

She knelt and folded onto his manhood, and J.B. thought Rance was hot and wet and tight and wonderful.

As they made love in the starlight, J.B. felt a stab of pain in his chest. His body went rigid. Rance didn't seem to notice. She just kept pumping her round rump up and down, sliding her smooth slick tightness up and down his rigid shaft.

The pain hit again. Worse. Like being shot. Or the way he imagined being shot would feel.

J.B. gasped. He was finding it hard to breathe.

He gripped her arms tight, but he couldn't hold on. He began to slide away from her into blackness.

"HE'S STARTING TO come out, Healer," Donal said.

Lindy Rao frowned at her assistant. His face, even darker than hers, looked concerned behind his gauze mask. His apron was dotted with drying blood, as she knew her's was.

She glanced down at the man she'd just operated on. Fortunately he hadn't lost enough blood to require a transfusion. She felt fatigue weighing her down. But also satisfaction. She loved her work and took pride in it.

"He should pull through fine now," she said, picking up a fresh needle strung with surgical thread from a tray. "He's strong. But we'll need to keep him under, and not just while I finish sewing him back up all the way. I don't want him straining the incisions any sooner than necessary."

"Right, Healer," Donal said. He reached for the chloroform.

He was an excellent assistant, and would make a fine healer himself someday. She felt mixed emotions regarding the fact that she would soon recommend to Baron Frost that he send the young black man away for advanced training. On the one hand, she was pleased and proud for Donal. On the other—she would miss him sorely.

Baron Ivan Frost and his wife were rarities: intelligent rulers, who *cared* for their people. They honestly seemed to regard the folk of Stormbreak as their family.

Rather than livestock.

"It seems a shame to patch them up only to send them out to get cut up or punctured again," Donal said.

"This one has seen his share of it before, by his scars," she said. "And, yes. That is the healer's curse. Yet, realistically, all we can ever do is stave off the inevitable. Even during the fabled time of plenty before skydark, people died eventually."

She shook her head. "And much as I hate it, I hope his friends are good at killing. As good as they seemed to be. Because poor Milya doesn't deserve what's happened to her. Nor do the baron and baroness. And should she not return—" Lindy shook her head "—I fear for what it may do to Lady Katerina. I'm frankly frightened by the way she looks lately. As if her physical condition is deteriorating along with her mental and emotional conditions."

Donal just nodded. Despite her concern, she smiled her approval. He showed the proper attitude for a healer: gentle concern, but no false soothing.

"I'm putting him back down deeper, Healer," he said.

"Good," she said, and came back to finish her repairs.

RANCE'S FACE HUNG smiling over J.B.'s. She held herself up with her hands braced on the blanket to either side of him.

He felt a vague recollection of pain. But the pleasure washed it out of him.

Her face was the most beautiful thing he'd ever seen: full, soft, feminine, yet strong, too. Her breasts swung back and forth, the nipples teasing across the skin of his belly.

It's just like a dream, he thought, feeling the urgency
bunch and gather itself within him like a big cat about
to spring.

But better.

And he wished it could last forever.

Chapter Eighteen

The liberated slaves stared at Ryan with a mixture of apprehension and cautious elation. He gazed back calmly.

The day was bright, though the sun wasn't warm enough to threaten the general snow cover that enveloped the now-silent woods, the clearing that surrounded the burned-out shell of the house and the rutted roadway. But icicles dripped from the eaves of the outbuildings, shed, barn and shitter, though their shake roofs showed some scorch marks from the previous night's burning.

By the house's stone back stoop, intact though partly burned, Alysa Korn washed her saber in the water from the hand pump.

Here and there, depressions in the snow were stained red, fading to pink toward the edges, in irregular patches. A couple still had bodies lying in them. Right where the road emerged from the brush, the leader of the party of four slavers lay on his back with arms outflung. His eyes stared from his bearded face at the cold blue sky.

"What about the wounded one?" asked the Stormbreaker woman.

"He croaked, too."

The slavers had led their party of a dozen captives, roped together in a shuffling, miserable coffle, down the road from the east and into the open with utter arrogant assurance. They were struck by surprise when they saw their objective burned to charred posts, heat-cracked stone wall-stubs and ashes.

Which was nothing to how surprised they were a moment later when the ambush sprang. They never had a chance.

Granted, the tail-end Charlie had been alert and fleet enough to escape the fire-sack formed by two longblasters aimed from good cover and aided by a quartet of handblasters. Alysa had been waiting on her blood bay, hidden in the brush not far from the road. She had taken him out.

Alysa shook water from the blade with a flick of her wrist and looked at Ryan in puzzlement. "Didn't we need at least the one alive for information?"

Ryan chuckled. "I reckon we got some people here inclined to be a lot more helpful."

He nodded to the slaves, whom Krysty and Mildred were still in the process of cutting free and examining. Ricky and Jak were on guard. Doc stood to one side. Clearly when the brief, one-sided fight had ended, he had retreated back into the sad, confused memory-mists in his mind.

"What do you mean to do with us?" called the most assertive-looking of the bunch, a tall, strongly built brown-haired woman wearing tattered overalls.

"Let you go," Ryan said. "We're not slavers. But we've got some questions we'd like to ask before you go."

"Narda, where will we go?" whined a slight, balding man with myopically blinking eyes and a lame left foot. He had to have been a drag on the coffle on the march here from whenever he'd been caught.

She waved a callused hand at him. "We'll get to that, Husker," she said. "Reckon we owe these folks. And in case you didn't notice, we're still at their mercy. They got blasters. We don't."

"When we go you can help yourself to what the slavers had," Ryan said. "We took what we needed off them. They still got knives, a hatchet, stuff to make fire. Blasters, too. You should make out."

Mildred shot him a look. He ignored it. His bunch didn't need to load themselves down with spare blasters on this mission. And the slavers' blasters didn't use the same ammo as any of theirs did.

"I'll talk," Narda said. "Not like I owe these bastards any favors."

A corner of her mouth quirked up, then. She laughed.

"Now that I think of it, what we *owe* them is to help you folks any way we can. Because I'm judging your notion is to fuck these taints good and hard? I don't believe you just freed us out of the goodness of your hearts."

"We hate slavers and look to cut them down anytime we can," Ryan said. "But, yeah. We got more reason that that to take it to these bastards. We need to know what you know about their operations."

"Ask away," she said. The others agreed. Even Husker, reluctantly.

Ryan did. Alysa joined in, using her knowledge of the country plus her own experience of the slavers to know what questions to ask. Doc and Krysty participated, too.

Ricky kept glancing toward them from where he stood at a corner of the ruin where he could keep an eye up and down the road. Ryan knew he was itching to ask about his sister Yami, who'd been kidnapped from their home island of Puerto Rico by slavers. He knew she'd been sold to other slavers here on the mainland.

The youth could ask if he wanted. Ryan doubted a random group of captives would know anything about a slave taken a few thousand miles away. He didn't mean to waste the air.

Mostly what they got confirmed what Baron Frost had initially briefed them with, plus their own impressions. The slaver operation was big—hundreds of men, spread out in units large enough to cause problems for any ville sec force, spread out across New England and up to Canada, too. They set up a temporary base and send out raiding parties.

Sometimes they put their captives on small boats, like fishing craft, to run them down the coast. Others, like this group, got marched overland.

As to what such a big operation was doing reaping such a large harvest, no one knew for sure, although the liberated slaves had several differing positions. Narda heard that some important baron needed plenty of labor down the coast toward Hatteras. Others said the labor was needed for sugar plantations in Cuba or tobacco ones on the Gulf Coast—both crops that could readily be sold for profit, or what passed for such in the present world.

A gaunt man with gray hair hanging over a gray face, who seemed dwarfed by his big tattered overcoat, said he'd heard some baron over cross the Lantic needed miners. Or maybe an army. Or an army and miners and other laborers to equip them.

"Did the slavers themselves talk about who needed so many slaves and why?" Krysty asked.

Narda shrugged. "Yeah," she said. "Plenty. Reckon that's where most of the slave-barracks rumors got their start. Problem is, slavers themselves didn't seem to have no better notion what it was all about than we did. Mebbe the higher-ups did. Do. But if so, they didn't tell the grunts. I believe the 'big baron down the coast needs warm bodies' story for the most part. I'd say he's some-body who wants to start a war."

One thing they were in no doubt about was that the slaves were being gathered at a spot on the coast not far south and west of their current position. There they were put aboard an old freighter, a big oceangoing ship, for transport to…wherever they were going. And the word was the ship was on its way back from its latest run to fill up again. If it wasn't lying at anchor already.

"Where is this base, or port, or whatever?" Mildred asked. She was antsy. She wasn't usually the most pa-tient woman. Worry about her lover, J.B., clearly set her teeth on edge.

Ryan didn't like it, either. He just did his best to put it from his mind. The only thing he could do for J.B. now was to get this kidnapped girl back to her parents as soon as possible and hope the tiny, dark, fierce Healer Rao knew her shit the way the Frosts thought she did.

"Down past a ville called Tavern Bay," said the larg-est person in the group, a powerfully built man called Givens. He looked like a blacksmith to Ryan; he had arms like most strong men had legs.

He also had an angry red burn, scarcely healed though not infected, on one bearded cheek. It looked about the right size and shape to be made by a red-hot iron. He didn't offer an explanation. Nobody asked for one.

"They dock it at this bay?" Ryan asked.

Givens shook his head. "No. That's just the nearest ville. The anchorage lies mebbe five, ten miles farther down, or so I heard. Next to some high granite cliffs where people can't climb up and down triple-easy."

"Makes sense," Ryan said.

"What about a young girl?" Alysa asked. "She would be fourteen. She would clearly appear…privileged."

"Skinny, kind of broad, high cheekbones, black hair cut short, pale green eyes?" Narda asked. "Lots of mouth on her?" She sighed. "Yeah. We seen her."

"Lyudmila," said the gray man. "Daughter of my baron, of Stormbreak, and his wife. They are good people. Scarcely like barons at all. They did not deserve such loss."

Alysa was now looking at him. It was clear that she had regarded the slaves as objects of pity rather than individuals and had paid little attention to them as anything other than potential information sources.

"You're Grave Loomis, from Winter Creek!" she said.

He nodded. "And you're the Korn girl, serves the baron and his lady. They sent you to bring her back, didn't they?"

"Yes," she said excitedly. "I apologize, I did not recognize you. You were a stout man."

"Long walk on short rations," he said.

A troubled look crossed his haggard face, making him look even more tired and worn-down than he had. He was another meal meant for the Bears, Ryan reckoned.

"She has spirit," he said. "Too much for her own good. And—for others."

"Yeah," Narda said. "Everybody knew her. Knew of her, anyway. She was kept at the same staging camp we were, ten, twenty miles back. For a while. She really gave the slavers what for. For a while."

"How so?" Doc asked.

"Well, she fought them as much as she could, which wasn't much, really. She's just a skinny little thing. But an obvious tomboy and had some pretty fast fists and feet on her. Hard ones, too."

"Baron Ivan and Lady Katerina trained her in combat," Alysa said proudly.

"Not well enough," Mildred muttered.

"Stand down, Mildred," Ryan said without looking at her. "A kid like that isn't going to do much against hardened slavers."

"Nope," Narda agreed. "But she was uncooperative. Plus, she cursed them at every opportunity. Even encouraged others to resist their captors."

"Well, good for her," Mildred commented.

"I get the feeling there's a 'but' here," Krysty said apprehensively. Her concern didn't stop her from eating a dried apple from the Bear family's winter stores, which had mostly survived the blaze.

"Of course there is," Ryan said.

Narda nodded. "First they stripped her naked, tied her spread-eagled on a kind of wood X thing stuck in the ground, and whipped her with branches. They didn't want to leave any deep marks, you see."

Alysa gasped. "They didn't—"

"Rape her? No. Slaver bosses made it clear that anybody who laid hand on her without permission would lose that hand and his balls. To a sledgehammer and a flat rock. But they wanted to humiliate her as well as cause her pain."

"How'd that work?" Ryan asked.

"She was kinda subdued for a couple days. Then she waylaid a slaver bringing food, kicked him in the balls and made a break for it. They caught her, of course."

"Yeah," Ryan said. "What they do then?"

"She had a servant girl with her. Not much older than she was. Mebbe eighteen. Blond hair but dark brown eyes. Pretty girl. Sweet."

"Darya Wilkes," Alysa said. "Her maidservant." She looked at Ryan. "We never found her body. Nor did she come home to her family. We surmised she was taken with her mistress."

Ryan grunted. "Nice of Ivan and Katerina to tell us that little bit of info."

She looked genuinely pained. "I am sorry, Mr. Cawdor. They—they must have thought it would have little use for you."

He waved it off. "That's spilled blood. So, this girl, Darya—they made an example of her, didn't they?"

Narda pressed her mouth shut tight.

"They made Milya watch," Husker said in a hollow voice. "They made everybody watch. They staked her nude on the ground and gang-raped her. Five men. They weren't gentle. Then, when they were done, they hung her by the heels from a strong tree limb and beat her with heavy clubs until she died."

Krysty drew in a sharp breath.

"Shit," Mildred said.

Alysa uttered a sharp cry of "Oh!" She turned and walked several steps away. Glancing after her, Ryan could tell her hands were over her face by the position of her elbows. Her shoulders shook with the effort of trying to hold in sobs. Which his ears told him was not a double successful effort.

Girl mostly acts like she's cased in tool steel, Ryan thought. That shot went right through her armor like it wasn't there.

He wondered why. But he didn't have the luxury to wonder much.

Krysty went quickly after the stricken sec woman. She put her arm around Alysa's narrow waist and cradled her head against her shoulder.

"After that," Husker said, "Lady Milya became far more cooperative."

Ryan let go a breath he didn't realize he'd been holding. "Yeah. Well, at least it sounds like they're taking good care of Milya. She still at that staging camp you came from?"

Narda shook her head. "No. They took her away in a wag, a couple days ago."

That didn't sound good. "You know where?" Ryan asked.

"Same place," Narda said. "They just reckoned they could take better care of her there. Or keep a closer eye on the goods."

He turned to his friends and saw Ricky staring with wide eyes at the liberated slaves. He looked as if he badly needed to pee.

Ryan knew he was fighting an urge that was almost as strong. And longer-lasting.

"Okay, kid," he said. "Say your piece."

"Have any of you seen a young girl? Beautiful, with long black hair?"

They stared at him. Finally Grave Loomis said, gently, "They're slavers, kid. They specialize in capturing beautiful women. Those are their big-ticket items. Not like us."

"What he's saying is," Narda said, "yeah. Lots. What good does this do you?"

"I mean—I mean, with dark eyes and olive skin like mine. Puerto Rican. About eighteen. Her name is Yamile—Yami, we call her. She's my sister."

The captives looked at each other. "Puerto Rico," Narda repeated dubiously. "Not ringing any bells."

"Monster Island," said Husker. "It's in the Carib. The Caribbean. People there are mostly Spanish."

"Like the Mex?" Narda asked. "My grandmother was a Mex, from outside the Shy-Town rubble. But no.

Nobody Spanish. Bunch of Frenchies from Kay-beck, couple of Portugee sailors off a ship that went down in a storm. That's it."

Ricky seemed to deflate.

"Thank you," he said, sounding as if he had a belly-ful of broken glass.

"Okay, people," Ryan called. "Time to saddle the horses and get going. How far away's this Tavern Bay again?"

Their Stormbreaker escort had recovered her compo-sure and detached herself from Krysty. Now she came back to the conversation. Ryan noticed her eyes were red. But dry.

"We can make it by tomorrow afternoon," she said, then frowned. "It is not a good place."

"How so, Alysa?" Krysty asked.

"They have a dark history. The town was built by slavers—long ago, many centuries, when such things were legal. When that was banned, it was said they turned to smuggling and another form of buying and selling human souls—kidnapping men and selling them to sailing ships in need of crew."

Mildred had started looking pretty thunderous at the mention of old-days slavery. Now, she shook it off like a buffalo trying to shed a horsefly.

"That was a long time ago," she said. "Even by my— That is, it's ancient history. What about now?"

"The people there…are strange," the blonde woman said. "They still have a reputation for sharp practice. People still talk about hidden ways and hint at midnight disappearances."

"Sounds like any ville with a gaudy," Ryan said, rub-bing his cheek with a gloved hand and hearing the bristles rasp the tough fabric. "Or with a baron, for that matter."

"And some say certain of the people of Tavern Bay conduct strange rituals."

"Great," Mildred said. "Cultists. The way our luck has run lately, they'll probably be cannies, too. Like our late hosts from last night."

Alysa shook her head urgently. "No, you must not think that! There are good people there. Very good. Our baroness herself comes from one of the ville's leading families. She is beyond reproach. Others, though—"

"Ryan's right," Krysty said. "That sounds like any-place."

"Not that *that's* encouraging," Mildred said.

"So we'll be pushing off," Ryan told the freed captives.

"Thank you," Narda said.

"What do we eat?" Husker said.

"There's a root cellar next to where the house was," Krysty said. "We replenished our food stocks. There's plenty left. They did well by themselves. Bread, vegetables, dried fruit, cheese, smoked fish."

"Don't recommend you go for any of the meat, though," Mildred said. "You never know who it's been."

Chapter Nineteen

By the blue-white light of a spotlight powered by a growling portable generator, J.B. squinted down into the tray of parts on the folding table and frowned. We've got a problem here, he thought.

"Trader," he said. "You need to come look at this."

Part of him, not too deep down, either, felt a thrill to be talking to the great man that way. Then again, that was implicit in the thrill of being put in a position, too.

Trader stood at one end of the table talking to the representative of the Science Brothers, who through some perverseness that bothered J.B.'s sense of rightness, was a woman. Her two companions, like the other Science Brothers who could properly be called *Brothers,* had shaved their heads egg-bald and wore round wire-rimmed specs whether they needed them or not.

The woman had hair. And not just hair—hair piled up on her head in a sort of swirl with what was probably a dyed-in white streak running up from the left side of her forehead. She also had outrageously made-up eyes and dark lipstick that might have been black. Or it may've been green, as the odd highlight struck off her hair suggested her's was.

She scowled dangerously at his interruption, but Trader came right over.

J.B. was doing the very job Trader had brought him

along for, which was why he was so swelled-up with pride it felt as if his chest and gut would just burst.

His skills and his resourcefulness at employing them—whether in improvising repairs and replacement parts out of damn near nothing or his diabolical booby traps—had won the respect of most of Trader's hard-bitten, cynical crew. And even the cautiously qualified approval from The Man himself.

He was doing. That was the key thing. He always felt good when he *did* things—made things, fixed things.

Even better—he was *learning*. Though a stern task-mistress, Rance Weeden was an excellent teacher, always willing to show J.B. where he'd gone wrong—and give him just enough information to figure out the *right* way to do something on his own.

And Ace DeGuello also proved a master worthy of following. After actually working under the man on the long and winding run across the Deathlands, J.B. had abandoned thoughts of supplanting Trader's weapons master. At least, anytime soon. More patient than Rance, Ace showed a breadth and depth of knowledge of metal-working and just plain weapons that made J.B.'s breath run short just to think about. And he treated J.B. as a sort of prize pupil.

To cap it off, tonight Ace had suggested J.B. go in his place to meet with the Science Brothers and evaluate their offerings as pertained to blasters and rocket launchers. Ace himself was tied up putting the last touches on Trader's new pet 20 mm quick-firer, the recently installed hardpoint atop the prow of War Wag One.

And Trader had agreed without a pause. So here he was, glasses pushed in tight over his eyes and his heart in his throat, conscious that he held the literal future of Trader, his convoy and his people in his hands.

J.B. held a thin dark-silver metal object up to the light. Everyone looked at him, including Marsh Folsom, who was inspecting the high-value wares the Brothers and Sister had set on the folding table.

"It's supposed to be a triple-fancy titanium firing pin for the Oerlikon 20 mm autocannon you just bought," J.B. said.

Trader nodded. "What about it?"

J.B. turned it. "It's not titanium. It's cheap electroplated junk."

Trader frowned as he saw the long scratch down the side where the shiny metal had been scratched to reveal duller gray beneath.

He turned back. "What's this, Vespa?" he asked the Science Sister.

"That's bullshit!" squealed the shorter of her male companions. "What does this fucking kid know?"

The Science Brothers were a group of about a hundred members who operated out of a hidden HQ somewhere in the Midwest. They liked people to think it was some kind of lost predark research facility, but nobody knew. Outsiders never got in to see. *What* they were was an open question. Some said they were no better than a coldheart gang with fancy trappings—certainly, their reputation for arrogance and truculence did little to dispel that, though J.B. wasn't sure if that might just be because they defended themselves when people messed with them.

That happened frequently. In a time when scientists, or as they were usually called, whitecoats, were nearly as universally distrusted and despised as muties, the Science Brothers openly professed not just an open admiration for science, but attempted to practice the ways of twentieth-century science—the thing that had caused, or at least enabled, the destruction of the world.

How successful they were was another open question. Marsh Folsom, who knew things—book things—called them a "cargo cult," claiming that they mostly acted as if they'd gain the secrets of the near-mystical powers of science if they could just imitate the old-days white-coats closely enough.

Seeing them here and now, at this remote site where they'd insisted on meeting with Trader and a small party in the middle of the damn night, J.B. was ready to believe they were coldhearts, right enough. After getting a close look at them he thought he might sign off on the "cult" thing, too.

"I'll show you," he said to the man who had challenged his knowledge. He picked another pin out of the tray set out among other displays of parts and components, mostly pretty high-tech, that they were trying to sell Trader. He examined it by the light, hefted it. Then he held it up.

"Looks like titanium, too," he said. "But check this out."

He flicked open his knife and carefully scratched down the side of the pin.

"Hey!" the Science Brother, who had by now moved obnoxiously close, shouted. "That's valuable merchandise you're damaging!"

He tried to snatch the pin. J.B. pivoted neatly away and never stopped working.

He was able after a moment's effort to dislodge a thin shard of what appeared to be titanium plating.

"See?" he said, holding his prize out so both Trader and the Science Brother could see it. "It's just a thin coating of titanium with monkey metal inside."

He tossed it back in the bin. "These parts'll last just long enough for us to be a hundred miles away from these bastard scammers before they bust. Probably in the middle of a firefight."

He looked at Trader, who did not look pleased. "I'm no big judge of the electronics. But I bet the same applies to everything they're trying to peddle."

The Science Brother turned to Trader. "Are you going let this little sawed-off shit queer the deal? He's trying to pretend he knows stuff to make himself look like a big man."

J.B. sucker-punched the back of the guy's bald head, hard enough to make the knuckles of his right hand sting. The man lurched forward.

J.B. jumped on his back, pummeling him.

"Take them out!" he heard the woman named Vespa scream.

Suddenly the scene flooded with dazzling white light. And Trader said, softly, "Oh, shit."

"NOT MUCH OF a tourist attraction," Mildred remarked.

She was not in the best of moods. Worry for J.B. ate at her guts like an ulcer. But she doubted it was *just* her disposition souring her view of their destination.

Tavern Bay lay where a gorge through hilly, heavily forested highlands suddenly opened into a wide valley that gave onto the sea. The cliffs wrapped around to the north and south to form headlands that protected the anchorage, which was a wide, placid extent of water that looked gray-green. A pair of dumpy fishing trawlers headed back toward the ville, drawing narrow V-shaped wakes behind them. A triangular white sail stuck up from the water like a shark's fin, way out where the haze ate the horizon. The sun was already threatening to fall out of sight beyond the heights behind them.

From the landward side the ville was surrounded by a broad, flat expanse of salt marsh. Big straw-colored patches of various aquatic reeds and weeds—Mildred wasn't a botanist—were interspersed with swatches of murky-looking water. She could smell the brackishness from where she stood, along with a glum, stomach-dragging hint of decaying sea life.

The ville looked like a collection of wooden structures, some just shacks and shanties, toward the outskirts, others bigger if not always less dilapidated. Toward the center of the ville, down toward the waterfront, the buildings turned more to brick, bluish-gray or a kind of grime-encrusted red, and grimy gray granite. Most of the buildings were two or three stories tall and narrow to the point of attenuation. The streets had to have been narrow, too, Mildred reckoned; that would account for the cramped, crabbed look to the place.

Though the afternoon was starting to turn ashy-yellow and dark, no lights showed from the ville.

"Does anybody even live here?" Mildred demanded.

"It's the most populous ville in this area," Alysa said. "It didn't suffer much damage from the war. The population came back fairly quickly after skydark. But it seemed to peak and began to dwindle perhaps fifty years ago, or so we're told. It still holds perhaps a few hundred souls."

Once more, Mildred wondered at the girl's odd turns of speech, many of which would have been archaic in Mildred's own time, over a century ago, before the Big Nuke. Then again, the phrase *it takes all kinds* was even more applicable to the world today than before she had gone into cryosleep—and with a fraction of the population to make up all those kinds.

She shrugged. Compared to the people where we picked up the new kid, she reminded herself, Alysa's mundane to the point of boring.

The human denizens of Monster Island lived in perfect amity alongside all manner of muties, including stickies, notorious for their vicious sadism and homicidal proclivities.

"We're not here to sightsee," Ryan said. "Let's get a move on."

"The road we're on," Alysa said, referring to the pair of parallel ruts through sandy soil clumped with sparse, knee-high yellow grass on which they had halted their horses, "meets up with the causeway into Tavern Bay."

"I don't like this," Mildred said.

"Not like, either," Jak said from the back of his penny-colored mare.

Krysty had ridden up alongside Ryan. They had used some of the jack they had taken off the slavers they ambushed, who had no further need of it, to buy her a new ride from a logging camp about ten miles from the Bear-clan cabin. This was a gray mare, a bit undersize to carry a woman of Krysty's size, and undernourished and depressive to start with. Or so Mildred judged, though she wasn't a vet, either.

The beast had both filled out and brightened up in the day and a half since they got it. Krysty just naturally got on with animals. As of course she would; she had the sort of nature that was strong enough to be kind in a blighted world like this one.

She laughed. "Would you rather spend the night out here?"

The breeze off the sea was warm. Ish. The day was

cold, but by comparison to the brutal bitterness of the
week and change since they'd jumped into the former
Maine—Mildred still wasn't sure why anybody would
stick a secret facility way up here in frozen-ass Stephen
King country—almost comfortable. But the failing light
was dialing down the celestial thermometer, turning
down the heat as it went. And the wind was rising.

For answer, Ryan nudged the flanks of his notch-
eared, black-and-white-splotched beast to get it walking
down the track. He did it firmly, and without unneces-
sary force, Mildred couldn't help noticing. She couldn't
call their one-eyed leader kind, really. She'd seen him
do some harsh things, even by the tough standards of
the here and now. But never any more forceful, or any
crueler, than he deemed necessary to survive.

And it's kept us alive, she thought. So far.

And she clamped down hard on the cold, dark place
where she kept fear for her own love.

Mildred hauled her mule's big, ugly head up from
where it had its snout buried in a clump of grass.

"It's not just a life, it's an adventure," she muttered,
and fell into line behind the shiny black rump of Doc's
gelding.

Chapter Twenty

J.B. froze in the act of pummeling the bald-headed Science Brother, and his adversary froze. As if their heads were fixed to the same transfer rod, they swiveled to look toward the source of the brilliant light.

The meeting place of Trader's group and the Science Brothers was a scrap of grassy shelf between a steep raw-dirt bluff and a wide valley belonging to a tributary of the upper Wabash River. A new sun had appeared at the bluff's top. It was a compound sun, made of a pair of square bluish headlights and multiple spots.

It was War Wag One, rolling into place just behind the line of sight. At some signal from Trader—even J.B. didn't know what it was—it had rolled forward to the edge of the bluff and hit all the lights at once.

Even as reflex cranked his neck that way, J.B. knew what he'd see. He'd been in on that much of the plan, anyway. Trader had not got where he was, or even stayed on his pins, by being overly trusting. And a powerful, arrogant bunch like the Science Brothers he didn't trust at all.

At least he had sense to wind his eyelids down to slits to save some of his night vision.

J.B. didn't need night vision, truth to tell, when he looked back down the shallow slope to see what had disturbed Trader.

It turned out Trader's mistrust of the Science Broth-

ers was justified. In spades. The valley below swarmed
with wags and bikes and dudes on foot, all bristling
with weapons.

An evil grin winching across his face, the Science
Brother whose back J.B. straddled turned his face back
toward him. J.B. met him with a right-hand punch to
the jaw. This time he remembered to clench his hand
tight and land with the last three knuckles of his fist
lined up with the bones of his arm for maximum struc-
tural strength—and damage, the way he'd been taught
by Abe, who knew old-days boxing.

As intended, the properly delivered punch didn't
much hurt his hand. It also had the intended effect. The
Brother's visible eye rolled up in its socket and his knees
buckled.

The other Science Brother had launched himself at
Trader, who lunged at him in turn, catching him by surprise and shattering his nose with a brutal head-butt.

As J.B. dismounted his own collapsing opponent, giving him a brisk knee to the side of his head as he sagged
downward from his knees, Trader caught that Brother
with a shin-kick to the balls. As that man folded, Trader
put right palm on left fist and pile-drove his elbow into
the back of his victim's unprotected neck.

A shockingly loud noise hit J.B.'s ear from the right,
followed quickly by two more. Marsh Folsom was standing behind the table with his hideout .38 snubby blaster
held in both hands in an isosceles stance. And Vespa
was wheeling to the ground with some kind of semiauto
blaster dropping from her hand.

Then dirt began to kick up all around them as the
Science Brothers waiting in ambush below opened fire.

J.B. dived for the cover afforded by the fact that the

coldhearts were shooting upward past a shelf. As he did, he snagged the SKS he'd left propped by a rock.

Trader and Marsh both hit the dirt. An M-4 carbine came cartwheeling over the table of dreck wares to be snagged by a now-prone Trader with one hand. Marsh had scooped it up and tossed it to his partner.

Somewhere below a machine gun began to rip. It sounded like a 5.56 mm, probably an M-249 Squad Automatic Weapon. J.B. fast-crawled on his elbows forward to where he could return fire with some cover by the edge. Since it was mostly sod, basically, it wouldn't afford that much cover. But he knew shooting at an upward angle gave the blaster a disadvantage, and he was never one to hang back from a fight.

Especially one, he realized with a rush of adrenaline to his heart, that he had started himself.

Crackling thunder came from above. Ace was cutting loose with the new 20 mm blaster in its armored mount atop the front section of War Wag One. From the green tracer lines streaking overhead, he was shooting at the M-249.

The first thing J.B. saw when he hit the edge of the cliff made his nutsack try to crawl up into his skinny belly and hide. It was the firefly flicker of a couple of dozen muzzle-flashes flaming his way. It was the giant yellow-white fire-blossom from below and left, and the blue spark streaking upward from it, that scared him to his core.

J.B. was never much for reading. Not for its own sake, though he knew how to do it. But one thing he did read was books about weapons—especially predark tech manuals.

He had never seen one before, but he knew instantly with no possible leeway for doubt that he'd just witnessed the launch of a BGM-71 TOW anti-tank missile that would burn through even War Wag One's stout front armor and blow the command section apart like a firecracker in an apple.

TOW stood for Tube-launched, Optically tracked, Wire-command guided missile. The big tank-killer needed an operator to guide it to its target.

All that flashed through J.B.'s mind as fast as a high-speed rifle round. He knew there was just one chance to save War Wag One.

He snugged the SKS butt to his shoulder and started squeezing off rounds at the spot where he'd seen the first flash of launching. He wasn't much of a longblaster man, not with his vision. Nor was the SKS especially accurate. But the missileer was about 150 yards away, and J.B. was ice-cold now, not even tempted to crank shots off wildly.

He fired until a flash lit the sky from above and behind.

He looked back to see brilliant sparks and smoke explode away from War Wag One's cab.

But not the compartment. Rather the missile had deflected upward—slightly. It had hit the front glacis of the 20 mm blaster's improvised-armor shield.

From way off to the right, well past the now-silent SAW, more bluish glare flooded a narrower valley running down to join the one where the Science Brothers had laid in wait.

War Wag Two had joined the fray, swinging down around the right flank of Trader's people, emplaced on the bluff, to take the Science Brothers on the left.

Or even more likely, J.B. realized, to do just what it had just done: provide a nasty surprise to a troop of Science Brothers blaster wags and bikes, clearly driving up the tributary valley to try to outflank the convoy on that side.

He tried not to think about the fate of the 20 mm blaster, and Ace and his crew, and the rest of the butcher's bill he'd run up by losing his self-control, and began picking out muzzle-flashes to shoot at. Because right now, he had a job to do, and that was always the best refuge.

"I HOPE THEY can give us information here that will allow us to recover the baron's daughter quickly," Alysa Korn said as the seven of them walked through the slanting yellow light that couldn't quite bring color to the gray and washed-out streets of Tavern Bay. "It is so urgent to bring her back home safely."

"Yeah," said Mildred, walking a few steps behind the sec woman. "The sooner we give Frost back his daughter, the sooner I get J.B. back."

If he's even still alive. Krysty didn't need to be telepathic to know that her friend was thinking that. The sturdy woman with the beaded plaits might as well have shouted it.

Alysa's shoulders hunched briefly beneath her bulky coat. Mildred blew out an exasperated breath.

"Sorry, kid," she said. "I didn't mean that as harsh as it sounded. We all want to get your girl back safe. Even Ryan, no matter how much he likes to play the hard-ass."

Swinging along at Krysty's side, Ryan scowled briefly. She suppressed a giggle.

The pair brought up the rear. Jak, restless at having been encumbered—as he thought of it—by a horse, was walking point with his pal Ricky, who clutched his blaster with both hands, trying to look alert as well as important.

Horses were not permitted in Tavern Bay, the middle-aged man and teenage boy who guarded the bridge that seemed to provide the only land route into the ville had told them. For an extortionate amount of jack they had stabled their mounts in a ramshackle structure on the ville-ward side. It was no more than a mile to the ville's center, anyway. They had been instructed to seek out the ville mayor. There had been an ominous tone in the older gatekeeper's voice when he'd said that, suggesting dire penalties if they disobeyed.

But lacking any better plan once they got to the ville, Ryan had decided the mayor was just the man they needed to see anyway.

"Where is everybody?" Ricky asked. "This is spooky. It's supposed to be a well-off ville."

Up close the place had a decaying look. Many roofs showed great gaping patches open to the long lead-and-rose clouds streaked across the near-sunset sky. Windows and doors gaped like the eyes and mouths of skulls. Even many of the buildings that showed signs of recent use and occupancy looked as if they were just waiting for the next strong wind as an excuse to lie down and give up.

"Plus I guess you're pretty broken up about what happened to Milya's maid," Mildred said. "Uh, Darya. So she was a pretty good friend of yours?"

To Krysty's surprise Alysa shook her head, making her pale yellow hair fly across the shoulders of her greatcoat.

"I barely knew her. She was a sweet girl. As Milya is, down inside her show of rebellion. I'm not close to the baron's family, really. Only the baron."

They walked a few paces down what seemed to be the main drag of Tavern Bay. Ahead of them several blocks opened a square, around which were set the biggest and most pretentious-looking buildings. According to the instructions reluctantly doled out by the older bridge guard, that was indeed where they'd find the ville's town hall and whatever help or otherwise the ville could offer them.

Krysty reached out, found Ryan's hand and squeezed it. It wasn't just to reassure herself; he did need it sometimes, which would surprise most of their companions, let alone the rest of the Deathlands that had One Eye Chill's boot-prints on it. But while she doubted there was anything here to make Ryan more than normally wary, she also felt curiously on edge at how deserted the streets were during the waning daylight.

Apparently Tavern Bay had resisted the wave of modernization that had risen and spread throughout the twentieth century. The main street of the ville was only two lanes wide, though generous for that. Some of the side streets, even narrower with buildings that seemed to lean together conspiratorially over them, looked like cobblestone.

They were in mostly good repair, better than many of the buildings. Also the streets were mostly cleared of snow, though gray slush gathered in the gutters and the alleyways and on the sidewalks, which were less well tended. Krysty smelled the snow and the slush, cold wet concrete and stone, mildew and rot, and fish, the seemingly inevitable stink of decaying sea life.

Though the air was quiet here at street level, a wind seemed to whistle among the peaked roofs. She heard random creaks from the structures that they passed, and groans, as if the ville itself felt disquiet in its guts and in its bones.

Krysty was not as allergic to urban settings as Jak

was—especially not as allergic as he pretended to be. Still, she preferred the direct sense of connection to Gaia that even the roughest sketch of civilization seemed to impair. And here in a ville that seemed to have escaped the ravages of the war, less those of time and neglect, the disconnect was especially strong. But the unease she felt now, like small animals running along her nerve on tiny clawed toes, was more than that.

She glanced up at Ryan again. Though he frowned, that was a common expression. They were headed toward something unknown, and that always meant danger.

And so did the known, as a general thing. She smiled and inwardly laughed at herself. Where isn't a certain amount of apprehension the appropriate thing to feel? she asked herself.

"You see," their guide said, speaking with her head down and not looking at the others, "when I was a small girl, my family…did not treat me well. I don't even know if they were my real family. They told me a dozen different stories. All I know is that the adults, my supposed parents and a few uncles, or so they called them, who drifted in and out of our shack, treated me as a slave from the time of my first memory. As they did my brothers and sisters, who also seemed to come and go mysteriously—and those who went were usually never heard from again.

"The man who called himself my father…used me. Again, from the time I was very small. He didn't even bother to hide the fact from the woman, or anybody else. He didn't have to. When I cried, the woman beat me with a heavy wooden ladle and withheld my food, calling me an ingrate and a whiny brat."

"That's awful," Mildred said quietly.

Krysty glanced at Ryan. His rugged face was unreadable behind the stubble, dusted with gray, that darkened his jaws. It wasn't exactly the norm in the Deathlands, that sort of thing. But it was common enough. And Krysty had to agree with Mildred's twentieth-century scruples: it *was* awful.

"When I was perhaps twelve—for I never knew my real age, either—a patrol attacked the shack. Apparently my so-called father and 'uncles' were bandits. I heard later they robbed a farmhouse a couple of miles down the road, killed four people and left a fifth for dead. She was found beside the burning house, and before she died she told the baron's men who had committed the crime.

"The baron himself led the assault. My father and two of my uncles were caught and hanged from trees nearby. My mother cut the throats of one of my brothers and one of my sisters. She had me with the kitchen knife at my throat, blade still running with the blood of Natasha and Jack, when the baron himself strode into the house. He called to her to let me go. She laughed. The blade bit my neck—"

She touched her throat, drawing down the wolf-fur collar aside far enough for Krysty to see a thread-thin white scar she hadn't noticed before.

"And then there was a blinding flash and deafening noise. The blade fell from my throat. I heard something heavy hit the planks of the floor. Then I was being cradled in the strong arms of the baron."

She sighed.

"When I turned and saw the woman who said she was my mother lying right beside me with the right side of her head blown off by Baron Frost's pistol shot, I felt nothing at all. Not triumph. Not relief. Certainly not sadness.

"I was taken in by a family of carpenters who lived near the castle. They were good people, kind even when it wasn't easy—as opposed to my former family, who were cruel even when it took effort. They were the Korns. I took their name proudly.

"And since then I have devoted my life to serving Baron Ivan Frost and his barony of Stormbreak. He and his wife, Lady Katerina, have always treated me well. Although they treat everyone well, except for evildoers."

Mildred turned back and mouthed the words *daddy issues* to Krysty. Despite herself, Krysty smiled. She certainly could find little blame in her heart for Alysa's devotion to the strong man who had saved her in person from horror, degradation and death. And, for a fact, Ivan and Katerina seemed almost too good for a baron and his lady.

They reached the square. It had grass that may have been tended, although it wasn't easy to tell, given that it was winter-yellow and sparse and partly covered by old snow. A dead fountain stood in the middle of it, a concrete basin surrounding an oblong of concrete that had probably served as pedestal to some statue or other, long since pulled down and scavvied for its bronze. Krysty could see the remnants of a plaque from one hundred feet, a discolored square on gray. The fountain basin was oddly swept clean of detritus, although a few leaves showed around the inside edges of the bottom.

They found themselves facing a building wider than others in the ville, with soot-and-grime-streaked pillars and a dome whose green color suggested it was at least copper sheathed. Either the inhabitants hadn't been able enough to scavenge that or the rulers of the ville had been strong-handed enough to stop them.

"This takes me back," said Doc, drawing himself up

to his full height and dusting the lapels of his frock coat. "The sort of pretension that characterized town halls in the small villages of the New England of my youth. I daresay we shall find those whom we seek within."

Ryan had stopped. His frown deepened as he eased the strap of his Steyr Scout longblaster onto his right shoulder. As usual the carbine rode beside his backpack on his right, muzzle-down for quick access.

He surveyed the square. So did his friends. There were no wags in sight, and no people.

To the left of the town hall was an equally large building that looked to have fallen in on itself. The tops of some pillars stood against the empty sky. Krysty wondered if it had been a library or museum of some sort. An important public building, anyway. To the town hall's right was a church, only slightly smaller and less ostentatious than either of the other buildings. Its steeple was broken off jaggedly halfway up above the colonnaded portico. Its doors and windows were boarded over. A bizarre figure had been scrawled on the plywood that covered the big double doors: it looked like a face with two huge, staring eyes, surrounded by eight wriggly arms, all in rusty brown.

"Is that dried blood?" Ricky asked breathlessly, looking at the image with wide eyes.

"Nonsense," Mildred said. "You're letting your imagination run away with you."

"Looks like blood to me," Ryan replied. He squinted at the sky, which was purpling like a bruise. "And speaking of blood, time's blood, and it's running out on us. So let's shake the dust off our boots and go talk to the man."

Chapter Twenty-One

Trader sat at an angle with one knee crossed over the other. The fingers of his left hand drummed the top of the map table fixed to the floor of War Wag One's briefing compartment. Given that Trader didn't like to waste motion any more than fuel, jack or blood, that tic, along with the double-hard set of the man's stark features, would have been enough to tell J. B. Dix that he was in shit up to his neck.

Except he already knew all that.

"You screwed up, kid," he said. "You got three of my people killed."

J.B. ground his jaws shut so hard his teeth squeaked. Any reply he made aloud would only deepen the hole he was in.

The battle hadn't lasted long. The Science Brothers' big play had been their intended flank attack. War Wag Two's flank *counter*attack nixed that. After that, they saw no reason to stand and fight. The Brothers cut their losses and fled, leaving a dozen dead.

But Ace DeGuello had died instantly in the 20 mm blaster emplacement. His assistant gunner, Earl Vore, had been so terribly injured that he had to be written off, and the only help that could be given him was a 9 mm painkiller. Ace's loader, Betty Lou Mirelli, had been blown out of the nest by the TOW warhead's blast. The patches of skin on her back and the backs of her hands were expected to grow back sometime, but she was basically intact.

Ace's assistants had been part of the bunch that had gang-stomped J.B. when he was a newbie what seemed a lifetime ago. And what really was, for Ace and Earl. It surprised J.B. even to remember that now. In a matter of weeks they had accepted him as a valued comrade. And him them.

Which made what happened hurt.

There had been two more minor injuries. And another wag-driver had taken a shot through the head and died. He felt bad about that, too, though less. He hadn't known the dude to talk to. Close-knit as they were, Trader's crew was large, and there was a certain amount of turnover. The things that mostly held them together were the sheer magnetic force of Trader's personality and his legend.

J.B. glanced to the side. Rance Weeden sat on the third side of the table with her arms folded beneath her small breasts and her chin sunk to her collarbone. The diffuse gray-white light that shone up through its translucent top underlit her features, making them look harsh and haggard, and her hazel eyes sunken. But those eyes were fixed on him without a hint of softness. They were currently almost brown. The only hint of color in her face.

He looked back to Trader. That was easier, somehow.

Trader looked down at his hand on the table as if not sure what triple-stupe bastard it belonged to. The finger-drumming stopped. He raised the hand to scratch at his chin.

"Then again," Trader said, "you tripped the Science bastards' trap before they were ready. That saved lives."

"But you knew it was a trap," J.B. stated. "That was

why you set War Wag One up on top of the bluff. And sent around War Wag Two on the counter-flank maneuver."

Trader cracked a brief lopsided grin. "They don't call me 'the man who never was taken' for nothing, kid," he said. "Still—you spotted their scam smart-quick. That showed your tech chops and your quick eye. That shows value to me. And again, you helped nuke their timing—which on balance probably helped us get away clean as we did."

"I still don't get why they'd bother trying to scam us with junk if they intended to jack us all the time," Rance said.

"That's because you're a straightforward bastard, Weeden, not a sneaky one like me. They probably reckoned to lull us without risking their real ace stuff to a firefight. Or mebbe they hoped we'd get hotter than nuke red and start a fight, giving them an excuse to take us down. Just not so early as J.B. here did."

He turned his weathered face back to J.B. "What came near blasting us all was the way you did it. Letting your temper get the best of you."

J.B. looked down at the tabletop. He knew the ax was fixing to fall. The only question was what it would chop off.

"The other thing in your favor is, you managed to make that tank-killer gunner flinch, when he had War Wag One dead to rights. Saved my mainstay machine as well as some of my best people. Those are solid ticks to the positive side of your ledger."

Trader swung his leg down, swiveled his chair to face J.B. Then he laid clasped hands on the map table and leaned his bearded face out over them. The highlights made him look like some kind of devil from campfire stories kids told to scare each other.

"I pay my debts, son," he said. "The whole Deathlands knows that. One day I'll pay the debt the Science Brothers incurred. With blood interest. But not this trip.

"So. The good news, I let you live. That's your payment for one service you did me, and us.

"The second one is, you still have a job."

Rance sucked in a sharp breath. J.B. cut his eyes to her. She didn't meet them.

"If Rance'll still have you, you stay with her," Trader said. "Turns out Ace's people don't blame you for getting your boss chilled. Be that as it may, you did, and I'm sure as shit's brown not gonna reward you by putting you on his crew. No matter how much talent you have for that work."

J.B. opened his mouth to protest.

"Before you go and run your face any further, Junior," Trader said, "you'd best hear the bad news, which is that you are stone out of chances. Fuck up again in any way, shape, or form—if I even *suspect* you seriously might fuck up—you're out. For good. And I won't guarantee you won't end your employment staring up at the stars."

He stopped and stared hard at J.B.

"Now, do you still got anything to say to me?"

"No, sir!"

He nodded. "You may be stupe, but you're not triple-stupe. Do you hear me? And do you understand me?"

"Yes, sir!"

Trader stared at him with eyes like tungsten carbide bits.

"Yes, *sir!*"

Trader nodded and sat back.

"So what do you say, Rance?" he asked.

She glanced at J.B. as if she'd found him on the bottom of her boot walking out of a gaudy-house crapper.

"As long as he does he job," she said in a voice as flat as an anvil.

Trader stood up. "That's it," he said.

With no further words he left, heading forward into the command compartment.

J.B. looked at his boss. He moistened his lips.

"Rance—"

"Shut it," she said in a voice that would've been hostile had it seemed she cared. "From here on, talk to me only when I talk to you first. Or you got something important to say to me. Work important."

He shook his head. His eyes stung.

"I don't understand," he said, promptly violating her instructions. "What— I mean—you and me—!"

"There is no you and me."

She stood up. He gaped at her. He felt his jaws working like a carp on a ditch's bank. He shut them.

"I hoped to help make you a man," she said in a voice that was almost soft. The way mild steel was to stainless, say. "Now I see I undertook a task beyond my power to achieve.

"You know steel. If it's triple-hard, it's brittle. It breaks easy unless it's tempered right. No one can temper you but you, John Barrymore."

He kept shaking his head as if he could make her words unsaid.

"I don't understand," he said again.

"A man controls his temper," she said. "Not the other way around."

A sense of hurt unfairness bubbled up inside him like acid vomit scalding his throat. She didn't understand.

He had to be that way! His willingness to throw himself at the face of anybody who got in his was the only way he'd ever survived to here and now. Couldn't she see?

He started to explain it. But the terrible urgency made him try to explain it all at once. The words, which had never come triple-easy to him to start with, all tried to get out at once. So all that he got out was a flock-of-geese stammer.

To her back. She was already walking out.

"WHAT DO YOU want in Tavern Bay?" the mayor asked.

"Information," Ryan said.

The mayor's office was a circle of light cast by fish-oil lamps in the center of the echoing emptiness of the building's rotunda. Mayor Augustus Thrumbull sat behind a large desk of some kind of hardwood, possibly oak, and looked across it at his visitors. It was finely finished, with only a few nicks and scratches in it, and polished to a bright shine. It held only a few writing tools. Ryan wondered where the mayor found an inexhaustible supply of green blotters. Unless he never actually used this one as such.

A windup clock stood by the mayor's right hand. It was a kind that Ryan reckoned was familiar to Doc from his former life, with a big round face and brass bells on the outside. It ticked loudly and remorselessly.

Thrumbull turned his large head, his jowls with their side-whiskers like gray wings spilling over the top of his stand-up collar.

"Cosgrove," he demanded of the man who stood invisible in the dimness beyond the ragged circle of illumination. Echoes of the syllables chased each other up the dome overhead like bats. "What do you mean, bringing them here?"

"Remember, Mayor," the aide said smoothly, "commerce is the life's blood of Tavern Bay. That's our tradition, after all."

The aide did everything smoothly, so far as Ryan could tell on their brief acquaintance. He had met them at the big double doors, opening to Ryan's knock. He acted as if he expected them, introducing himself as Morlon Cosgrove in an oil-on-water voice and inviting them inside out of the evening chill before even asking their names. He was small and slim and neat, like a weasel in a brown suit. But an immaculately groomed weasel with chiseled, almost too-handsome features not spoiled by receding dark brown hair slicked back from them. He seemed to be in his middle thirties.

It hadn't been that much less chilly inside the foyer than out. It was scarcely warmer here. Ryan could sense the presence of a woodstove in the shadows not far behind the mayor—mostly by the smell of smoke, since he felt barely a hint of warmth on his nose and cheeks from it. It had to have had some sort of stovepipe cobbled up to an outlet in the dome, likewise unseen, to chimney out the smoke.

That turned the emptiness and ache where J.B. belonged into an active pain, like a knife in the ribs. J.B. would've been fascinated by exactly how the smoke exhaust was handled—as opposed to Ryan, who merely noted such a thing had to be. J.B. always had to know how things worked.

Can this geezer tell us something that'll get him back? Ryan wondered. It was the best shot he could see, other than to explore blindly along the coast, which would eat more time, and double or triple the risk of discovery. And disaster.

The clock ticked.

"Harrumph," Thrumbull said, turning back to glare at Ryan with rheumy brown eyes. "Commerce. These look like vagabonds out of the wasteland, not merchants. Very well, I shall play along. What do you offer in exchange for this information, then?"

That was a tricky question. "We have jack," Ryan said.

Thrumbull's scowl deepened. He seemed to sense his guests weren't talking about copious quantities of jack.

His oldie face was well-suited for scowling, but his body still showed wide shoulders beneath his black coat. The garment was much less dapper than his aide's, and it seemed to have both shrunk and sagged away from a large frame. But his dome of balding skull was imposing, for all the liver spots splotched across it, and the mayor's vanity apparently denied him the absurd yet common expedient of combing lank gray strands over the top of it. His long upper lip seemed to press his mouth into a line of sheer disapproval, even at rest. His eyebrows, though—they were awesome gray wings sweeping outward from formidable shelves of bone and flesh and fit to intimidate a stickie on jolt.

Still, there was something pathetic about him, as if his furious demeanor was a show to help him deny some awful truth to himself.

Ryan gave his head a tiny shake. He had no time for fancies like that. They didn't load any blasters for him. And now Alysa Korn stepped up beside him to confront the old dragon.

"I am Alysa Korn," she announced, standing as straight as the barrel of her rifle. "I am a sec woman in the service of Baron Frost of Stormbreak."

"Ahh," the mayor rumbled, though less openly skeptically now. "The Rooskie ville up the coast."

"Yes, Your Worship. Stormbreak trades regularly with your ville, is it not so?

"It is," the mayor said, a bit begrudgingly.

"Baron Frost and Lady Katerina have need of your help in a matter most urgent," the girl said. "In return they are prepared to offer trade concessions as well as other considerations."

The mayor sat back and folded his big hands across his sunken chest and still-rounded paunch.

"Indeed. What is the information they prize so highly?"

Ryan saw her pale green eyes flick sideways toward him. "Slavers have kidnapped their daughter and heir, Lyudmila. We know they brought her this way. We have been told they have a sea base not far from here. We want to know where it is. Also, if you have heard anything about Lyudmila herself, we would very much like to know what."

The clock ticked. The eyebrows rose into bristling arches. "You think we have commerce with slavers?"

If it wasn't for the fact Doc often talked that way, Ryan would have had a hard time catching his meaning. This whole ville seemed like something out of the distant past. Not so far as Doc's day, perhaps, but older than Mildred. It struck him as early twentieth century, somehow.

"You have to have some information on the slavers, Mayor," he said, "if only to protect yourselves against them."

"Do they ever attack Tavern Bay?" Krysty asked, slipping up to stand a half pace behind Ryan's other shoulder.

"Ha!" the mayor said. "No. They have reason to fear us. We have means of dealing with intruders!"

"You're quite correct that we do receive intelligence about the slavers and their movements, Mr. Cawdor," Cosgrove said. "While we get few travelers from the landward side, we deal regularly with people from the surrounding countryside. For various reasons the slavers no longer prey on them directly, at least not much. But our farmer and woodcutter neighbors have no reason to love them, and frequently report their movements."

"We don't have a firm offer in hand, Cosgrove," grumbled the mayor.

"Leave the negotiations to me, Your Worship," the aide said. "No need to trouble yourself. I'm sure Baron Frost will be openhanded to any who help him recover his child. And certainly the slavers are disreputable types whom we owe few favors."

The mayor uttered a rumbling sound. His jaw, which was visibly broad beneath the loose gray flesh of his face, sank toward the top of the vest he wore beneath his coat, as if fatigue was overcoming him.

In the stretching silence the ticks of the clock seemed to fall like hammers on Ryan's heart. He wasn't sure why he felt such tension. Worried about J.B., he told himself. That's all. Natural enough.

"See them off, Cosgrove. Give them what they want and send them on their way."

"But it's *cold* out there!" Mildred exclaimed.

The man's big head snapped up, and his old eyes blazed with anger.

"What concern is that of mine?" the mayor snapped. "Tavern Bay is no place for strangers to spend the night. Be off with you!"

The ringing of the clock, startlingly loud in the large emptiness of the rotunda, seemed to chase them as Morlon Cosgrove led them out, mocking their hopes and dreams.

Chapter Twenty-Two

The Trader took his convoy up north to the ville of Erie, a port in Sandusky Bay at the southwest end of Lake Erie. It was uncomfortably close not just to the Toledo ruins, but to fallout footprint from the wrecked Davis-Besse nuke power plant in the uninhabitable ville of Oak Harbor. The rad detectors in Trader's war wags registered radiation far higher than background. Strange things were said to happen around there. Marsh Folsom said the rad emissions likely played tricks on people's eyes and even brains.

J.B. didn't know if that was true, but he did understand the place was named for more than just the big-ass lake it was situated on.

J.B. rode in disgrace. He suffered in silence. He'd learned as a kid that complaining never did any good. If anybody even noticed, it was likely to bring you even less of what you wanted and more of what you didn't.

He responded the only way he had, when fists and fury hadn't served—he threw himself into work and learning. It was the best way to lose himself.

It was the best way to distract himself from the feelings that had betrayed him.

They'd always been uncomfortable companions, anyway.

But he still felt them. Too many. And bad ones.

Especially where Rance Weeden was concerned.

As she promised, she had frozen him out completely—
except for work, where she remained a good if now-
distant boss.

But that distance ate at him. He'd been totally caught
up in her—the torrid nightly sessions of lovemaking. Not
enough to detract from his work, but enough to absorb
him otherwise thinking of her when he wasn't having
sex with her.

Now, to be shut off from the vigorous, avid strength
of her long taut body—even any sign that he was more
to her than just another part, like a carburetor or mani-
fold—ate at his belly like a mob of hungry rats.

He'd tried talking to her—even sweet-talking, though
he knew he wasn't any good at it. It didn't matter. If it
wasn't work-related, she didn't acknowledge his exis-
tence, much less his words.

Once, before they hit Erie, he decided to take the
manly course and just grab her and make her kiss him.

The swelling in his jaw went down after a couple of
days. He was able to eat food other than soup through
a straw. But the hinges of his jaws still creaked when, a
week after leaving the rad-ridden ville, they hit the Lantic coast in what had been Maine, to park the convoy to
landward of the wide stinking salt marsh that guarded
a seaport ville called Tavern Bay.

"WE SAW SURPRISINGLY few folk abroad on our way
through your fair town," Doc said. Mildred frowned.
She was *not* in the mood for his archaic pomposities.
"None, in fact."

"People tend to keep indoors after dark here," said
Morlon Cosgrove, as he led them away from the rotunda
down a corridor inadequately lit by candles flickering on
pedestals that seemed to Mildred to be made of things

like improvised hat-racks. "Especially in the depth of winter. Also, the people of the ville tend to be wary of strangers. They have reason, as you can certainly appreciate."

"You have trouble with outlanders?" Ryan asked. "I'd judge you were pretty well protected, what with being surrounded on three sides by salt marsh and one way in from the mainland."

The mayor's aide laughed briefly, as if he paid for it by the heartbeat. "You of all people should realize how imperfect even the best defenses are."

Mildred frowned again. Granted, she was doing that a lot lately. But this time it was because she was puzzled. She wasn't the heavy tactical mind in the group—but not even she thought a makeshift barricade guarded by a fat middle-aged guy and a skinny adolescent boy would keep any even moderately determined malefactors out of Tavern Bay for long.

But what the oily aide said next drove thought of anything else right straight out of her brain.

"Remember, we do have to deal with the slavers passing by on a distressingly regular basis, which is why we have, in fact, heard about the baron's abducted daughter."

Her heart jumped up to her throat in excitement. J.B.! she thought. How I miss you.

"They're reports," he added. "Nothing more substantial than rumors, I must admit. But persistent ones."

Which only threw a bit of cold water on Mildred's flaring hopes. Half a bucket, say.

They came into the foyer. The cold now beat from the door; if the area was heated Mildred couldn't feel it. To one side what had to have been the curving information desk moldered under dust. Mildred wouldn't have been surprised had a security guard's skeleton still sat behind it, cobwebbed in its final doze on the job.

"And now," said Cosgrove, with something Mildred doubted even naive newbie Ricky would take for actual amiability, "it's time to discuss the *quid* to the *pro quo* you mentioned."

Mildred barely caught the reference. She hardly expected her companions to do so.

But Ryan nodded.

"Yeah. That's how it works. Korn, I think you're on."

The platinum blonde and the smarmy factotum negotiated briefly and calmly. Mildred tried to rein in her distinctive distrust of the man. He seemed to be just professionally unctuous; there was no reason to suspect that covered anything more than concern for himself, and little for others, which was scarcely an uncommon trait.

In the Deathlands it was just closer to the surface than it had been in her time. The terrible truth was, the more hard lessons the savage present taught her, the better her own times looked in retrospect.

Mildred tuned out the actual terms. Her distaste for commercial transactions had faded since her reawakening. Or maybe just been pushed way into the background by lots of things that were lots more distasteful. But she still had little interest in them. The girl may have sometimes seemed to show the affect of a robot—not surprising to Mildred, now that she knew her to be an abuse survivor—but it did give her at least the appearance of calm strength here.

Though Mildred also knew that they didn't really hold the hammer hand here, either. As close as she could reckon, though, Alysa managed to satisfy the oily little functionary without giving away the whole farm.

Alysa started to hand over the agreed-upon amount

of jack to seal the deal. Mildred noticed it wasn't all the amount Baron Frost had entrusted his sec woman with to procure assistance on their quest—explicitly including information. She had to nod. The girl's not much more than a child, she thought, but damn, she can handle herself well. And not just with a horse, sword and blaster.

But Ryan held out his hand. "Right," he told Cosgrove. "You got your terms. You've seen the color of our jack. Before we hand it over I think it's time we got the *pro quo*."

Cosgrove smiled thinly and it was quickly gone.

"You are clearly an educated man, Mr. Cawdor," he said. "You also make a sound point. As I told you, we have received reports from several sources. While details inevitably differ, there are consistent strands. All suggest a young woman fitting the description you gave us was taken past here in the last week, headed for the slavers' sea base."

"Anything else?" Ryan asked.

"She was spotted in a wag that looked as if it was a predark. She was held under heavy guard and appeared the only captive being transported. She showed no sign of injury and appeared in good health, albeit unhappy, which is scarcely surprising, after all. At the very least, the slavers would seem to consider her extremely valuable merchandise."

He looked at Alysa and performed a slight bow. Mildred couldn't tell if it was mocking or not. Indeed, that summed up just about everything this dude did. Whatever else he may or may not have been, he was smarmy.

"I apologize if that sounds insensitive. But they are slavers. And the value they obviously put on her does suggest they have treated her well, and will continue to do so."

Mildred and Krysty swapped looks. Yeah, the physician thought. At least until some major perv buys her for a ton of jack.

But they wouldn't let it get to that point. Ryan was on the case. And his friends. Motley a crew as they were, they were good at tracking and chilling. And they were all acutely conscious J.B.'s life—or at least his freedom—lay at stake.

"Can you tell us where this slaver base is?" Ryan asked. "Where their big ship puts in?"

"Yes." He looked at Alysa. "How well do you know this coast?"

"Not intimately," the slim girl said. "I have served as onboard sec on trips by boat as far down as New Portsmouth. Additionally, I have maps."

"You probably won't need them. Are you familiar with the small sheltered anchorage about seven miles from here? A sort of nook or inlet among high granite cliffs?"

Her brow creased briefly. Then she nodded. "I remember our captain urging me to stay alert. Sometimes raiding ships lie in wait there, to rush out to attack passing vessels. No one molested us, though."

"That's the place," Cosgrove said, nodding. "It's called Smuggler's Cove."

"For crap's sake," Mildred said with a snort.

Cosgrove laughed. It seemed the most genuine thing he'd done. "The people of what once was Maine have long prided themselves on being blunt-spoken. Especially the coasters. Although others might as easily call them unsubtle."

"You can find the place from here?" Ryan asked the sec woman.

"Yes."

"Well, then, let's save the discussion of quaint local customs for another time. Right now I reckon we need to shake the dust of this place off our boot heels in a hurry, so we have a chance of finding someplace to lie up the night without freezing solid."

"May I suggest the Carcosa Arms? It's our local hostelry. It lies right across the square from town hall. You passed it on your way in."

"Your boss said we weren't supposed to stay here," Ryan said. "Why do you even have a hotel, if you don't let outlanders stay the night?'

"We do entertain regular guests, usually merchants and commercial travelers of one sort or another. It is not that we are actively hostile, or even inhospitable. We do tend to be suspicious of outlanders, and for adequate reason. Far from everyone who visits Tavern Bay does so with benign intent."

"Still," Krysty said, "the Mayor seemed pretty emphatic we should go."

Cosgrove laughed again. "His Worship is a man much weighed down by his concerns. He can sometimes seem abrupt in his judgments. It seems to me that in this occasion he was overhasty. Especially in the light of the benefits this transaction had brought us."

"You're sure?" Krysty asked.

"Not like," Jak said.

"You never like," Ryan said. "But I'm not sure we won't be better off moving along. It's not healthy to stay in a place where we aren't wanted."

"Ah, but I won't hear of it!" Cosgrove said. "You are honored emissaries of a highly esteemed and powerful baron. We can do no less than provide our best accommodations—free of charge. Or shall we say, free of further charge?"

"Are you sure it won't get you in trouble with Mayor Thrumbull?" Krysty asked.

"Our plainspoken common people have a saying—'what he doesn't know won't hurt him.'"

Chapter Twenty-Three

Floorboards squeaked beneath J.B.'s boots as he walked back down the darkened corridor.

It was gut-deep night in the old hotel. Though the Northeast coast's early-summer night wasn't too hot, inside the Carcosa Arms Hotel it was stuffy and it didn't seem as if any of the windows would open. It smelled musty and of old paint, and something else he couldn't quite put a finger to, along with the inevitable smell of fish and rotting ocean creatures that pervaded the whole ville of Tavern Bay.

Still, the place had a functional lavatory here on the ground floor. J.B. was returning from the facilities to the room he shared with five of Trader's people, having been roused from his bed by the need to pee.

He was not happy. Even being one of the team of ten Trader had hand-picked to follow him into the decaying old coastal ville and back him up on whatever secret business he meant to transact there didn't much mollify him.

For one thing, he was among the group left behind in the ville proper while Trader took four of his top people with him, including Marsh Folsom. They were meant to back up Trader some way, somehow, when the deal was done. Whatever the nuke it was. The rest of the crew was laagered in with the wags on the solid ground where the valley started to widen out at the base of the ravine. In the meantime, all Trader's second-string could do was hole up in the room they'd been given in the hotel across from the town hall and grab some shuteye so they'd be fresh when Trader's call came.

For another thing, one of the men Trader had picked to accompany him, his top aide, and two of his ace sec men to his meet with his mystery trading partners was the man who'd taken Ace DeGuello's job as chief armorer for Trader's convoy. It was Tully, a rat-faced red-headed guy not much bigger than J.B., the guy who had straw-bossed the crew Rance had stopped in the middle of gang-stomping J.B. to lifeless mush.

As with the other armorers, Tully had accepted J.B. as a comrade once Ace recognized his skills. While he could nurse a grudge as well as any, J.B. had at least some idea of when to let bygones be that. Or, anyway, was glad enough to have his abilities acknowledged that he was willing to let some of the rage and resentment that smoldered in him go out.

And Tully was good enough at what he did. No question of that. One thing J.B. never had a problem with, temper or not, was summing up a 'smith's skills and according him the respect those entitled him to.

But good wasn't great. J.B. also knew he was better than Tully, who was near to twice his age. Which meant better than Tully would ever be.

In his mind he knew why things had happened as they had. Trader was not about to reward the person who'd gotten Ace DeGuello chilled by handing him the man's job. Not when Ace had been doing his duty and double-well at the time. Johnny's brain accepted that.

His balls didn't. And like an alcohol-lamp, their heat kept the resentment in his gut at a constant simmer.

And the other thing was Trader apparently saw nothing wrong with sticking him in a room with his former lover, Rance. Yeah, there were four others bunking with them in the big dorm-style room, and one rotated out of the sack every couple of hours to keep watch. But that didn't make young J.B. yearn less for the woman who had once been his bed partner.

He paused at the door to the room, down at the far end of the hallway near a window.

That had been perhaps the purest, most unalloyed pleasure of his life, the sex with his boss. At least, aside from when he was making something or fixing something with his hands, or figuring out a clever repair or fiendish booby. But Rance had shut him off cold and kept him in the cold.

He gritted his teeth and shook his head. He still wanted his gig with Trader. He needed more than ever to show everybody how good he really was. How *valuable* he really was.

Maybe then Rance would take him back.

He reached for the knob, which seemed outsized by way of layers of enamel painted on it over the years, the most recent coat being a white that was stained yellow as a smoker's teeth by hand grease.

Funny, he thought. I don't remember that fish smell so bastard strong.

The door opened.

Because there were two windows in the long room, the light was better there, though still dim. The first thing he saw by the star-glow, since he had his eyes down to the doorknob and hadn't yet raised them, was a body sprawled facedown on the floor almost jamming the door. A flash glance registered that it was male, tall, pretty spare, with a bald spot in the middle of dark hair.

That made him Joe Slammer, the ace driver who'd been standing sentry when Johnny left to hit the pisser.

The back of his head under the bald spot seemed kind of sunk-in and gleamed as if with moisture. A black pool spread out around his head like a halo in some predark religious print.

J.B. looked up, and his gut constricted to a fist.

There were *things* standing in the room. Hunching, more like. They weren't much taller, if any, than he was, but much more massive, with giant deep chests and massive huge-jawed heads thrust forward from stooped shoulders without visible benefit of necks. Their legs were bowed but unnaturally muscled. Their eyes were huge and glittered like gelatin in the starlight.

Two stood by a hole gaping in the floorboards of the room. One was helping a third who had big clawed-flipper hands wrapped around Rance Weeden. One was clamped over her mouth. Her eyes rolled wildly as she struggled. But strong as she was, the mutie monster's power was clearly too much for her.

The other beds lay empty. One was actually overturned. Everybody was gone, down that hole to horror.

Rance's wild eyes lit on J.B. standing like a simp in the doorway. Somehow they got bigger. She managed to wrench half her mouth clear of the muffling claw.

"J.B., run!" she screamed. "Warn the others!"

That was the smart thing to do. No doubt about it. There was clearly no helping her otherwise—one lone kid against hulking, shambling monsters, with only a lock-back folder knife for a weapon.

Hollering, "Rance!" Johnny launched himself to the attack.

The nearer frog-shaped mutie met him with a brutal backhand sweep of his right flipper-hand. He didn't even bother to look at the lunging youth.

The impact on the side of J.B.'s face caused his world to go darker and distant and blurry. He had the sense of floating backward.

Then his skull cracked hard against the doorpost, red lightning lanced through his brain and that was that.

RICKY CAME AWAKE to a hand on his mouth.

"Rrmph!" he said urgently as his eyes snapped open to darkness. He tried to sit up on the bed in the room he shared with Jak and Doc.

A weight came down his chest. By the moonlight through the frost-furred window he made out a pale glow floating above his face.

Jak Lauren grinned at him.

Ricky rolled his eyes down over the snow-white hand muffling it. He squealed in outrage.

"Not talk," Jak commanded firmly.

When Ricky nodded, Jak removed his hand.

"You're *sitting* on me!" Ricky said in outrage.

"Stop jumping and acting like feeb," Jak said.

Like the rest of them Ricky had gotten used to Jak's bizarre shorthand speech. Or at least learned to extract meaning from it. It was still annoying to him sometimes.

The hand went away. So did Jak's narrow jeans-clad ass. Ricky belatedly sat up.

He looked around. They were alone. The third bed lay empty.

"Doc on watch," Jak said.

"And you're waking me, why?"

Though they were alone now, Ricky kept his voice low. They were sandwiched between the room Ryan shared with Krysty and the one where Mildred and

Alysa slept. From what Ricky had heard of Ryan and Krysty's activities before he pulled his pillow over his head and sheer exhaustion finally pulled him down to sleep, the walls were not soundproof.

He still wasn't sure where two people that old got that kind of energy.

Jak's grin got wider. His white brow creased hard above eyes showing hints of ruby glint to the moonlight.

"Explored," he said. "Found something."

Instantly Ricky nodded. He knew whatever Jak had in mind was probably not a good idea. At least for Ricky, though the way Jak could move through any setting like the ghost he resembled meant he'd likely get away with whatever bad craziness he had in mind.

But even after weeks with the companions, Ricky was still thrilled that his pal Jak wanted to include him in his escapade. And despite growing up sheltered and pampered, as he now realized, in the little ville of Nuestra Señora—a seaport town much like this one, except neater, more lively and smelling much less nastily of must and decomposing mollusks—he found he had a taste for adventure.

Perhaps *because* of that sheltered life.

"What?" he asked quietly.

Jak held up Ricky's utility belt, with his Webley handblaster hanging from it in its flap-covered holster, and Ricky's silent-shooting DeLisle carbine.

"Follow, see," the albino said.

"Now," Jak said softly. He slipped out into the hall.

Walking as lightly as he could in his socks, with his boots slung around his neck by their tied-together laces, Ricky followed. He was almost trembling. He was so keyed up he forgot even to be cold.

He glanced right. A tall, narrow shadow was walking deliberately away down the threadbare runner carpet, silhouetted by moon-glow from the window at corridor's end. Doc was pacing up and down the corridor, possibly to stay awake.

Ricky wasn't sure how much difference that might even make. Doc had a tendency to wander off inside his own head when left alone. Who knew where he was now?

Still, Ryan let Doc take his turn on watch, as he was doing now. And they were all still alive. So Ricky wasn't about to question his adored leader's wisdom.

Jak, meanwhile, was creeping the other way, toward the T-juncture where another corridor crossed this one. In one direction it led to the door to the lobby at the front of the run-down hotel. In the other it headed to a door into a dining room that had probably been closed since before the Big Nuke, so far as Ricky could tell.

Jak went down to the very end, just before the cross-passage, and turned to his right. He disappeared inside a room.

Ricky followed.

"Shut door," Jak commanded.

Ricky obeyed, as quietly as he could. He winced when the door mechanism engaged with an inevitable metallic clack.

Jak was hunkered in the middle of the floor. This was a two-bed room. Both beds were empty. The bureau and single chair weren't deep in dust, so Ricky gathered it saw use fairly recently. Not this night, though.

"Smelled something funny," Jak said. "Tried door. Then found."

He tapped the floor. In the faint light from outside, Ricky, by straining, could make out a line along the floor. It was darker than the normal ones between the bare polished hardwood planks.

Then he made out a right angle in the black line. He was looking at a trapdoor improperly shut.

"Smell came out here," Jak said. "Sea, dead sea stuff."

Ricky couldn't smell anything more than the usual nastiness of the ville itself, which at least was muted in here. Admittedly, it was muted by the hotel's stuffiness, as well as the general smell of mildew, dust and age. But he trusted Jak's nose. He had a wild animal's keen senses.

Ricky came over to squat beside him, studying the trapdoor. "Shall we open it?" he asked.

Jak gave him a look.

"Okay," Ricky said. "Dumb question." He started feeling to see if he could start the trap open with his fingertips. Though his hands were still relatively soft, lots of detail work on metals had made them strong.

Jak stopped him with a couple of fingers on his forearm. "Boots first," he said.

The albino youth already wore his customary sneakers. Johnny nodded. He sat down, pulled on his boots, quickly tightened the laces and tied them.

Then Jak helped him pry up the trapdoor. It made surprisingly little noise.

Even Ricky could smell the saltwater in the breath of air that rolled up from the blackness and hit him in the face. It felt so warm he thought they might have opened a passageway to a furnace, although there was none in evidence in the hotel. It didn't even have radiators, those obviously having been salvaged for scrap decades before. Then Ricky realized the air was warmer because it was insulated by the Earth itself from the chill that made his nose numb and his breath mist white before his eager face.

He reached to his belt to unlimber the flywheel flashlight he carried in a small holster there. It had been made by hand by his Tío Benito, who sold them on the side to augment his income as armorer and general tinker.

"No," Jak said. He nodded down the hole. "Light."

Ricky frowned. Then his eyes picked up a faint glimmer of yellow.

"Follow," Jak said, and eeled down into the hole.

Ricky followed. There was a wooden ladder there. He pulled the lid shut behind him, trying to make sure it seated properly this time, then he descended to stand beside his friend on a damp floor of cut stone.

He was able to see now, just a little. The tunnel, which was just high enough that the two not-very-tall young men could stand upright, obviously continued along parallel to the building front. That meant, he realized, that it ran *under* the other rooms on that side of the corridor.

"You mean *our* room—?" he asked in an alarmed whisper.

"Shut," Jak said sternly.

Ricky shut. The glow came from the other direction. He realized that it had to intersect beneath the cross-passage, then open into a larger chamber directly underneath the lobby.

Jak stalked toward the light. He carried a hunting knife with a clipped point and a five-inch blade, not the trench knife or one of the butterfly knives he usually favored for battle—and, of course, not one of his specialized leaf-bladed throwing knives. Ricky had no idea where he carried all those damn knives, concealed on his wispy frame. He never quite got up the nerve to ask, either. It just seemed too personal.

After a moment Ricky unslung his DeLisle from across his back. Unlike Jak he wasn't a master of the stealthy blade, but he trusted himself and that blaster. And the fact was, its locked-up action and subsonic projectile made it little louder than a knife was.

Crouching, Jak peered into the large chamber, then he stepped out. Ricky followed without hesitation. For all his propensity to do balls-out-crazy shit like this, Jak retained the paranoid instincts of an old tom alley cat, as well as its senses.

It was a big empty room with ladders leading down from the lobby and where Ricky judged the kitchen had to be. There were a few old crates and barrels stashed by the back wall, near that second ladder. He couldn't make out much of them since they lay too far from the single lantern hung from a bracket in the wooden ceiling, which was a little higher here. Enough a tall man like Ryan or Doc might be able to stand upright without braining himself.

Ricky saw that another tunnel opened up toward the back. The rooms on the other side of the corridors had to host concealed trapdoors, too. He shuddered.

"Shouldn't we warn the others?" he asked, realizing it was even now probably a little late to be asking.

"And say what?" Jak asked. Then without waiting for the answer he knew was not coming, he padded off into another, wider tunnel that led out past the front of the hotel.

Ricky followed, glancing back nervously over his shoulder. His nutsack was trying its level best to crawl up inside his belly, and Jak seemed to be leading them into the utter lightless dark of underground.

"Not look back," Jak said. "Spoil vision."

Ricky set his jaw for fear of somebody—*something*—

creeping down the tunnel after them. He followed Jak by the light that came from behind. Ricky realized quickly there was more faint glow shining from ahead.

They came to a place where another wide tunnel crossed this one. To the right lay total blackness. From the left came a faint yellow glow—and a hint of moving air.

Before them the tunnel continued. Clearly it ran on beneath the town hall. And to the sea, judging by the way the smell had gradually gotten stronger.

Jak headed to his left. About forty yards ahead another fish-oil lantern hung from a bronze bracket sunk in the dressed-stone walls.

As they neared the lamp, Jak stopped. He held up a slim white hand.

Ricky frowned. Then he heard.

"Is that someone chanting?" he asked, remembering to speak in a low voice rather than whispering. As J. B. Dix had taught Ricky, a whisper actually carried far, and was more liable to catch the notice of the very people, or other creatures, you didn't want to hear you.

And speaking of other creatures, Ricky realized there was something wrong with the distance-muffled voice he heard and the chorus of other voices that rumbled a low response.

Jak moved forward. He was crouched, going slower and more cautiously. Shaking off a pang of fear and lonesomeness for his wounded, missing mentor, Ricky followed.

They came to some stone steps that were wide, slick with condensation and led down.

Ricky tapped Jak's shoulder, gingerly, since he was afraid of what his friend and that knife might do if he startled him.

But Jak merely glanced back.

"We're under the old church," Ricky mouthed.

Jak nodded once, then he put a white finger to lips so pale they were barely pink.

He led them down the stairs. Past him Ricky could see that at the bottom was some kind of landing, apparently unlit. From behind, as they reached the bottom, came the dancing glow of nude flames.

Jak slipped onto the landing and to his left, so that his slight form wouldn't be lethally silhouetted against the light at the top of the stairs. Ricky had almost reached the bottom himself when he caught a glimpse of what lay beyond the landing.

There was a vast chamber lying perhaps a story below the landing, which turned into a kind of gallery. It was full of light from two bonfires and a number of torches—and a myriad of hunched bodies shadowed and swaying against the light.

"Santa María, Madre de Dios," Ricky breathed. "Frogs!"

Chapter Twenty-Four

Ricky almost shrieked in reflexive terror when a hand grabbed his left arm. Then he realized it was Jak, leaning back into the opening to pull Ricky's stupe ass out of the light. He'd have been clearly visible if any hostile eyes had turned his way.

Actually reassured by the gallery's darkness, Ricky overcame his urgent desire to run screaming back to their friends. Bent low over the reassuring heft of his longblaster, he followed Jak forward to the rail that ran along the gallery.

The lower level was *full* of frogs. The man-size muties hunched or swayed in place, waving their long misshapen arms above their heads. There were at least a hundred of them packed into a rough circle around the open, man-high fires.

The ones with their backs to the young men in the shadows were shadows themselves, grotesque and horrible. The ones on the far side were worse. Ricky could see their faces—their sunken cheeks and lantern jaws filled with long, curving needle teeth, their enormous eyes, the vertical slits that almost completely supplanted noses. What was worst about them was that, underlit like this by capering flames, those faces clearly showed the *human* in them.

Ricky noticed that some of the creatures had blue eyes. He crossed himself and begrudged the second or

two it required him to take his hand off the foregrip of
his longblaster.

So mesmerizing was the sheer horror of the mob of
frog muties that it took Ricky—a healthy adolescent
male who liked the opposite sex—a good half minute
to notice that in the middle of the stone-floored circle
were two naked women.

For some reason Ricky's first thought was a terrified,
I hope one of them's not the baron's daughter!

But he quickly realized neither could be. They were
both fuller-bodied, thus obviously older, although neither
was what he'd call overfed. Each showed ribs down her
bare sides. The blonde one had pink skin and nipples.
The rangier redhead had olive skin.

Both were done up like gaudy sluts, eyes staringly
outlined in black and showing hints of green and purple,
cheeks unnaturally pink and mouths painted as red as
fresh blood. For gaudy sluts, though, they looked surprisingly young and fresh. Not that Ricky had…intimate
experience of such. But in the time he'd spent crisscross-
ing the Deathlands with Ryan and his companions he'd
seen his share of them.

And they were both busy pleasuring a naked young
man spread-eagled face-up on a stone or probably concrete slab set between the bonfires.

Ricky turned to look at Jak, who crouched beside
him peering over the stone rail. He felt oddly relieved to
see the albino was watching the scene with ruby eyes as
avid as Ricky's. But they were still attuned to the slight-
est flicker of peripheral motion; the foxlike white face
turned instantly to his companion's.

"So why is he chained down like that?" Ricky
mouthed. He knew *he* wouldn't need to be restrained
to let himself be pleasured by two girls like that. De-

spite the scrotum-tightening existential dread of so many man-eating muties packed together—some almost within reach of his arm over the railing, and stinking horribly of fish—a raging hard-on threatened to explode the fly of his jeans.

Jak nodded as he turned his attention back to the scene. He wasn't tunnel-visioning on the naked girls, though obviously he was as aware of them as Ricky was.

A tall and rather narrow-looking frog stood on the far side of the altar. With another gut-shock Ricky realized that was the only thing the slab could possibly be. Around his neck the frog had a big gold medallion decorated with a weird staring-eyed face surrounded by wiggles like tentacles. Ricky remembered that symbol suddenly: it was the same one he'd seen daubed on the front of the church by the town square.

The one they were hiding beneath.

The frog mutie was chanting something in a deep and sibilant voice. The mob of excited muties croaked responses in ragged unison.

The young man had his eyes closed and was tossing his head side to side as the women worked on him.

And then the mob fell silent. The only noise was the beguiling moans of the women and the captive youth's answering and increasingly urgent groans.

Another creature stepped from the shadows on the far side of the sunken temple. It was tall and also somewhat gaunt for a frog mutie. It possessed a pair of small but unmistakable breasts protruding from either side of its keel-like breastbone. The green nipples were erect.

"Santo Niño de Atocha," Ricky breathed.

As she approached the altar a pair of naked—and obviously male—frogs came from both sides to seize the naked human women around the waists and drag them away from the young man. They struggled and screamed.

The young man's eyes were still shut, his head whipping back and forth.

Climbing onto the pedestal, the frog-woman mounted the young man and the mating ritual continued.

As the young man clearly spent himself in the frog-mutie woman, she threw her head back and uttered an ecstatic roar. The onlookers went crazy, hopping and dancing and shaking their talons in the air as if they were all getting off, too.

As the spasms of his orgasm subsided, the captive opened his eyes and uttered a shattering scream.

The frog-woman swung her body around so that now she straddled his bare, hairless chest. She bent down toward him. He stared up at her with eyes bulging from his young face. She thrust her face toward him as if to kiss him.

At the last instant she opened her huge jaws and bit his face off with an audible crunch. His body spasmed.

Ricky's mouth filled with sour vomit. He tried to raise his DeLisle. His only thought was to blast the frightful creature.

Jak placed his hand across the built-in silencer that shrouded the barrel, stopping Ricky. As cryptic as the albino usually was, Ricky had grown adept at reading his friend's expressions and body language, which could be downright eloquent.

One upraised white eyebrow loudly told him, You aren't triple-fucking-bright, are you?

He lowered the longblaster.

The nude women were struggling futilely and screeching shrilly, also without effect on their burly captors. Their bare breasts flopped in a way that almost distracted Ricky from the awfulness of what he'd just seen—and was continuing to see.

"You promised when you bought us you'd let him go when you were done with him!" shrieked the blonde.

Ricky's heart, trapped in mid-throat like a pigeon flapping frantically to fly out his mouth, plummeted to the bottom of his stomach like that same bird shot full of lead buck.

Bought! he thought. They're trading with the slavers!

The frog priest turned an unmistakable and ghastly smile on her. "We lied," he said in his sonorous bass croak.

The blonde glared at him defiantly. She opened her mouth to say something furious.

Then her blue eyes shot wide and her companion's scream blasted out fit to shatter glass. Ricky realized the male frog who held the blonde had just reached around to slash her throat.

"The hell with this," Ricky said to Jak. The frogs were croaking fit to bring the low-domed ceiling down. Jak could barely hear him.

"Go now," Jak agreed.

He turned and rabbited back the way they'd come. Ricky gulped and followed.

THERE WAS NO ONE on watch when they burst back into the corridor from the unoccupied room where they'd entered the tunnels.

"Oh, *no,*" Ricky moaned. "We're too late."

Jak trotted down the hallway to the door of the room Ryan shared with Krysty. As he reached it Ricky sprinted to his side and raised a fist to hammer frantically on the door.

Jak turned the knob and opened the heavy hardwood door.

Their friends were standing in the middle of the floor by the empty, rumpled bed, shrugging into their well-stuffed backpacks. All except one.

"Where's Ryan?" Ricky yelped.

He found himself thrust out of the door he stood blocking by a hard hand on the shoulder. "I was arranging a little diversion," the one-eyed man said.

"You found the fish-oil stores, then, Ryan?" asked Doc, who stood with his huge LeMat in one knobby hand.

"Affirmative," Ryan said, as Krysty swung his heavy backpack off the bed as if it were as light as a newborn baby and held it up to his back.

Ricky stared with his mouth hanging open. As he threaded his arms through the backpack's straps, Ryan grinned at him wolfishly.

"What?" he demanded. "Did you think J.B. was the only one who could improvise incendies?"

Chapter Twenty-Five

Consciousness landed on J.B. like an anvil. It brought with it a skull-busting headache and awareness of a gut that tossed like storm-blasted sea.

Then terror and loss and rage.

"Rance!" he croaked, snapping up to a seated position.

His head reeled. The back of it banged against the door, which he'd been knocked against, he recollected now. His head was still sore.

His stomach turned over. He only just managed to stop himself from puking.

Dark night, he thought. I got a nukin' concussion.

His eyes, now open, cleared to the sight of an empty room. That much he could make out without his glasses.

Feeling sick fear—laid atop the nausea—that the frog mutie might've busted his glasses and left him just a little less blind than a bat, he groped around for them. Almost at once his fingers felt the familiar hardness of cool curved wire and ground glass. He fumbled the specs onto his nose.

He let out the anxious breath he'd been holding. The lenses were intact, though the frame needed a bit of careful warping to fit correctly on his face. But at least he could see.

The floor looked intact again. He might have believed the whole episode had been some kind of hallucination, cooked up by his brain after he'd tripped and addled it by banging it against the door frame, if not for the sight and smell of the dead body lying just past an arm's reach away.

Digging with his heels, he pressed his back up the wall and away from the chill, who obviously had crapped his pants when he bought it.

For a moment he just leaned back. While his blood sang with urgency to rescue Rance—and his other companions, too—the very dizziness that made it obviously unsafe to move forced him to focus his aching brain and think.

First: *observation*. One man had been chilled and four people taken from their beds without much sign of struggle, which meant they'd all been caught sleeping except for Slammer: Gonzalez, a wiry little Indian-looking guy who was an electronics wizard who usually worked comms and sensors in War Wag One. Under Ace he had taught J.B. the rudiments of electronics as well as weapons-control and sighting systems. The others were a couple of Trader's burliest cargo-handlers, who doubled as drivers—along with most everybody else—named Zap and Stang. And, of course, Rance.

He noticed there were wet patches on the wooden floor. Some gave a vague impression of footprints, from the front ends of clawed feet. He remembered the creatures seemed to stand on their toes. So the weird frog-like muties had come from water. Reasonable enough. Maybe the sea, which was just a few hundred yards past the town hall?

They hadn't bothered to ransack the room. J.B. could see his own pack, as well as a Remington 870 pump 12-gauge lying on the floor beside Joe Slammer's body.

Experimentally he pushed off from the wall. His head

still hurt like hell and his legs seemed to be made out of boiled noodles. But after a little swaying back and forth his legs solidified some, and his stomach at least started acting as if it meant to stay put.

Now: *action*.

Keeping his mind focused, he went quickly through the things Rance and the rest had left behind when they were taken. There were some things he needed, including Rance's EAA Witness handblaster and a pair of spare double-stack mags of .40 S&W rounds. And, of course, the shotgun. He was never going to be a long-range marksman, not with his weak eyes. But he always favored the heft and firepower a longblaster gave him.

As he got ready to leave, he spotted Rance's fedora lying under her bed. He bent and picked it up. He tried fitting it experimentally on his head.

Surprisingly, it did fit him. Though Rance was taller than he was, he'd always had a big head for his frame.

He didn't delude himself she'd take him back for bringing her her cherished hat. He was beyond that now. If rescuing her didn't do the trick, the thing could not be done.

Of course, first he'd have to rescue her. And hopefully his other friends.

And, he was realizing—mebbe even Trader himself. J.B. distrusted coincidence, and that the same ville Trader had chosen to do a secret deal was just incidentally also home to a tribe of horrible fish-frog-human muties who had a secret tunnel network connected to hotel rooms by trapdoors was just way too much to swallow. That meant that Trader, Marsh, Tully and the convoy's two ace blaster-handlers, Sciabarra and Morrison, were either captives, too, or chills—or in immediate danger of becoming one or the other.

As for the convoy itself, J.B. dismissed it. The majority of the crew were still with the wags. They wouldn't go down without a bastard fight, and they were just the bastards to lay one down. They could take care of themselves.

He went to stand beside the trapdoor. Then he squatted. The light in the room was too dim to make out detail, least of all with his eyes, glasses or not. But he had a small flywheel flashlight that was powered by squeezing the handle to generate juice. It was one of the things Trader apparently bought from the Science Brothers; they did do some pretty fair fabrication, whether or not they sometimes decided to go into the grand larceny end of things.

He took it out now and began to pump it with his palm. It made a sort of wheezy grinding sound along with a spatter of faint light the color of old piss. Then it lightened and brightened.

The light was enough for him to make out where the trap was fitted. That was good work, he had to admit. Though he also had to admit he was no kind of carpenter. He wouldn't think that fine a separation would allow the door to open easily and without making much noise, as obviously it had to take even the watchful Slammer by surprise. Though obviously the sentry was focused on the door when the frogs took him down by stealth. But it took all J.B.'s fabricator's knowledge and intuition to make out the hair-thin lines where the door was cut out crosswise to the run of floorboards.

With his pocketknife he pried up the door. As expected, it came readily and quietly. No frog monster sprang out to rake his face off with its claws.

He eased the door down beside the hole. Cautiously he shone the flywheel light inside.

A ladder with wide and double-sturdy wooden rungs led down about six or eight feet to a floor of polished flagstones. He could actually see some puddles of water at the bottom where the muties had dripped.

He needed a plan, but without more information he had no grounds to make one. So taking a deep breath, he lowered himself into the hole and pulled the lid shut above his head.

He was well and truly stuck in it now. With no clear idea of what *it* really was.

He only knew it was bad, and that it'd probably chill him.

But he never thought of backing out. Setting the hat firmly on his head, he swept the flashlight beam around his new surroundings. It was a tunnel, not a sewer, and it seemed to run along the line of rooms.

The wet patches and marks of frog-mutie feet led toward the area beneath where the lobby was. He headed that way.

Quickly he found himself in a larger chamber, low but much wider. Other tunnels opened off it.

A larger one led in a direction that, if he was oriented right, went under the square toward the town hall. The wet marks led that way.

By the entrance he spotted something dark. He knew right off it was unusual. The tunnel and subterranean chamber were clear of trash, even any accumulation of dust and muck, although some of the crates and casks stashed toward the back showed dust.

He went to it and hunkered down. He primed the flywheel light, which squeaked. He was glad his hands were strong, though the truth was he felt his palm muscles tiring. His hands, capable and used to doing as they were, weren't accustomed to doing *this*.

He reached for the dark item on the ground. It was a little scrap of black. Brown fragments fell out of it as he picked it up with his free hand.

He thought he recognized it. A sniff made him sure. It was a piece of one of the cheroots his boss and former lover smoked.

Rance, he thought. Stuffing the chunk of cheroot in his pocket, he steeled himself and walked into the tunnel's black mouth.

"UGLY," RYAN SAID, as Ricky finished gasping out the story of his and Jak's exploration and their horrifying discoveries.

And it was. Ugly even by the standards of what Ryan had seen and heard in his travels.

Weapons in hand, they were trotting through the ville toward the bridge inland. Not down the main street, but down a cobbled side street so narrow Ryan felt as if he could stretch out both arms and brush the soot-smeared brick and stone facades with his fingertips. He didn't like moving through surroundings that made things this easy for would-be ambushers, but he was relying on what lay below the yellow glow that was visible behind them, down by the waterfront, to give the frogs something better to do than chase them.

All a man could do was all he could do. Trader had said that, often enough. And like many things Trader habitually said, Ryan lived his life by those words.

"But don't you *see?*" Ricky gasped.

He and Alysa were bringing up the rear. He clutched his longblaster in both hands. At the very tail of the line, the Stormbreak sec woman had her saber in her hand and her pale eyes were wild in her paler face.

"The ville is full of muties!" Ricky said. "And they're dealing with the slavers!"

From right ahead of him in their single file Mildred shushed him.

"We figured something was dirty, kid," she told him—gently, given how the stress she was under was amping up her normal grumpiness. "Why else do you think you found us getting ready to bolt?"

"We didn't know the details," Krysty said from right behind Ryan. "But we knew our hosts planned something."

"Ryan suspected," Doc said. "He smelled out the trap. Our white wolf, Jak, is not the only one with that gift, either. A sly, black wolf is Ryan."

"When we came in across the bridge the only sec they had on the one and only land route into the ville was guarded by a fat middle-aged dude and a weedy teenage boy," Ryan said. "And if Tavern Bay didn't have some kind of top-notch defenses against attack from the sea, the slavers would own this place. The locals weren't staying off the streets because they were afraid of outsiders invading. They had reason not to want to be seen."

"Ryan went out for a quick recon," said Mildred, who was right ahead of Ricky in their single file. "And what should he see but *frogs*. Hopping across the square right out in front of God and everybody, headed for that boarded-up old church of yours. Like they had no reason to give a shit if anybody saw them or not."

The she added, "Eyes front, kid."

Glancing briefly back Ryan saw the boy was walking backward, obviously staring back at the brightening yellow glow.

"Did you set fire to the hotel?" Ricky asked, reluctantly facing forward again.

"No," Ryan said. He already had his face swiveling again, his lone eye skinned, scoping the buildings on either side for signs of danger. "I found a warehouse full of cloth, a couple blocks down. I poured the cask of fish oil I happened to have along all over the stuff, left a lit cigarette I rolled out of the tobacco and paper we carry to trade on a crate beside it, so it'd fall down in the oil when it burned down to a butt."

Behind them a bell began to ring with frantic urgency. Ryan allowed himself another glance back. The yellow fire-glow had just gotten visibly brighter.

"And *now* the hotel's on fire," Ryan said with just a flash of satisfaction.

"The old church retains its steeple bell," Doc said musingly, "despite the profane purposes to which it has been turned."

"Yeah," Ryan said. "Well, we best power out of here now. If we're lucky, the frogs'll reckon we're heading for the docks to steal a boat, instead of taking the long, slow way out of this ville."

He led them into an easy lope. Until they had evidence of direct pursuit he saw no reason to blow everybody's wind running full-tilt. Plus a fast pace would make it hard to spot incidental danger.

As it turned out they were going too fast anyway. Or not fast enough.

They were within a couple of blocks of where the street played out into the weeds of the salt marsh, which were ghost-pale in the starlight. The moon had set about half an hour before. The light of the fires behind them was spray-painting a sullen burnt-orange glow on the underbellies of storm clouds rolling in low off the sea as if in pursuit of the fugitives.

Over the clip-clopping of their boot-soles on the uneven cobblestones, Ryan heard Alysa scream.

He stopped and spun, raising his SIG-Sauer handblaster.

At least a half dozen dark, shambling shadows surrounded the young woman. Ryan saw one reel back with its face spurting black from a slash of the girl's curved sword.

"Run!" she shrieked after her companions. "Save Milya!"

A frog hopped at her with arms wide to clutch. She ran it through the chest. It uttered a dismal croak and fell flopping. But the blade was caught in its sternum. Its weight wrenched the hilt from her hand.

Another grabbed her from behind and picked her up off the pavement.

Other frogs were emerging from a side street—what had been Alysa's right, with the main drag two blocks to their left. Apparently a whole passel of the muties had been making for the main street in answer to the church-bell alarm and had spotted the fleeing group at just the wrong instant.

Another frog went down. Facing the mutie mob, Ricky worked the action of his DeLisle to chamber another round. And short-shucked it, jamming the empty in the breech before the ejector had a chance to kick it free.

Mildred grabbed his collar from behind. "Come on, kid!" she yelled. "We can't help her!"

With a deep hollow tolling like a parody of the perverted church's bell, a manhole cover was pulled open by the frogs. They clustered around the thrashing captive. Ryan could see her blond hair flying as she battled them.

But it was hopeless, as were the shots Krysty, Doc

and even Mildred sent into the growing mutie pack as some turned to chase the others.

"We can't just let them take her!" howled Ricky. He didn't even flinch as Mildred's ZKR blasted off right by his ear a second time, though unburned propellants from muzzle and cylinder had to have stung his face and the muzzle-flare scorched his hair. *"I know what they'll do to her!"*

A louder blaster shot cracked between the buildings. With her body halfway down the manhole Alysa's blonde head snapped back. A black spray hung briefly in the air above her and her stooped captors.

By reflex Ryan worked the bolt of his Steyr Scout carbine as he brought it back down on target. The echoes of his shot were still rattling up the multi-story buildings that seemed to lean above them.

Alysa Korn's body, now lifeless, vanished into the depths beneath the ville.

Most of the muties had already gone down the hole, or followed the sad, slim chill some of them still clutched. A half dozen hopped in pursuit of the others. But their short, bent legs, powerful though they were, weren't meant for speed. At least on land. Three more went down to blasterfire, two of them to Ryan's big 7.62 mm slugs. The rest melted back into the doorways of the dark buildings to either side.

"*Now* run," Ryan shouted.

THE MIDDLE-AGED MAN stood by the entrance to the guard-shack. He held what looked like a single-shot shotgun in his hands and swiveled his head as he stared toward the flames that shot into the sky above the town square. For some reason, the shack showed no lights. In the improvised tin-roofed stable nearby, horses stamped and whickered in agitation at all the noise.

And, thought Ricky, crouched at a shadowed corner a block to the side of the bridge entrance, from the smell of smoke that was now strong in his nostrils.

Overhead the storm clouds slid across the stars like a black curtain being pulled by God's own hand.

By the barrier that blocked this end of the highway bridge that connected Tavern Bay to the causeway through the marshes, a skinny boy at least two years younger than Ricky stood clutching what looked to the Puerto Rican youth like a Ruger 10/22 carbine. The guards were the same pair who had passed Ryan's party into the ville in the last hours of the day.

As he switched his view over his carbine's iron sights back to the man, Ricky thought they looked more piteous than anything. He felt bad for what was about to happen, in spite of everything he'd just seen.

He covered the older sentry just in time to see a pallid blur appear behind his forward-slumped left shoulder. A ghost-white hand grabbed him by the forehead from behind, yanking the balding head backward.

Blood gushed like a black river from a throat slashed open to the neckbones by the hunting knife expertly wielded by Jak Lauren.

Ricky aimed his stocky longblaster back at the boy. Don't do it, he willed the kid. Don't make me—

But the youth raised his blaster. Even from fifty yards away Ricky could see it quiver as he drew a fast, deep breath and let half of it out.

The metal plate sheathing the DeLisle's wooden butt punched his shoulder. This time he worked the short bolt action with his customary smooth skill as the weapon recovered from the mild recoil.

He had already seen the dark blood-brain spray in the air in front of the young sentry. When he collapsed bonelessly to the cracked asphalt, Ricky knew he wasn't faking.

A horse neighed in alarm, then it settled down. Ricky knew Krysty had gotten into the stable and was soothing the nervous animals.

He flinched, then, as Doc, who'd guarded his back, slapped his shoulder from behind.

"Time to be on our way, lad," he said. "Though our escape was seen, it seems our hosts have better things to do than chase after us. Perhaps they are glad enough to see the last of us for the nonce."

Ricky cast what he hoped was his last glance ever back over Tavern Bay. The fires Ryan had lit as a diversion blazed brighter than ever.

Then he followed the oldie's flying coattails in a mad dash for the horses and freedom.

Chapter Twenty-Six

J.B. crouched in blackness as complete as any he'd ever known. His heart hammered at his ribs as if trying to break free of them.

He actually felt it more than the pounding at the back of his head. At least his balance had come back, and the strength in his legs. His nausea had subsided to a low slogging unease that wasn't hard to ignore.

The enclosed space and the sense of tons of earth and concrete right on top of him, ready to trap and crush, had aroused his mild claustrophobia, too. That, at least, he kept in check. There was just too much else to get upset about.

He saw light. It just didn't illuminate where he was. The trouble was, it came from two directions.

One led off to the left. From the ochre glow he could tell it went downward. The other went straight ahead, and widened into a pretty big chamber. Air flowed from both—and in both cases smelled of salt water, and nasty sea muck, like the whole bastard ville.

That had to be under the town hall, he reckoned. By counting his paces he knew he'd made it at least to below the entrance.

He had already passed a wide tunnel that led off left—to the old boarded-up church he'd noticed when Trader led them to the hotel, apparently. But just beyond its opening another chunk of cheroot was lying in the main tunnel heading toward the town hall and the waterfront beyond. That showed him the way the frogs had taken Rance and the other captives.

Somehow his boss had managed to get hold of one of her smokes and break off bits to drop to mark their trail. That was just like her, cool and resourceful, even at a time like this. That would've made him love—

Nuke that, he told himself savagely. Feelings got me into this mess with her. Feelings got my head half-busted.

Fuck feelings.

He didn't need emotions to drive him. He had a job to do. And really, that was all Johnny B. Dix had ever needed.

He turned left.

At the bottom the tunnel went off at an angle. Still toward the bay, he figured, but perhaps toward the north end of the waterfront.

It curved. He thought he could make out the faintest glimmerings of light along the outside wall. Not enough to see by, but he was reluctant to make any light right now. He sensed, amid the residual turmoil in his belly, that he was getting close to his destination.

He knew well that any light illuminated its source even more surely than whatever it shone on, which, he'd noted, a power of other people tended to forget.

Hanging his flywheel hand-lantern off his belt, hefting the shotgun by the grip in his right hand, J.B. forged on. He navigated by trailing his outstretched left fingers along the stone.

The urgency to find and save his friends—not to mention get the nuke *out* of this reeking death trap—filled and shook his skinny body like electricity.

The walls grew smoother and clammier to the touch.

Condensed moisture started trickling down the back of his hand. The tunnel here seemed to be bored through rock, not stone-reinforced the way the ones under the hotel and the town square were.

The glow brightened. There was a *lot* of light coming from somewhere ahead, which meant there was no need to run his hand along the wall anymore. With relief he shook the water off and gripped the pump-action 12-gauge with both hands.

Ahead the passage opened into a huge chamber. Though the curved ceiling was well lit by what were probably a boatload of lanterns, burning fish oil by the smell, he could see that the floor area was illuminated only in patches. The crates and plastic barrels stored to both sides of a path that led on to open space were especially shadowed.

Where the tunnel began to widen, a set of steel rungs led down the wall. Glancing up, J.B. saw a circular shaft. It was too black to see up inside it.

He shrugged and crept forward. He saw no sign of activity. It occurred to him that if he had to fire the blaster, its roar would bring all the muties stuffed into what he realized was a natural cavern system right down on his head.

Again, he acknowledged the fact and stuck it back out of his consciousness. He wasn't getting caught, that was triple-sure. He didn't know what the muties wanted with human captives, though their webbed talons and long curving fangs raised unpleasant possibilities. He blasted-well sure wasn't letting it happen to him. If that meant he died fighting, so be it.

But he was determined not to do that. Not because he was so attached to life—which, frankly, kind of sucked, both in general and specific. At least, not only that. What really made him steel his jaw and firm up the grip on the shotgun he hoped not to have to use was that dying, fighting or otherwise, would mean he'd failed.

He would have once more let down Trader—and Rance. He refused to let that happen.

Hunched over the shotgun, J.B. advanced cautiously toward the boxes.

The blaster was snatched right out of his hands. A strong hand clamped over his mouth. Another caught the collar of his jacket and yanked him into the shadows.

RYAN'S PINTO GELDING reared. Just beyond its elevated hooves the flat ground, tan grass wind-blasted free of snow, fell abruptly three hundred feet or more toward an unseen roar of surf.

He leaned forward, patting its neck and doing his best to speak soothingly to it. He wasn't sure what had spooked the animal.

Ryan knew what had excited him. If not exactly spooked him.

They'd found the slaver base. It lay spread out to the south of them in a sort of broad, squared-off U demarcated by granite cliffs. The one on the far side fell sheer, as this one seemed to. The cliffs behind the level grassland and gravel beaches, at least a quarter-mile high, were less precipitous, although they still didn't make it easy to approach from the landward side.

He got the horse pulled back from the edge and settled down.

Overhead the sky was blue, spotted with clouds. The storm that'd helped blow them on their way out of the mutie-controlled ville of Tavern Bay had passed before morning. Fortunately it dropped snow rather than rain, which would have made an already uncomfortable night worse.

But another storm was blowing in across the Lantic. From the black rampart of clouds piling up higher and higher in the eastern sky it was going to be a bastard.

"You think they saw you, lover?" Krysty asked anxiously. She rode her gray mare close, but not too close, evidently out of concern for provoking Ryan's horse into more risky behavior. Like dancing around on its hind legs right next to a cliff.

Ryan shook his head. "Doubt it. Anyway, I'm not sure that it makes much difference. People must wander by all the time."

The redhead didn't look convinced. Ryan, for once, felt unsympathetic to her concern. It wasn't as if they were going to raid the rad-blasted slaver base without running any risks. Why should that be any different from the rest of life?

"I know," she said. "I'm starting to feel more and more anxious about J.B., too. And the girl."

He laughed and shook his head. "You amaze me sometimes."

Her smile was sweet—and promised more than that. "Only sometimes?"

"Look out there!"

It was Ricky, bouncing up and down on the back of his palomino pony, which had long since learned to take his antics calmly.

Ricky was pointing out to sea, where a ship was standing in to shore from the north. It was a big battered freighter, riding high in the water, with white superstructure towers rising at bow and stern.

"Good timing, Ryan," Mildred said.

He shrugged. "Yeah, well. It's time we hit a little

luck. Let's shift out of here to a different scenic over-
look, people. Just in case the slavers *do* send a patrol up
here to check."

A STRONG FEMALE hand clamped over his mouth, J.B. noticed. It felt familiar, too. And he could smell the tobacco
still pretty fresh on the fingers that had crumbled it.

"Rance?" he said. Although it came out, "Mnnss?"
with the palm on his mouth and all.

"What took ya so long, kid?" she asked.

And there, standing in a small open space between
wooden crates stacked higher than his head, holding
J.B.'s scattergun and grinning wickedly through his
beard, stood the Trader his own bad self.

"What?" the Trader said. "You thought they'd take
me? There's a reason I'm called the man who was never
taken, boy. That isn't just advertising."

"Rmmph?"

Trader nodded past him. "Turn him loose, Rance. If
he didn't have sense not to squall right here and now, he
wouldn't have made it this far."

The hand came off. He spun and threw his arms
around her neck and hugged her tight.

After a moment she hugged him back. It made him
warm to feel again just how strong her arms were.

After a moment he noticed just how warm *she* was.
Maybe it was just the sea-cave chill made her seem so.
But still…

She kissed him hard. Her tongue probed against his
teeth. Almost of their own volition they parted. Her
tongue darted into his mouth, caressed his once, then it
withdrew and she broke away.

"You still let your damn temper get the best of you,

John Barrymore Dix," she said. "But good job anyway, you sawed-off little fucker."

"You're naked?"

Actually she wasn't. She had on the heavy red plaid wool shirt she'd been wearing to sleep in the cold hotel room. Of course, the temperature wasn't the only reason they all slept in their clothes.

But the shirt hung open to reveal the smooth, pale skin right down the inner swells of her boobs to her trim brown bush. She twitched it shut and paid no mind when it promptly fell open again.

"Buttons all got torn off when the frogs stripped me," she said. "Clawed off my jeans and scratched my damn legs like a bastard, too. Seems like boy frogs like human girls. And also have parts like human boys. But bigger."

"Don't sound so disappointed, Weeden," Trader said. He handed J.B. the shotgun.

She laughed quietly. It reminded J.B. of somebody. Somebody male, with a face the color of fresh snow on Pike's Peak in midwinter. But I don't know him yet, flashed through his mind.

Before he could process that, Rance snapped his attention back to the terrible present.

"Turns out the muties react the same as human men do when you give them a hard shin in the balls. They dragged me off down a side passage to some kind of workshop. Tried to rape me on a worktable, can you imagine that? The two holding on to my arms were so surprised when I busted their pal in the nuts I broke loose and got my hands on a nice four-foot length of bar stock. After that it was all over but the brainpan smashing. Bastards."

She turned her head away and spit on the floor. "Don't think they were supposed to do that. Think they jumped the gun, decided to have a little fun on the side without waiting to say Mother May I. But the other frogs just dragged Gonzales, Stang and Zap onward without noticing when the three of them slipped off with me. They seemed pretty stupe, actually."

"But they got humans working with them," Trader said. "And they're bastard smart."

Rance picked up a steel bar. It still had blood and brains stuck blackening on one end of it.

"I decided I'd head back, see if I could help you. Then, if your sorry ass was still alive and not room temperature, send you to the convoy for help. But before I could, this skinny old bastard found me."

Trader nodded. "It was a trap all along, though they do have the goods. They showed me before they jumped us. I think they were just so proud they had to show off. Fortunately, I had a flash-bang palmed. When the cold-heart cocksuckers I was dealing with, in their fancy high collars, pulled blasters out of their suit coats, and the frog muties made their appearance, I lit it off. Blasted two frogs with my 625 and tossed a frag gren behind as I ran. Couldn't do anything to help the others but get caught. Or die like poor Tully did. He jumped a frog three times his size, and the taint turned his head right around on his neck with a single swipe of his paw."

He shook his head. "That's two big deals turned out to be honeypots in one trip," he said sorrowfully. "I must be getting old. Losing my touch."

"Why aren't they crawling all over the place looking for you?" J.B. asked nervously.

"They met us at the north end of the waterfront," Trader said. "Like they agreed to. There's a stone pier built out into the water. There was a little shack there, with a steel lid in the floor. It covered a ladder down here. We're under the actual bay. The way they took us lies northeast a ways. And the cavern system is bastard huge—and seems to keep going down deeper.

"I ran back the way they took me, went up the ladder and opened the hatch. Then I hid out, crouched in the rocks at the end of the pier, when a couple of the humans I'd met and a dozen or so frogs came boiling out. They never even glanced my way, just assumed I'd headed straight back to the ville and took off that way.

"Then I came back here. Got business to settle. First to rescue my people, including the three grabbed with Rance. Then to get what I dark-dusted-well came for."

"Which is what?" J.B. asked.

He realized he might've been giving into impulse again here, speaking out of turn. But it also struck him it might be good to know what had led the canny Trader on a frantic drive across the Northeast—and, at the end, to walk with both eyes wide open into what he obviously more than half suspected was a trap.

"Sky bomb," Rance said.

J.B. frowned. "You don't mean—"

"She does mean, son," Trader said. "A Sov SS-N-21 sub-launched cruise missile. Complete with a 200-kiloton warhead. A nuke."

Chapter Twenty-Seven

Ryan lay on his stomach on cold gray rock and watched through his Navy longeye. The wind had picked up and it plucked at the backs of his pants legs.

The camp was big. He already knew that, but he still felt surprise at quite how big it was. There were dozens of tents of various sizes and shapes, and ramshackle structures cobbled together out of bits of lumber and plank and random scavvy—like a lot of villes across the Deathlands, actually, but even less well put-together.

"Must be a bitch at night," said Mildred, who had shimmied up beside him. "Trying to keep warm."

"Yeah."

They had shifted around to the cliff that walled the southern side of the little cove sheltering the base. The compound was a good ten acres in size, ringed with razor-wire tangles, a couple of rickety-looking guard towers inland and a gate on the single road that led down the slope to the west. As Ryan watched, a panel wag was waved through the barricade by bored-looking guards with remade AKs.

"More captives?" Mildred guessed.

The others had come up to join him, peering over the edge. They were on a brushy outcrop—down from the crest, which sported a gnarled scrub-oak sprouting from amid a jumble of rock that would make ideal cover. Therefore it would be an ace target for scrutiny by suspicious slavers.

But if the slavers in the camp were suspicious or alert the least little pinch, they hid the fact completely from the eye of Ryan Cawdor.

"I think not," Doc said. "It would seem more likely the trucks bring supplies. So many people have many needs and consume much in the course of a day. And while I cannot say much for the quality of housing provided, they dare not starve their prospective merchandise. Far less deny them fresh water."

Ryan watched the wag trundle to a concentration of more solidly constructed buildings, possibly prefabs, toward the middle of the waterfront where the freighter had tied up close to a makeshift dock. It was built up at the bow, with the bridge clearly atop that superstructure. A second rose aft. Judging by the stubby stack sticking out of it, it housed the engines as well as a second bridge. The name *Serge Broom* was painted on the chipped black paint of the prow.

Though he had a lot more experience of smaller watercraft than the large seagoing kind, Ryan judged this one at seven hundred feet or so, and it might weigh forty thousand tons fully loaded. You could pack a lot of slaves into that hull, he thought, if you cared as little about their comfort as these coldhearts do.

A group of shabbily dressed men began to unload crates of some sort from the wag's box under the eyes and blasters of several slavers. They carried them inside a large tent that obviously served as either warehouse or commissary.

"Supplies," Ryan said.

"You'd think they'd get those from the sea," Mildred said.

"Didn't unload anything from the freighter, though," Ryan said.

Mildred shook her head. She hated slavers like nuke death.

"Who would *trade* with scumbags like that?"

"People trying to get by any way they can," Ryan said. "Like pretty much everybody is. People who don't want the slavers just taking what they want by force."

"So why don't the coldheart bastards just take what they need, then?" Ricky asked through gritted teeth. The new kid seldom cussed. But the way he felt toward slavers, who had butchered his family before his eyes and carried his beloved sister off to captivity, made Mildred seem all warm and fuzzy by comparison. "Why should they pay when they have blasters?"

"And raise the countryside against them more than it is?" Doc asked.

"Yeah," Ryan agreed, moving the longeye toward the gangplank that ran from the ship's deck to the dock. A couple of slavers packing handblasters were sauntering up it. "Ever heard the phrase 'don't shit where you eat'? This is their big, long-term base. If they try just raiding for stuff, the people hereabouts will either bushwhack their foragers or take their stuff and go. Leaving the cupboard bare."

"So it ever has been," Doc said.

"So what do we know, lover?" asked Krysty, snuggling up close to his other side.

"Well, the slavers have no uniforms to speak of," Ryan said.

"Slavers got blasters," said Jak, hunkered down the inland slope watching his friends' backs.

"Indeed," Doc said.

"And no women slavers I've seen so far," Ryan stated. "Speaking of women—"

Another important-looking slaver, with a shaved head, an imposing black mustache and a black, fur-collared coat that made his big frame look bigger, was walking from the more-solid buildings that obviously housed the slavers toward the dock. Behind him came a quartet of blasters, who walked surrounding a rather tall but stick-slim captive with a shock of black hair. There was little to see, even through the longeye, to identify the sex of the slave, who obviously had the highest value. But the way the captive walked, with skinny shoulders back and head defiantly up, told Ryan all he needed to know.

"That's our girl," Ryan said. Relief flooded him in a warm flow he could only compare, with brief amusement, to pissing his pants.

"Ah, thank God," Mildred said.

Haughty, as if she were already ruler of Stormbreak, Milya marched up the gangplank and into the superstructure. Her coldheart escort was following by a sturdy woman, obviously an attendant, who from her hangdog posture was a slave rather than a slaver matron.

"So, now all we have to do is make our way past two hundred slavers armed to the teeth, aboard a well-guarded ship, and steal away their most valuable treasure," Doc said with what seemed like relish.

"Ace on the line," Mildred stated glumly.

Ryan uttered a brief, guttural laugh. They were all keeping their voices low, which wasn't rational, since the base lay hundreds of yards away and upwind to boot. He approved of the practice, though. Letting yourself slip into bad habits—like poor noise discipline—was an ace way to wind up staring at the stars.

"We got this," he said.

Mildred shot him a look of disbelief. "Ryan Cawdor, how can you say a thing like that? Have you lost your freaking mind?"

"Lover, are you sure?" Krysty asked.

Ryan lowered the longeye and gazed east across the sea. "Storm coming," he said. "Gale, by the looks of those clouds. Should start hitting here by nightfall. That could cause us problems, but I think we can use it."

"But how are we ever going to get *in?*" Ricky asked. He sounded almost ready to cry. Ryan knew the youth hero-worshipped him. Now his faith had to be badly shaken.

Jak laughed softly at their backs.

"Get in easy," he said. "Slavers care people not get out."

Ryan grinned. "Right the first time, Jak. I have a plan to get us, if things fall into place, right straight to where they're keeping Princess Lyudmila."

"It looks as if they are beginning to rouse the slaves from their barracks," Doc said. Despite his apparent age, there was little wrong with the sight in those winter-sky eyes. "They are about to commence loading the slaves onboard, it would appear."

"Ryan, we've got to do something right now!" Mildred said from the ragged edge of panic, to judge by her voice. "They're going to leave."

And that meant they would take the girl with them. There went any chance Baron Ivan Frost, Milya's loving father, would hand over J.B. If he was even still breathing.

Yeah, he is, Ryan assured himself. That healer, Rao, knew her stuff. And J.B.'s as tough as wound wire and boot leather.

"No rush," Ryan said. "They won't get that many slaves loaded shy of midnight. And that's only if things go smoother than they ever do. These slavers have a fairly slick operation—professional. But in the end, they're just coldheart scum."

He slithered back from the precipice, rasping his thighs and belly against the rough rock.

"But you're right, Mildred. It is time to shake the dust off our boots and move like we've got a purpose."

"But Ryan," Krysty asked. "If everything goes as you plan—how will we get out?"

He grinned at her. "One thing at a time, Krysty," he said. "I'm working on it."

"A NUKE?" J.B. breathed. He couldn't believe he'd heard right. Or at least understood.

"That's it," Trader said. "You aren't as dumb as you look, kid."

"But why?" Johnny asked. "What do you want with a nuke? You wouldn't sell it, would you? Give somebody else that kind of power?"

He blinked. "Wait—you aren't looking to make yourself King of the Deathlands, are you?"

"Trader, we got no time," Rance said, standing on her tiptoes to peer over some crates back at the main cavern. Even as het up as he was, J.B. couldn't help noticing how sweet-shaped that made her long, strong legs, and the way the apple-round cheeks of her backside peeked out under the hem of her shirt....

"Got time for this," Trader said. "I won't ask a man to risk throwing his life away like I'm about to without giving him some idea why."

He fixed a surprisingly calm and steady gaze on J.B.

"It doesn't work that way, kid," he said. "I'm not looking for power. If I wanted that, I'd have it already. I'm just looking to travel around and do deals."

"And mebbe help people get going again," Rance said. "*Doing*. Instead of just slowly sinking into nothing."

"Yeah, you were always the sentimentalist, Weeden. No, Dix. Nobody on Earth needs that kind of power. And Earth doesn't need that dreck brought back into it. Aren't things bad enough without a nuke running around loose? Or in the hands of some crazy-mad blood drinker who'd try to conquer an empire with the threat of that thing? Or set it off to watch the pretty mushroom cloud? Which thank you so much for thinking might be me."

"No—no—" J.B. caught himself before his tongue stumbled over any more of an apology. He knew in advance anything he could say would be lame. "But what were you trying to do?"

"Buy it," Trader said, "and deep-six it. Make sure nobody gets it. Ever."

"What were you gonna pay for something like that?"

Trader chuckled. "Most everything. Except my people and the war wags. I can get more trade goods from different stashes.

"I got a hot tip in Erie that claimed a sunken Sov missile boat had washed up briefly off the old Maine coast. Long enough for some triple-stupe bastard to haul a missile out of it before it slid under again. Hopefully to come up no more. But nothing I can do about that, one way or another.

"So, as you noticed, I hustled our asses here triple-fast. Made preliminary contact and agreed to do the final deal on the docks here at Tavern Bay. I took along the two people I reckoned had the best shot at helping me judge the merch at first examination, plus two shooters—who were mainly there because the people we were dealing with would've been suspicious if they weren't, whether they were on the level or not.

"Four of us was all they'd agree to. So I had the rest of you waiting as backup in the hotel, to help me handle the thing if the deal went down.

"And make no mistake, they got the goods. Nice, shiny missile. Not even any sign of corrosion. They even let me run a Geiger over it, see if it was too hot to handle. It's not, though I wouldn't sit astride the son of a bitch for all the tea in China.

"Like I said, I was dealing with norms. Or what seemed like it, anyway. Though there was something a little off about them—but it's not like that's as rare as a well-wiped asshole these days. All I can reckon is they wanted to show off their shiny sky-bomb missile before they grabbed us."

"What was the point?" Johnny asked.

"It's not like they discussed their evil plans with the man," Rance said.

"They do in the old vids!" J.B. said. Then his cheeks flushed hot. Control, he reminded himself.

"Reckon they figured to use me somehow to take the convoy. With War Wags One and Two, *and* a nuke, well, they could make a pretty big noise if they wanted. But we'll never know now.

"And now you know enough to decide. You in, Junior?"

J.B. blinked from one to the other, then he took off his glasses and began to polish them on his shirttail.

"What's your plan?"

Trader laughed softly. "Free my people. Make sure nobody ever uses the warhead. Power back to the wags and get the hell outta Dodge. Sound good?"

"Sounds double-stupe," he said, which wasn't giving in to impulse but his own damn reasoned judgment.

"You in?"

"Dark night, yes!"

Rance yanked the hat off his head and settled it on her own with exaggerated care. Then she stooped to pick up the steel bar from where she'd leaned it against the crate. She didn't seem to even notice that her shirt fell open to fully expose her body.

J.B. did.

She slapped the inch-thick steel rod against her palm. "Then let's go bust some mutie heads."

WAVING HER ARMS, sentient red hair flying from more than the wind, Krysty rushed into the path of the wag as it trundled along a well-worn dirt road toward the place where it began slanting down to the slavers' camp. "You've got to help me!" she cried.

It was a well-battered wag, faded from olive green to gray in places to bare metal in others. It was a predark military truck with a covered bed. The fabric cover had clearly been replaced by recently manufactured canvas, though not recently, judging by the holes in it.

There was plenty of room for the wag to go around her. The road had two lanes with a shallow ditch running on either side. No doubt the slavers had made their captives improve the road and keep it from rutting out badly.

Of course, the white-haired driver could have run Krysty down easy enough. But she was nimble and trusted her reflexes to spring out of the way at need.

Just as she was about to do that, the wag shuddered to a stop with a squeal of brakes and a cloud of biodiesel exhaust.

Inside the cab the younger, skinnier man riding shotgun turned to the red-faced driver. Krysty could hear him angrily shout, "Why'd you stop for, Pa?"

The older man smiled and gestured Krysty around to his door. He rolled down the window as the woman approached.

"Oh, thank you so much," she sobbed, clutching the bottom of the window with both hands. "You don't know what I've been through."

A hard hand clamped on her wrist. "Sorry, missy," he said. "See, if we help you get away from them slaver boys, and they find out about it, they'll chill us and hang us up either side of the gate to make an example of us. If, on t'other hand, we hand you back to them, they'll reward us double-good for a pretty little redheaded thing like you."

With his other hand he started to open his door. "So, now you just slide your pretty little fanny in here between me and Colten, miss."

As the door cracked open, the black barrel of a long-blaster poked right through it. Blue eyes went wide in the old man's weather-seamed and reddened face, crossing slightly as they stared down the muzzle.

"Not today, Pops," Ryan said.

Krysty yanked her hand free of the driver's now-slack grasp.

Colten goggled, then turned to yank open his own door, apparently looking to dive out. He froze as he found himself staring through the mud-streaked glass of his own window down the two barrels of Doc's absurdly huge LeMat handblaster.

"Just keep coming out, lad," Doc instructed him. "Only nice and easy, like."

"You're talking like a character from a B movie," said Mildred, emerging from behind a cluster of rocks on the passenger side of the road. Jak came with her. "That's what you're doing, isn't it, you old coot?"

"Allow a fellow chronic traveler his indulgences," Doc said.

"Don't look at our faces," Ryan commanded sharply as the two piled out of the truck. Go stand by the ditch, facing away. And keep your hands where I can see them."

He gestured with his Steyr toward the passenger side of the vehicle. As Krysty stepped back, the older man got out and shuffled around the hood of his wag. He was a big guy, heavyset. He wore canvas overalls over a wool shirt. His son had a mottled tan linsey-woolsey shirt and canvas pants cinched by a rope.

With Mildred and Jak covering the pair with their handblasters, Doc backed around to peer into the shaded bed of the truck.

"By the Three Kennedys!" he exclaimed. "I do believe they're carrying kegs of beer!"

"Shame we can't crack one open," Ryan said. "I've worked up a thirst, I'll tell you."

Holding their hands up by their heads, father and son obediently went and stood by the ditch, looking resolutely away. The rising wind made their baggy clothing snap and flap. The day was getting black, and not just because the sun was already sinking into the heavy hardwood forest to the west. The storm was coming, hard and fast.

As Ricky emerged from his own cover on the driver's side, holding down on the pair with his big Webley revolver, Ryan slung his Scout carbine.

Then he drew his SIG-Sauer handblaster. Two fast shots cracked out. Colten and his white-haired father flopped face-first in the ditch with 9 mm holes drilled in the back of their skulls.

"*¡Nuestra Señora!*" Ricky yelped.

"Ryan, did you have to?" Krysty asked quietly, though she already knew the answer.

"Bastards had it coming," Mildred said, tucking her ZKR 551 handblaster back in its holder. "Bottom line, they were feeding slavers."

"I didn't chill them on account of their character flaws," Ryan said, putting his own semiauto handblaster away. "I did it because it's the only way to make sure they wouldn't rat us out."

Without being asked, Jak dragged the bodies out of the ditch and behind some brush. Ryan nodded.

"Right. Everybody got what they need? Packs all cached? Ace on the line. Pile into the back. Ricky, hand off that novelty longblaster of yours to the people riding in back, and haul your ass into the cab."

The youth's brown eyes shone. "Can I drive?"

"No."

Chapter Twenty-Eight

J.B. stepped out from behind a pile of crates. The Remington scattergun bucked hard against his hip bone and roared like a bastard.

A frog mutie, running triple-fast despite its short bandy legs, threw up its webbed and taloned hands as the charge of double-0 buckshot caught it square in the keel bone. It toppled backward and lay kicking its clawed hind feet on the stone floor of the entrance to the cavern system.

Then the youth's eyes got big. "Dark night!" he yelped. "There's dozens of them!"

Trader ran past J.B. between the piles of crates. He had his stainless-steel 625 in his right hand. His other supported Marsh Folsom, who was dragging his right leg as if it didn't work anymore. The leg of his jeans was dark. Despite the fact they were running a three-legged race, the two made good time.

Right behind came Rance Weeden, still bare-ass beneath her hat and shirt, turning back to loose shots at the hopping, croaking horde from her .40-caliber handblaster. Trader had passed her supplies and she'd buckled a web belt with magazine carrier around her waist.

Next came Stang, the burly cargo handler, who was cranking out shots from a lever-gun. A .30-30, J.B. made it by the sound. Bringing up the rear were the two blasters who'd gone with Trader and his top aide, Sciabarra and Morrison.

As J.B. watched, the black, broad-shouldered Sciabarra turned to fire back at the frogs with a hand-blaster. He kept walking backward as he did so.

He put his heel on a round piece of debris. It and his boot shot out from under him, and the man went down hard on his tailbone.

Worse by far, the frogs swarmed him instantly. One knocked his blaster flying from his hand. Then he spun Sciabarra's head sideways on his bull neck with a back-hand swipe. The muties surrounded the man as he fell back supine on the stone.

"No!" Morrison shouted. He ran toward his comrade, yanking shots off furiously from his Browning Hi-Power blaster at the shambling horrors that blotted Sciabarra completely from view.

"Leave him," shouted Trader, who had stopped just back of where J.B. stood with his 870. "He's done for!"

Long arms glistening with fine scales were swung high, flinging sprays of blood from the talons. The fallen man wasn't making a sound. His slide locked back on an empty mag, Morrison turned and ran to join the others. His bearded face was twisted with grief and help-less rage.

"Let me down, Trader," Marsh said. "I can shoot."

Trader shot, too, then they all did. A quick barrage of blasterfire dropped six of the muties, leaving them thrashing on the cavern floor. The rest turned and hopped back out of the line of fire behind a bend.

"I didn't know they were smart enough to run away," J.B. said.

"Now we know," Rance replied, slapping him on the shoulder.

He looked at her. She gave him a grin and a thumbs-up. That made him go warm in the cheeks, the pit of his belly and parts south.

Among the fallen frog muties lay Sciabarra. Even from twenty yards off could tell there remained no life behind the eyes staring unblinking at the ceiling.

"I hate like glowing nuke shit to leave a man," Trader said, "but I won't spend blood to buy a chill. You finished here, Dix?"

"Almost," J.B. said simply, not defensively. Because he didn't *feel* defensive. He had done what he could as fast as he could—and Trader himself had told him that doing a proper job was the most important thing of all.

J.B. hadn't been thrilled at being told to stay behind while Trader and Rance went off to save their friends and zero out the Sov warhead. But he had done it. In part because it was Trader who told him to. In part because he knew it was the right thing.

It didn't mean he liked it. But that didn't much matter. From now on, he was resolved to give mind only to the job at hand and nuke what he was feeling.

"Good," Trader said. He had the cylinder of his Smith & Wesson open. Ejecting the moon clip that held the six empties, he replaced it with another full of fat, round-nosed .45 ACP cartridges.

Slamming the cylinder decisively shut, he said, "Rance, you go watch our way out. Make sure none of the bastards catch us from behind. Rest of you make sure you're all loaded up. Those frog muties won't hold off a heartbeat longer than it takes to take reinforcements."

"Frogs got no blasters?" J.B asked. He was concerned about the ammo they'd just burned through, much less how long they could put up a firefight against a concerted attack. But given that he'd made up his mind to keep his trap shut except for asking necessary questions or giving necessary info, he held off from asking Trader about the ammunition situation. Having done so, he realized Trader was at least as aware of the problem as he was, and that would be a stupe question.

The one he'd asked wasn't, though.

"Muties don't use them, that we've seen," Trader said. "But the humans working with them do, which is why we have a couple extras, and some more ammo. Not enough to get frisky with, though. I reckon the frogs are waiting for more humans to turn up and tell them what to do."

J.B. got back to the job of inserting blasting caps in the plas-ex charges he'd been placing as high on the walls as he could climb on the crates. The claylike Composition 4 blocks, caps and coils of fuse made up most of what he'd stuffed into his backpack back in the room, before setting out to find his friends.

"We're gonna need a Plan B," Trader said, moving to cover behind the crates.

"Didn't disable the bomb?" J.B. asked, crimping red fuse to a cap.

"Never got close enough to look," Trader said. "Rance and I found the storeroom where they had our buddies stashed double-fast and chilled the frogs guarding them. But not quietly. They landed on us pretty quick—a dozen or so of the hopping fuckers, led by Cosgrove, the slick bottom-dealer I was here to trade with, and one of his pals named Spode. We all had blasters by then, and we gave them a worse surprise than they gave us.

"But Gonzalez, who I brought along hoping he'd be able to work out a way to futz the nuke's initiator or otherwise make sure nobody was gonna be setting that rad-blasted thing off anytime soon, he got his head popped like a zit by a mutie. Poor bastard. Zap got it, too. You 'bout done up there, Dix? I'm starting to see signs of movement down the way."

"Got it," J.B. said. He turned and started to clamber down the crates.

From the darkened place where the cavern narrowed to tunnel landward came a startled cry. Then a thump, and a wet and ripping noise.

Rance Weeden screamed. Though it vibrated with sheer agony, it rang mostly with fury and frustration.

"Rance!" J.B. yelled.

Like a feeb he'd left his shotgun propped against a crate beside Trader. He had no other blaster or access to one.

Not in time to do Rance any good.

He launched himself off the boxes. He hit hard and banged one knee. But mere pain never did deter J.B. much. He launched himself at the hunched, ridged back he glimpsed in the shadows where Rance was.

The frog-mutie sensed the skinny youth's headlong approach. It spun with surprising speed for its bulk, lashing out with its talons. The rising blow caught J.B. on his chin, laid it open to the bone and knocked him skidding backward on his backside.

Muttering to itself in its weird half-human voice, the monster turned back to its victim, only to be silhouetted by a bright yellow flash that briefly illuminated the whole mouth of the tunnel. The eye nearer J.B. blew out in a spray of gore and ichor.

The monster dropped on its face. J.B. scrambled up once more and darted for Rance even as he heard Trader shout, "Here they come!"

"Rance," he yelled. "I'll save you!"

The woman was mostly obscured by shadow. She stood funny, with hips cocked sideways and knees together. The hand that held the handblaster she'd chilled the mutie with hung by her bare leg.

Her left hand was splayed against her middle. It was drenched in blood. To his utter horror Johnny saw the gleam of entrails she was trying to hold into her torn-open belly.

"You can't," she said, in a voice taut with pain.

"Rance?" Trader yelled. Blasterfire cracked out behind Johnny's back.

He didn't turn. He could only tear his eyes off Rance's gut wound to look into her pain-filled eyes.

What he saw was steel-hard determination—yet also softness of a sort.

"Trader, I'm done," she said. "Leave me some blasters. I'll stand the fuckers off while you get Marsh and the rest clear."

"But you can't—" J.B. began, then he shut his trap.

What she couldn't do was survive that wound. Not here, not now. He saw there was no point in talking nonsense.

She nodded. "Ace," she said through gritted teeth. "You're finally learning to think, not just react. Keep... at it."

She looked around. Blood was pouring down the fronts of her bare legs.

She found her fedora lying nearby and kicked it toward J.B. with the blood-free side of one foot. She gasped at the pain.

The hat flew up at J.B. He caught it and stared down at it as if he didn't know what it was.

"Something to remember me by," she said, shuffling toward the boxes and the light.

J.B. stood as if rooted to the stone of the underwater

cavern floor, polished smooth by unknown hands and an unimaginable number of feet.

As she made her tortured way past him, she clapped him briefly on the shoulder with the hand that held her blaster.

"We sure had us some times. Take care of yourself, John Barrymore."

He frowned. The scene was blurring out around him. His mortally wounded former lover was starting to recede from him.

"Go, you rad-blasted fool," she said. And her face as it dwindled was the most achingly lovely sight he had ever seen. "Go now. Your friends need you—"

"YOUR FRIENDS NEED you, Mr. Dix," a feminine voice said. "You have to wake up now."

J. B. Dix found himself in a world of hurt. His chest felt as if it had been worked over with a cold chisel and sledgehammers.

That's not exactly how it happened. The words ran through his brain. *But she did trigger the charges, dropped the cave ceiling and half the bay on those bastard muties. Of course, Trader and me and the others came within a hair of being sucked back down when the water came surging up the tunnel all around us....*

He opened eyes that were older, sadder and infinitely wiser than the ones he'd been seeing through—in his mind's eye.

A woman's face hovered over his. After a moment his eyes focused on it; he didn't need his specs to see this close up.

It was a beautiful face, with huge luminous dark blue eyes framed by black hair sparsely threaded with silver.

Yet it was also haggard, with oddly exaggerated cheekbones and jaw.

"What happened to me?" J.B. asked.

"You have been healed of your wound and the attendant infection," she said. "I am Katerina Frost, wife of Baron Ivan Frost of Stormbreak. Our healer, Lindy Rao, operated on you, saved your life and brought you to the path of healing. We have kept you sedated, longer than she thought was wise, in order to allow the healing process to begin. We know you are an active man. Your friends told us. We feared you wouldn't stay put long enough to start to heal properly if we let you waken."

"Where are my friends?"

He looked around. He was in a room with walls painted stark white, packed with tables of medical-looking gear. He smelled the astringencies of alcohol and other disinfectants.

"In danger," she said.

"Gotta get to them," he said. He tried to sit up. It felt as if that same sledgehammer that had generally pounded him whacked him right in the middle of the chest, below the sternum.

He lay back down. "Right," he said. "Not a good idea."

He rolled his eyes toward her.

"Reckon that's another reason you had this Rao keep me under so long," he said. "To keep me from busting out and going after them."

"This is also true," she said, straightening. "Nor are you healed yet. Far from it. But—enough. You are a hardy and resilient man. The scars your body already bears prove that. And now your friends need you more than you need rest."

He managed to struggle up to his elbows on the bed. It hurt like nuke fire. But this time he was prepared for it.

He sat up, gasped, swayed, but held himself upright.

So that was all an anesthetic dream, he thought. It was me, but it wasn't me. I was never so bold or mouthy. And Trader put me right to work on blasters. I never was a wrench, but there was a Rance in my past. Part real, part dream.

He felt his chest, tentatively. Just because he could handle pain didn't mean he was eager to handle more of it. His torso was well-wrapped in bandages. Otherwise his skin was bare. The room was just on the edge of cool. He realized by the feel of the air and the smell he was underground.

"Well," he said out loud, his thoughts still refusing to come into their usual razor-edge focus, "half memory, half hallucination."

"Fortunately," the baroness said, "your incisions are healed. They will not break open under exertion. At least the external ones. So Healer Rao tells me, and I trust her skill."

She glanced aside. For the first time J.B. realized she was dressed to go outside into the sort of brutal Northeast winter night that was the last thing he remembered with any clarity before starting on his drug-fueled voyage to the past. She had a tall black curly-wool hat on her head and wore a long, heavy coat with a collar of what looked like the same stuff.

"Sadly, I had to have her locked away long enough to allow us to leave. She was unwilling to release you from her care. Nor can I risk having her alert my husband."

"Dark night, why? What's going on?"

"The change," she said, which hid more than it revealed, and not just because his thoughts were still socked-in by anesthesia fog. "It comes. And I feel it coming fast." She shook her head. "I will explain later. Now we must go quickly."

"Where?"

"To help your friends, as I told you. They are in terrible danger."

"I can believe that," he said.

"Can you walk?"

"I got to," he said without hesitation. "So I can."

"Lady Katerina," a calm, masculine voice said. "All is in readiness."

"Excellent, Caine," the woman said. "Thank you."

J.B. glanced toward where the voice came from. A tall, thin, distinguished-looking man with silver hair stood there. He was also dressed for outside, in a bulky parka with the fur-lined hood thrown back.

"Mr. Dix," the baroness said, "I have had your gear and weapons taken to the motor launch. Now you must dress. And as quickly as you can. We have no more time."

He nodded. This time the effort stabbed him in the chest like an ice pick. Where the bullet hit me, he thought.

"Then give me my hat, please," he said. "I...earned it."

Chapter Twenty-Nine

The rain screamed down through roaring wind. The gangplank bucked and twisted beneath Krysty's booted feet. The freighter's hull boomed and moaned as waves threw it against the immense tires, maybe twice as tall as Ryan, that had been roped to the dock to act as bumpers. Seen from this close, in the faint radiance of the storm lanterns at the landward end of the gangplank, the hull showed patches of obvious rust where the paint had flaked away.

Overhead the clouds boiled like lead.

The rain felt frigid. It wasn't hard to keep her head down, as if in numb compliance, fixed on the nylon rope that allegedly bound her wrists together before her. The rain felt like little spears when it hit her eyes. It plastered her hair to her head—and also, she knew, muted its distinctive radiant color, which could come in handy if any of the slavers they had brushed up against had survived to make it back to base carrying tales of the triple-hard band of wanderers they'd had the bad luck to encounter....

"What's that?" called a harsh voice from the freighter's storm-tossed deck ahead and above.

"Got some specials to deliver," Ryan called out. His voice sounded slightly muffled by the hood of the coat he'd found and put on over his own greatcoat. Also he put a hoarse rasp to his voice to make it harder to rec-

ognize, should anyone here have heard it. It was a long
shot. But since they could defend against it, why not?

All had gone as Ryan planned. Easier, as far as Krysty
was concerned. By the time they reached the compound
gates the rain had started, cold and hard from the out-
set. The guards had barely glanced at Ryan and Ricky
from the shelter of their shack before hauling open the
barrier and waving them through.

They'd found their way to the storage structures Ryan
had observed from above, which were dark and deserted.
They parked the truck and sneaked into a back one to
prepare for their next move.

"What about the black one?" a second guard's voice
asked. "She don't look special to me."

"How would I know?" Ryan snarled. "I just do what
I'm told. Mebbe you better do likewise."

He put a genuine snap in the words. "Hey, man, no
problem," the second guard said hastily. "No problem.
We're all just out here doing our jobs in this freezing-
ass shit."

Aft, which seemed to Krysty to be a mile away, another, larger ramp led to the deck. For a while, slaves
had been herded up that and into the hold. But when the
gale really began to rock and roll, that ramp had been
shut down. Whether the slavers were unwilling to risk
having their merchandise flung wholesale into the water
and crushed by the hull slamming the tire-buffered stone
seawall, or if they just didn't want to expose themselves
to the danger or the discomfort, Krysty didn't know.

Ryan walked behind her, prodding her occasionally
with the muzzle of his longblaster. He had goosed her
once, just as they started up the ramp. She hadn't reacted
to it, but silently promised to pay him back for that one.

Doc shoved Mildred along at the point of his handblaster. Behind came Jak. All three of the men were well muffled and hooded in garments Jak and Ryan turned up in a quick search of the cargo area.

The flexible gangplank got steeper as it approached the deck. Krysty was glad of the ropes that ran along either side at about the level of her short ribs. She wished she could grab on to them. But her tied hands, as fake as the bonds were, were necessary to the deception.

When Ryan told the companions that the only visible sign that distinguished slavers from slaves was the weapons, he hadn't just been making idle conversation. Not that he often did. It was on little more than the strength of that fact that they'd made it this far.

But a few feet from the deck of the *Serge Broom* everything started to unravel. "Hey, now," the first guard who'd spoken said. "Something don't smell quite right. I think we better call the officer of the watch to check this out."

"I wouldn't do that if I were you," Ryan said. He held up his left hand with forefinger raised.

Krysty knew that, because lifting her face long enough to see past her rain-weighted lashes, she saw the guard to her left jerk back his head slightly. His eyes rolled up as if to look at the third one that had neatly appeared between them and his knit watch-cap. Then he folded to the deck.

Krysty and Mildred both went to one knee. The other guard opened his eyes and mouth wide as if to shout a warning. Then his face went even whiter and he shut his mouth abruptly as Ryan, Doc and Jak aimed their imposing blasters at him above the women's backs.

He raised his hand away from the funny-looking submachine gun hanging horizontally in front of his hips on a long sling.

Jak eeled between Krysty and Mildred to slip around behind the guard. He put away his big, gaudy, loud .357 Magnum Colt Python and instead held the belled blade of a hunting knife against the guard's throat.

The rest hustled up onto deck. Once there, Ryan turned and waved back toward the dock. Ricky appeared around a stack of the monster tires a few feet from the gangplank and hustled up it, carrying his carbine in one hands and clutching the safety in the other.

Ryan knelt beside the guard Ricky had silently chilled with a shot from the DeLisle. He checked for signs of life as Krysty and Mildred shucked their loosely wound bindings, nodding in satisfaction. Then, picking up the man's Ruger Mini-14 longblaster from the deck, Ryan jerked his chin at the living guard.

"Truss him and take him. We've got questions."

"Will he give us answers?" asked Mildred, who was gagging him from behind with a rag they'd snagged from the cargo hootch for that very purpose.

Krysty didn't think Ryan's answering smile was very nice.

"Yes, he will," he said. "Won't you?"

Rolling his eyes from one to the other, the guard nodded so hard it looked as if his head would pop off.

ANOTHER BUCKETFUL OF salt spray hit J.B. in the face. It felt like a handful of pebbles. Keeping one hand clamping the fedora on his head and the other locked on to the cockpit rail, he shook his head like a dog to clear his glasses. At least for the handful of heartbeats before they busted the crest of another wave and he got blasted in the face again.

The lunging, rolling, yawing motion of the twenty-odd-foot motor launch made him feel as if he were getting stabbed in the chest with each and every random motion. He reckoned they couldn't be moving at anything resembling a safe or sane speed. Not that he had a snowball's chance in hell of judging it with anything like accuracy.

I hate water wags, he thought. The ground at least stays put when you drive on it. Mostly.

Standing at his side, Katerina Frost piloted the craft with a look of grim determination and evident skill. As they set out, J.B. had asked how she knew how to drive one of these things. She said that as a girl she had accompanied her uncle on trading voyages and learned to handle powerboats then.

He did notice how she steered parallel to the waves as much as possible, and when it wasn't, tried to climb their faces at an angle before they broke, which at least managed to keep them on top and the water on the bottom. Mostly.

The tall gray-haired man she called Caine stood behind them in the little cockpit. He spoke with what J.B. recognized as a Brit accent. The mat-trans system had jumped him and his friends to England once or twice.

Though it wasn't common, ships did make the perilous crossing of the Lantic, and thus so did men. And women. Whether to trade or because one of the other continents had become to hot for them was always an open question. J.B. reckoned Caine had to have spent years serving on a ship, let alone ridden one over. The man stood with his gloved hands folded behind his back and legs braced, and needed no more than that to avoid going over.

Unlike J.B.

It came to J.B. that it was no coincidence his anesthesia fantasies had wound up in the very ville they were bashing through waves toward right this moment, Tavern Bay. He'd known they were within about fifty miles of the place the first time the sky cleared enough for him to shoot their location with his mini-sextant.

But the path Ryan chose for them didn't take them anywhere near there. So J.B. had never thought to mention his earlier visit with Trader, at least a year before Ryan joined the convoy. Nor was J.B. in the habit of reminiscing out loud. Any more than he was in the habit of saying *anything* without due cause.

But his subconscious was well aware how near they were to the end point of his tumultuous first trip with Trader. And now he was heading back to that mutie- and memory-haunted ville.

"Why now?" he asked.

"I beg your pardon?" she asked without looking away from the churning violence of the sea. She had the gift of making her voice penetrate without shouting.

"I said, why wake me now?" yelled J. B., who didn't.

"We have received intelligence—terrible intelligence, which only I in all the barony truly understood. Indeed, I fear that's what triggered the change, though no one really knows why that happens, any more than they can foresee the hour appointed. So I dosed dear Vanya with sleeping meds and browbeat Rao until she roused you.

"So what is this danger my friends have gotten themselves into this time?"

"They are threatened by *lyagushki,*" she said. "The so-called muties of Tavern Bay—the frogs, as you know them."

"How'd you know about that?"

"You spoke in your drugged sleep."

He grimaced, then chuckled. He had almost blurted out the question, *What* else *did I say?*

It was as if he was still channeling his young, impulsive self in ways. From before he learned to clamp down his emotions tight as a workpiece. Now Mildred was always after him to let his feelings out more, after all he'd gone through to get them under control.

He shook his head. There was just no pleasing some people. Although, he remembered with a pang, he pleased her triple-well in other ways. And she him.

He shook that off. He ached to see her. His other friends, as well. Now he was on his way to do just that.

So, no point bothering fuddling up my brain with irrelevant details now, he thought. It's already messed up enough from the anesthetic.

"The *lyagushki* plan a sacrifice to their dread undersea god. I believe it is nothing but superstition. And yet I feel myself starting to feel the horrible impulse to worship him. Among other things.

"Apparently the drive is genetic. Engineered. We were made that way, you see. What…befalls us is no accident, no chance mutation."

"So who did all this? Whitecoats before the Big Nuke?"

"Yes. They were devils. People today are right to fear them. Though some are fools and fear learned healers like Rao."

Only then did J. B. say, "Wait. '*We*'?"

"We. I come from Tavern Bay. And—I am one of them. The accursed.

"You see, we all start as humans. Then at some point in our lives—it differs for each one—we change. Our bodies begin to transform. Sometimes it takes weeks or months; sometimes it happens overnight. Our minds also change. Likewise our emotions, which become…

dreadful. I can feel them now, like demon voices gibbering in the night. I can keep them at bay."

She raised her head toward the horizon. Or where J.B. reckoned the horizon likely had to be, given that any farther than a strong man could toss a gren it was impossible tell the sea from the sky. It began to rain again, harder than it had before.

"But keep them at bay I shall," she said. "For as long as I must."

J.B. glanced over his shoulder at the silent servant.

"Caine knows," Katerina said. "He is my sole confidant. He is as loyal to me as he is to his baron, and his loyalty to my dear husband is absolute.

"But still—he kept my terrible secret for me all these years. Because though our marriage was arranged, dear Vanya came to love me with all his heart. And I him, which is why I now must part with him forever."

Despite the rain and spray J.B. saw unmistakable tears welling in her eyes, to be whipped away by the rising gale.

"So you feel, like, this compulsion?" he asked.

"Yes. Even now. To join my kind. And…to serve. I believe we were made to instinctively serve our makers, who were mere men, if of perverted genius. But they are long turned to dust and ash. And that doglike loyalty has become…transferred to our god."

And deep in her throat she made a strange rumbling noise. To J.B., above the crash of wind and waves, it sounded as if she were growling the letters, "E.A.," several times.

His natural curiosity made him want to ask what they stood for. And the judgment, the cost of obtaining that which he had just relived—in however fouled-up a form—made him decide to keep his trap shut.

"So what do we do?" he asked instead.

"Warn your friends," she said. "Or save them. And my daughter. So they can get her back to Stormbreak safely."

"What about you?"

She looked at him. For all the curious gauntness of her face, the hollowness in her cheeks, he saw the beauty that had to still captivate the baron.

"I will never become one of them," she said.

He nodded. "Roger that," he said.

J.B. looked ahead, as if it would do any good. At least his specs kept the rain from blasting his eyeballs, although they ran with so much water he couldn't have seen much even had there been anything to see.

"How much farther?" he asked.

"Not far," she said. "We're passing Tavern Bay now, in fact."

She nodded to her right, evidently at something she could see that he couldn't, that helped her keep her bearings.

"We should come in sight of the slaver anchorage in fifteen minutes," she said. "I hope we come in time."

"Yeah," he said.

THEY FOUND AN unused stateroom on the deck below the main one, beneath the superstructure there by the bow where the bridge was. Locked inside, out of sight of any passing slaver, Ryan took the captive's gag off, having first impressed on him that the cost of trying to holler for help would be swift and painful.

He needed no further encouragement than the half-dozen faces staring at him in grim expectancy. Well, them and the blasters that went with them.

"That special girl is up on the deck below the bridge,"

he said. "She's the prime package for this whole run. I hear she's daughter to some hayseed baron up north along the coast a ways."

"Do tell," Mildred said.

With deliberate speed Ryan fired questions at him, terse and to the point. Their captive showed a tendency to babble, until Jak jabbed him in the cheek with the tip of his hunting knife, hard enough to start him bleeding. That got his mind right and his sentences short.

"Ace," Ryan said. "We got what he knows. And what we need to."

"How do you know he's not lying?" Mildred asked. She was clutching the Mini-14 longblaster Ryan had taken from the guard Ricky had chilled and glaring at the one he hadn't. The carbine had a banana magazine holding thirty 5.56 mm rounds in the well. She had several reloads stuffed in her belt.

"Because he knows if he lies, some of us might make it back here to settle up accounts with him. Which you know you wouldn't like, right?"

He grabbed a pinch of the man's cheek and twisted hard. The man nodded energetically.

"Gag him again, tie his feet, then stash him in the closet," Ryan said.

"Why not chill the bastard?" Ricky asked. "The way you did that driver and his son?"

"Because, unlike in their case, I see a way to stash him," Ryan said. "And because I don't have time to go chilling people solely on account of their moral failings."

He turned away. "Anyway, a few more questions may occur to me. Don't worry. You'll get to chill a load of coldhearts before the night is out, I don't even doubt. Speaking of which—Krysty, take this."

Ryan tossed her the blaster Jak had taken from the

captive. The redhead fielded it with her usual catlike reflexes. And promptly almost dropped it, despite the manlike strength of her arms and hands.

"Gaia, lover, it's heavy!" she exclaimed. Her big emerald eyes stared down at it as if it was a dead fish, not a black tube covered in peeling black enamel, with a pistol grip and a skinny box magazine stuck on the bottom, and a thinner barrel up front. "What *is* it?"

"M3A1 grease gun," said Ricky, his dark eyes shining. "Submachine gun, blowback operated, fires from an open bolt. Uses the same .45 ACP ammo my blasters do. America mass-produced them during World War II because—"

"Enough," Ryan said.

"Anyway, it's easy to use," Ricky said. "You'll love it. It's sweet. I'll show you how."

Frowning dubiously, Krysty nodded. Ricky bustled up to show her its workings.

"They call it the 'grease gun' because it looks like one," he couldn't resist adding. "You know, like what mechanics use—"

"Ricky."

"Yes, sir. So anyway, this lever here drops the magazine out of the well…"

"So, what's our plan?" Mildred asked.

"Sneak up into the superstructure. Chill the guards. Steal the girl. Not what you'd call complex."

"I mean for getting out of here."

"You got me."

He had to grin at the look of sheer amazement she gave him, with her eyebrows crawling halfway up her broad forehead toward her beaded cornrows.

"What do you mean?" she demanded.

"I mean I don't know," he said. "Yet."

"You have *got* to be shitting me. You still don't have a plan for getting out?"

"We lack sufficient information to formulate any kind of rational plan," Doc offered helpfully.

"Yes. So. I'm working on that. All right?"

He heard Krysty haul back the heavy bolt of the grease gun to cock it. Ryan *did* know what the weapon was. He only wished, with a hastily suppressed twinge in his chest, that J.B. was here to see it.

"Ace," Krysty said. "You're right, Ricky. It is easy."

"So you're good to go now, right?"

"I'm good to take Mildred and start freeing the slaves aboard," she said. "Right."

Ryan felt himself getting angry. "Step back away from the trigger of that blaster, Krysty. Has that soft heart of yours started softening your brain, too?"

Her eyes flashed green fire, but she answered evenly as well as briskly.

"Part of it's compassion, yes. I want to help these poor people—as much as I can without endangering our mission. Or my friends."

Ryan was getting the sinking feeling he'd really stepped in it with that one. Well, I gotta survive to take the consequences, he reassured himself.

"And I strongly suspect," Krysty went on, "that when the slavers realize we're here, as they are sure going to and at the worst possible time, you want them to have something to think about other than running us down. Right, lover?"

He held his hands up in surrender. "Okay, okay. You win."

"Of course."

"Who are you taking?"

"Mildred."

"Which of the others, Jak or Ricky?"

"Just Mildred," Krysty said.

He gave her a look.

She tossed her hair. It hadn't really dried out after that soaking it had gotten—it was too humid inside the ship for that to happen anytime soon—but had gotten some life back.

"We women can handle our job just fine," she said a bit tartly. "Right, Mildred?"

"Um—right? Right."

"Four of you males aren't too many for stealth," Krysty said. "And not too many for what you'll be facing."

Ryan sighed. "Yeah." Then he smiled.

Krysty and Mildred both looked at him suspiciously.

"What?" Mildred demanded. "I hate it when you get that look."

Ryan laughed. "I just figured out our plan for getting off this death trap. These slavers must have boats. A launch or two, mebbe. Certainly lifeboats."

"Slavers?" Mildred said. "You think they care that much about—"

"About their own personal asses? Nuking straight. So we grab the girl while you two spring as many slaves as you can as a diversion. Then we hop in a boat, lower it to the water and power out of here."

Both women stared at him.

"That plan sucks," Mildred said. "There's a storm coming, Ryan."

"Fireblast, Mildred! Do you have a better plan? Would you rather swim?"

Krysty came up to kiss Ryan briefly on the cheek. "We'll go," she said. "And trust my resourceful wolf to come up with a decent escape plan."

She winked at him.

"Right. We best get going now. Time's blood, and right now," Ryan said, "it's spurting out like an artery's cut."

Chapter Thirty

Holding a longblaster down by his side by the grip, Ryan strode down the passageway as if he belonged in it. Jak trotted at his side. He had his black watch cap pulled low and his chin pressed down in the turned-up collar of his purloined overcoat to hide as much of his albino skin as possible.

The deck rocked beneath Ryan's feet to no knowable rhythm. The ship's mass dampened the effects of the waves but couldn't cancel the ocean's power. The vessel's hull and structure boomed and creaked as the chaotic stresses came and went.

The pair of slavers on guard outside what they hoped was Lyudmila Frost's stateroom/cell were way more suspicious than the pair atop the gangplank. One had greasy dark hair, a beard and a gut hanging out the front of a black leather jacket. The other was lean, mean, graying and buzz-cut, with round glasses that reminded Ryan of J.B. as the two swung to confront them with their blasters. Beard Man had a double-barrel shotgun, Buzz Cut a battered folding-stock AK-47.

"No passage here, asswipes," Buzz Cut snarled. "Only those with business go farther. And you ain't got no business, so fuck right off."

"Hey, now," Ryan said easily. "No worries. Been a change of plans."

"That little dude!" Beard Man exclaimed. "He's snow white! He's a mutie!"

Ryan swung up the blaster. It wasn't his usual Steyr, but Ricky's homebuilt DeLisle replica. It chuffed once. Ryan felt even less recoil than he would have from his lower-caliber handblaster, with all that mass to soak up the .45 round's energy.

So quiet was the shot, he heard the 230-grain copper-jacketed ball smash through Beard Man's breastbone. He dropped the blaster with a clatter and staggered back, clutching his chest.

Jak made a blur-fast motion with his right hand. Buzz Cut dropped his AK-47 to grab with both hands at the steel hilt of one of Jak's throwing knives, sticking out of his left eye socket. It had punched right through the lens of his glasses.

"Good job, Jak," Ryan said. "Take them inside to finish them. Less blood."

Jak grinned and nodded.

Ricky and Doc trotted down the corridor behind them. Ricky toted Ryan's Scout carbine.

"Need me to pick the lock?" the youth asked.

Jak moved close to Buzz Cut. The man had fallen back against the door, and he was too preoccupied by pain even to notice. Jak grabbed his chin and slammed the back of his head against the steel door, then snatched the ring of keys off his belt and brandished them.

"Think we got it," Ryan said, exchanging weapons with Ricky. "This blaster really is pretty sweet, you know."

"Thanks!" Ricky said.

"Too easy," Jak said as he worked the stateroom lock. "Not like."

"Not too easy," Ryan replied, with a lightness he didn't feel. "We haven't got to the hard part yet."

Scowling, Jak opened the door. Ryan drew his panga and went in.

The stumpy older woman whom they had watched board with the baron's daughter was kneeling at the foot of the bed, sobbing into her hands. A weight descended on Ryan's back. Skinny but strong legs wrapped around his waist. Someone began screaming in his ear and clawing for his eyes.

Then the shrieking creature was gone. Ryan spun to see a girl with black hair and fury-red face, windmilling gangly arms and legs as Doc, who was stronger than he looked, held her up off the deck from behind.

"Fireblast, girl!" he said. "What the nuke is wrong with you? We're here to rescue you."

"It's true," Doc said reassuringly. "Your parents sent us. Baron Ivan and Lady Katerina Frost."

The furious girl subsided. "And I was supposed to know that how? Put me down."

Ryan nodded. Doc complied.

He had carried her into the stateroom. Immediately Ricky and Jak dragged the two guards inside by their collars. Both were still breathing. Briefly.

The girl stood and watched as Jak slit each man's throat with a butcher's expert hand.

"Bastards." She spit on Buzz Cut and then went up and kicked the feebly moving slaver in the side. "He was one of the ones who…hurt Darya. You should have let me take care of him!"

Ryan was starting to see why her mother and father had decided to ship her off somewhere. Still, he had to admire her fighting spirit.

He looked around. The chamber was spartan: bed,

lamp, table, writing desk, a chair. A closet built out from the bulkhead.

The *Serge Broom* uttered an especially loud groan, followed by three loud knocks, like a giant whaling on pipes with a claw hammer.

"¡Nuestra Señora!" Ricky yipped. "Do ships always make such sounds in a storm?"

"Yes," Ryan said.

"So it's not breaking up?"

"Probably not."

Milya was staring from one to another. She was wearing a T-shirt, jeans and sneakers. They were clean, or at least seemed to have been worn no more than a day or two.

Her blue eyes fastened on Ryan. "Who are you?" she demanded.

"Your rescue party, Lyudmila," Ryan said. "We need to move now."

Though Ryan's skin was crawling right up his back in his anxiousness to be done with this gig—or at least onto the still-sketchy part, which was getting off the damned tub with Lyudmila plus all their parts—they had hidden out and given Krysty and Mildred a ten-minute head start to start freeing slaves. Then they'd had to be careful working their way up the stairs to the deck right below the pilot house.

At least they hadn't needed to chill anybody on the way, with the attendant risks of noise or somebody stumbling onto chills.

"Anything here you need?" Ryan asked Milya.

She shook her head. "Just give me a blaster."

Ryan hesitated, then he remembered Alysa mentioning the girl had gotten combat training. Plus the story the freed slaves had told of her vigorous if futile, and painful, defiance.

"Take the AK," he said. "You know how to put the rad-blasted safety on, right?"

She stood up with the weapon and with a glare at Ryan worked the big selector lever with her thumb. It moved with the trademark Kalashnikov clack.

"Like the slavers ever do," she said.

"Right." He turned to the servant, who had turned away from the now-dead bodies and the considerable red pools they had bled out and was sobbing louder than before.

"Get up," he said. "We're not going to carry you."

"Sandra, please," Milya said. "Come with us." She had put a parka from the closet on and was slinging the longblaster's strap around her skinny neck.

But Sandra just shook her head, moaned and waved her hand for them to go.

"Right," Ryan said. They weren't getting paid to take her anywhere. As far as they knew, she wasn't even from Stormbreak.

From somewhere a siren began to wail. A moment later a Klaxon joined in, deafeningly loud, from the flying bridge right overhead.

"Told," Jak said. "Too easy."

Ryan shook his head. "We knew it was coming."

"No doubt the slaves the ladies have set free were spotted escaping," Doc said.

"Alarm start on land," Jak said. "Not boat."

"Whatever," Ryan stated. "Right now we need to get down the stairs and start looking for a ride home.

"SHIT," MILDRED SAID AS blaring mechanical noise filled the stairway where she and Krysty crouched.

The redheaded woman winced. The noise ricocheting up and down the steel passage hurt her ears.

At least they had managed to free fifty or so slaves before the alarm went off. They had asked the slaves to free as many of their fellow victims as they could before trying to flee the ship. She hoped some had listened.

How they'd fare if they got off the gangplank and into the slavers' base she had no idea. They seemed eager to try, at least. And if she and Mildred were turning them loose to get slaughtered like sheep—well, at least they'd have a chance at freedom.

Mildred craned her neck to peer briefly through the little window in the door. On the other side the hold had been divided into huge pens by metal partitions bolted to floor and ceiling. Whatever you were supposed to call them on a boat. Or a ship.

"I see three of the bastards," Mildred said, ducking back, holding her Mini-14 muzzle-up. "Thirty yards or so out, coming this way. Got blasters in hand but look mostly puzzled."

Krysty frowned as she considered their options. They weren't good.

"Fuck it," she said.

At her nod Mildred opened the door. Krysty stepped through and began blasting away.

JAK AND RICKY raced up the companionway from the main deck as fast as their legs could carry them. Their thudding footfalls echoed in the stairwell. Obviously they weren't worried about being heard. Ryan doubted anyone could be heard over the racket made by the storm tossing the ship around with increasing force violence, and the grinding yammer of the Klaxon.

Ryan led the small group that had been following a

landing or two back while the younger men scouted the way. Behind him came Milya. Ryan didn't feel comfortable having a fourteen-year-old who had an attitude *before* the slavers pissed her off hotter than nuke red right behind him with a full-auto blaster. Then again, she did have the safety on. Last he checked. Doc brought up the rear, with both blaster and sword in hand.

"Slavers?" Ryan called. He saw no reason to keep his voice down. He couldn't, if he wanted to be heard.

"No," Ricky screamed. "Frogs! They're swarming onboard and fighting with the slavers!"

Chapter Thirty-One

Even over the growl of the twin engines and the rising bellow of the storm, J. B. Dix heard sirens and Klaxons as Katerina Frost drove the motor launch toward the black bulk of the slaver ship.

Lights began to blaze up in the slaver base ashore, big, bright electrics, obviously generator-powered.

By their blue-white glare J.B. could see shapes climbing the enormous cables that made the ship fast to the dock. They were horrifyingly inhuman—and even more horrifyingly familiar.

"Lyagushki," Katerina said, glancing up from the wheel. "It has begun."

J.B. climbed into the cargo compartment aft of the cockpit, where Caine opened a chest bolted to the deck. From it he took a vest with pockets laden with shotgun shells and long narrow magazines. With unspeaking courtesy he helped J.B. shrug into the vest, then handed him his Smith & Wesson M-4000 shotgun and his Uzi. He checked both to make sure they were loaded with a round chambered, and slung them.

Still silent, Caine produced a double shoulder rig. A pair of blocky Glocks rode in the attached holsters. Both straps carried multiple mags.

"Lady Katerina," he said in his clipped Brit accent.

She nodded. She was fighting the boat through the waves now, which had gotten less choppy and violent but bigger since they passed the headland cliffs. But she kept them on course, as steady as the tiny vessel could be, as she took first one hand off and then the other to allow her servant to strap the harness on.

He stepped back. "You know what to do," she said.

"Yes, my lady."

"Get the grapnel gun ready."

"Yes, ma'am."

She flashed a quick glance over her shoulder at J.B. He was shocked at how much her face seemed to have changed. Her blue eyes were bulging now, her face longer and the cheeks even more hollow. She still retained a wild beauty, if not entirely human.

"Ready to climb?" she asked. Her teeth looked shockingly sharper than human teeth should.

"No," he answered honestly. "But you know I will."

"Yes." She flashed him an alarming smile and turned back to the controls. The black stern of the ship already loomed like a cliff, but a cliff that rocked and slid to the irresistible fury of the storm waves.

"You are a good man, John Barrymore Dix," she said. "Whatever happens, I am happy we could save such a man as you."

He didn't have much to say to that. So nothing was what he said.

"THEY'LL BE WAITING for you fuckwads on the bridge," snarled the slaver with the right forearm swinging unnaturally in a blood-soaked sleeve. A .357 Magnum bullet from Jak's Colt Python had broken both radius and ulna. "They'll blast you the second you show your bastard faces."

Ryan crouched on the metal steps just below the open hatch to the pilothouse. He held the slaver in front of him with his left hand and the AK he'd forcibly borrowed from Milya in his right. Behind him waited his companions and six or seven of the high-ticket slaves they'd freed. They were all young and good-looking, and some so young even Ryan was shocked. Many of the freed slaves had opted to try their luck on their own, either hiding in their former cells or trying to get off the vessel. Likely they were all chills now.

"That's why you go first," he said, and bodily threw the slaver up the last steps and through the open entrance by the collar.

The slaver was dead right. At least three blasters opened up on him the second he appeared, one of them snarling on full-auto. He did a brief spastic dance and fell forward, dead.

The only people on this rad-blasted ship Ryan gave half a fuck about were his friends and the baron's daughter. And they weren't on the bridge. Ryan simply poked the Kalashnikov up above the bottom of the hatch with both hands and cut loose blindly on full rock and roll.

He blasted through the thirty-round banana mag in four ragged bursts. The only reason he let off the trigger at all was to keep from blasting about twenty rounds up through the roof. The Kalashnikov was built to be fired by some shit-scared peasant conscript who was lucky if he could speak Russian, much less read it. He wasn't about to get its barrel burned by letting the whole mag go at once.

Ryan dumped the partially spent magazine and slammed in a full one. Then he launched himself up and over the lip.

He sprayed an even wilder burst as he flew into the room. He still managed to get a shoulder down and roll.

He came up with his back against the console at the front of the bridge, with the wheel on his right.

Several bodies were lying around. A bearded dude was standing up to Ryan's right, wildly cranking off shots from a Beretta. The one-eyed man gave him a quick burst that sawed his face in two and sent the windscreen panel behind him cascading down five stories to the main deck.

As wind whipped sleet into the bridge, Doc led the others out. He fired his LeMat twice, and stabbed one unwisely persistent wounded slaver in the face with the sword. That ended that fight.

The bridge was kind of crowded. Some of the freed captives stood with their backs pressed against the periphery, doing their best to stay out of the storm's direct blast, staring at the chills and obviously trying with all their might not to flip right out. Not Milya, of course; she had got a knife from somewhere and was making sure the seven fallen slavers were dead with a glee that even Ryan found a bit excessive. He decided to hold off a spell before letting her have the AK back. Even though the heavy blaster was kind of a pain to tote with the Scout strapped to his back, his SIG-Sauer and panga.

The captain was still alive. Ryan could tell it was him because he wore an actual captain's uniform, with a blue uniform jacket and even a hat with scrambled eggs on the front. It was faded but looked as if it was clean and regularly mended.

Or it had before the captain had taken a steel-jacketed Sov 7.62 mm round through the chest. Basically the same wound his slaver mates had dealt J.B., except nobody was in a hurry to tend to him. He sat with his back propped against the command console to the left of the wheel, glaring at Ryan.

"The muties betrayed us," the captain wheezed. He had a slight accent Ryan couldn't identify, beyond that it was vaguely Mex-sounding. "After we traded with them so profitably for so long. We should have known. What else…can one expect from monsters? But at least they'll chill you all to sacrifice to their god!"

And he laughed. That had to have hurt like blazing nuke death. Ryan had to give him that.

"Shut up and die."

The slaver captain laughed at Ryan, his teeth bloody.

Neither Ryan nor anybody else had any idea how to pilot this huge rad-blasted boat. He wasn't even sure how important any of the shot-out panels and screens were. So Ryan was trying to set up a better defense of the pilot house than its previous proprietors had managed, while hoping like a bastard to find a way out that didn't involve dying.

It's not going to be bastard easy, he thought, standing beside the open hatch he'd sprung through. It stood aft of the bridge. The windshields wrapped around to either side of it gave a view astern. They were intact. Only the forward windows had gotten starred by hits, and the only panel completely gone was the one on the starboard—landward—side that Ryan had taken out with the Kalashnikov.

The problem was, there wasn't any cover. Except for some chairs bolted to the deck.

We're going to have to suck it up and make some ramparts out of chills, he thought.

"At least the slavers and their erstwhile batrachian allies have something better to do than lay siege to us," Doc said, glancing down at the expanse of deck between the fore and aft towers.

"Just a matter of time before one or the other comes for us," Ryan said.

Ricky had hunkered down beside the captain and was speaking to him urgently. To Ryan's surprise the man actually answered.

"A menina bonita?" he said. "The wild girl from Monster Island? *Sim.* I saw her. She was…worth all the trouble she gave us. Given the price paid for her by the lecherous…baron of—"

His words ended in a rattle. His head lolled to one side. He eyes stared blankly at the deck.

Ricky grabbed him by the blood-soaked jacket and shook him. "Which baron? The baron of what? Tell me. Tell me!"

"Kid," Ryan said. "You shake a body in that condition, usually the only thing you get out of it is blood and other ooze you'll like even less."

A figure burst onto the bridge. Even Ryan was taken by surprise.

But the figure made it only halfway across in obvious blind-panic flight before Doc triggered his LeMat right into the man's throat almost at contact range.

The man fell spraying blood. Ryan set his jaw as hot droplets spattered across his face. He heard voices echoing up the stairwell—the ladder, he supposed. They started out surprised but turned quickly to anger.

"Get ready," Ryan said. After a moment's hesitation he tossed the AK to Lyudmila. She fielded it with one hand despite its weight and grinned.

"Careful where you point that thing before you light it off," he said, drawing his SIG-Sauer.

"Ryan," said Jak, who stood next to him looking aft across the main deck, which was mostly a battlefield of slavers, hunched, shambling muties and the occasional freed captive darting from cover to cover trying to keep out of harm's way.

Jak pointed a white finger dead astern. "Look," he said.

"AT LEAST NOBODY'S shooting at us."

Mildred shouted to make herself heard over the howl of the wind.

"Ryan," Krysty cried. She was jumping up and down at the rail of the top level of the after superstructure, waving frantically with both hands at the bridge up front.

Since that looked to be a good two football fields away, Mildred wasn't even sure how Krysty hoped to see or be seen. Then again, Mildred was having trouble keeping the hard-driving rain from impeding her vision. Maybe the redhead was having better luck.

There was plenty of shooting going on below them. Even with all the other noise, which at this point was about like being inside the throat of an erupting volcano, Mildred could hear the shots snap, crackle and pop like the famous and now-fossilized breakfast cereal. But it was all going on beneath them.

The slavers had found something much more interesting than the two marauding women. Or even the slaves they'd liberated.

Or rather, that something had found them. The frogs had started coming up out of the bay and swarming aboard. There were dozens of the hopping bastards.

They had seen flashes of obvious blasterfire in the distant pilothouse since climbing up here to avoid the battle between two sets of their deadly enemies. Mildred wished she could share Krysty's wholehearted faith that that meant their companions had captured the freighter's bridge.

Mildred glanced down to her right. She swallowed and looked quickly away.

"Okay," she said. "I'm not doing that again. It's hard enough dealing with the sway up here without *seeing* it. Looks like the slaves have quit even trying to make a break for it across the loading ramp. I think the frogs've gotten spooked more than the slavers."

"That's a shame," Krysty said. "Mebbe we can get them to start putting lifeboats down at the stern— Wait! I see somebody waving back. It's Ryan! I think."

Mildred blinked and wiped her eyes clear enough for a brief squint at the forward superstructure. "I see motion," she grudged. "That's pretty much it."

"It's Ryan! I know it is."

"If you say so, Krysty."

"He's— It looks as if he's waving us away. No, no! We'll come and join you."

"No, we're not," Mildred said. "All the slavers and frogs on Earth will eat us if we try."

She bit back the impulse to say he couldn't hear her, since Krysty—who was very bright, however carried away by optimism—no doubt knew that as well as she. Truth was, if it was her, and J.B. was up there, she'd do the same thing.

It doesn't look as if I'm going to be seeing you again, John Barrymore, she thought. Hope you get better and have yourself a fine old life.

"You're right," she said. She waved once, dispiritedly, toward the pilothouse. Then she turned away.

"Let's go around to the back and see what the deck looks like behind us," she said. "One way or another, we'll have to get a lifeboat away and go rescue the others. Might as well see how hard we'll have to fight."

"Right," Mildred said.

She also wished she had Krysty's faith they'd ever get that far. She was having a hard time seeing anything beyond that *fight* part.

But she wasn't about to go down without one, any more than Krysty Wroth was.

They started to their left on the walkway that ran around the after superstructure. They'd scarcely turned the corner, after quick wary looks to make sure no enemies lurked around it, when out to sea a siren pulsed three times. Its acid whine ate right through the tumult of storm and firefight and the giant ship's tortured frame.

Mildred cringed. She saw Krysty's face pale two shades.

"Oh, dear," Krysty said.

"Well, damn!" Mildred stated. "What fresh hell is this?"

Chapter Thirty-Two

Ryan leaned into the stairwell and blasted off four quick shots. Below him somebody screamed. The sound of a return shot crackled up, but Ryan didn't hear or feel the bullet go by.

The slide locked back. He tossed the blaster down the well for good measure. It was the Beretta he'd taken from the guy whose head he'd chopped in two with the Kalashnikov. There were no spare magazines, and nobody was going to take time out to reload that one.

He ducked back, shaking his head. He drew his SIG-Sauer. So far nobody'd made it past the landing immediately below the bridge, except the one slaver who'd caught everybody by surprise.

He could hear shots, screams and inhuman croaking echoing up from the lower decks. It was only a matter of time before they got bull-rushed. And whether by slavers or muties, Ryan knew for sure they could bring more bodies than he and his crew had bullets.

He heard a tapping from behind him. "Knock that shit off," he snarled without turning.

After a moment, a child's voice said, just audible above the wind howling in the broken windshield, "Sir, it wasn't us, please."

He turned. A figure stood at the side of the pilothouse, outside, looking in.

It was a familiar figure, complete with one hand doggedly clamping a fedora atop his head.

"J.B.?" Then, "What the fireblast are you doing out there? Levitating?"

With his free hand the Armorer pointed right aft. He mouthed something.

"Door," Ryan said. "What door? There's a door?"

The Armorer went the way he'd pointed. A moment later Ryan heard, "Don't shoot," and his long-lost best friend stepped onto the bridge.

He and Ryan clapped each other on the shoulder. "What took you so long?" Ryan said.

"Overslept," J.B. said with a brief smile. "Won't happen again."

"How did you get up here?"

"Steel ladder right up the side of the tower. There's a catwalk that runs right around this level. Must be to wash the windows or something."

"But the hatches on the lower levels are welded shut," Ryan said. "You mean the top one isn't?"

Ryan felt triple-stupe. He hadn't given the hatch from the bridge level so much as a glance to see if it showed the same inexpert weld marks the ones below did. Granted, he'd had other things on his mind, like blasting his way onto the bridge without getting blasted in return.

Still, he'd made an assumption. That was an ace way to get dead.

J.B. swayed, then toppled forward. Ryan caught him by the shoulder.

"You fit to fight?" he asked, then silently cursed himself for asking such a stupe question.

"Be fine," J.B. said, in a tone of voice that clearly

wasn't. "After I sit down for a moment and catch my breath."

As Ryan eased him down to the rubber mat that covered the pilothouse deck, a voice said, "The slavers saw no need to prevent escape to the outside from this deck, Mr. Cawdor. Inasmuch as they were the only ones who used it."

He glanced up. "Lady Katerina?" And then, "What's wrong—"

"Mother!" A black-haired rocket streaked past Ryan to collide with the baroness.

Ryan winced as the AK Milya had dropped clattered on the mat. Not even he could hold that carelessness against her. Much. Not when she was running into her mother's open arms. But one thing bothered him.

Lady Katerina had her face pressed against her daughter's shoulder. Between that and her Astrakhan he couldn't see much of her face. He put a hand on her arm and gently pushed.

"Don't want to stand right in the doorway," he said. "Never know what might be coming through it anytime now."

He didn't add, Or going into it—such as bullets. The expected rush hadn't materialized yet, but the sounds of battle were getting louder. Lyudmila pushed away from her mother. Ryan saw the girl's shoulder tense as she got her first good look at the baroness.

She asked the question that had just bubbled back to the surface of Ryan's mind. "Mother? What's wrong with your face?"

Katerina's Frost's face no longer looked fully human. Somehow it had become elongated, exaggerated at cheekbone and jaw. Her nose seemed to have sunk into her face. Her eyes were wide and round.

Strangely, horribly, she still retained more than a touch of beauty. But it was a frightening beauty.

"My fate," Katerina said. "The shadow over Tavern Bay. Decreed for me by men a hundred years dead. I'm turning into a *lyagushka,* Milya."

Milya made a noise like a stepped-on mouse.

"Don't be afraid, my darling," the baroness lisped through teeth whose sharp points protruded through her lips. "You will not share my fate. Only the direct offspring of a mating between human and *lyagushka* can ever change. Believe me. My family has been trying for generations to find another way to perpetuate our…breed."

Milya started to turn away from the mask of horror her mother's features had become. Then she turned and hugged her fiercely.

"Don't give in, Mother!" she cried. "Fight it."

"I have been. And I have lost. But never fear. I will die your mother. The mother who loves you."

"Don't talk that way!"

A boom blasted out of the stairwell. J.B. leaned back out of the entrance cradling his shotgun as the reverberations still sounded. He had shifted to put his back to the bulkhead beside the opening.

"We're all going to die if we don't figure out a way to get down safely double-quick," he said. "The frogs're driving the slavers upward. And if we try going down the ladder, the slavers can just lean out and blast us like birds sittin' on a wire."

He shook his head. "Hurts like a bastard when I shoot," he said.

"Fighting down there," observed Jak, who had shifted to look through the portside windows.

Ryan went up alongside the albino. A glance down

at the deck confirmed his words. Not that Ryan ever doubted them.

"So," he said, turning back. "Looks like we'll have to make a break for it and take our chances regardless. Slim chance is still better than none, as Trader used to say."

"No," Katerina said. Grimacing in pain as if her fingers had grown to her daughter's arm, she tore herself loose from her. Still fully the regal baroness, despite the awful change overtaking her, she swept to the helm with a swirl of her coattails and began to work controls.

The engines, whose near-subliminal hum Ryan had been aware of since setting foot aboard without really noticing, began to come to life. Despite the constant, seemingly random three-dimensional movements, the howling gale was putting the big ship through, and the frequent impacts of her black hull on the tire-buffers protecting the dock, Ryan felt a distinct shudder run through the vessel as her huge screws began to bite water.

"You know how to pilot this thing?" he asked.

He was keeping his focus soft. His eye caught motion in the corner of its peripheral vision. A pale oval blur popped up above the level of the floor. He snapped a handblaster shot across his body. Red sprayed. The face vanished.

"She went to sea as a girl," J.B. said helpfully.

Katerina pealed a wild laugh. "I sailed in this ship! She was originally a Great Lakes freighter, did you know? The slave trade goes back generations in Tavern Bay. And now this new set of slavers is learning the cost of doing business with the *lyagushki,* as others have before."

The deck moved beneath Ryan's boots as, almost imperceptibly, the ship began to move forward.

"What are you doing?" Ryan asked.

"Increasing your chances as much as I can. My daughter must not fall into *lyagushki* claws. They have no concern for ties of family—and those who are not them, or cannot change, they see only as breeding stock. Or food."

A little tremolo ran up through Ryan's boots, followed quickly by another.

"The cables have parted fore and aft," Doc said from the starboard window. "But how does this help us escape with your daughter, Lady Katerina? We might escape the base, but we still face a ship full of slavers and muties, each eager to see the color of our insides."

"I will drive the ship onto the rocks by the cliff to the south. It is a lee shore. If the impact doesn't break her back and send her to the bottom, the waves and wind pounding her against the rocks will."

"And that helps us get away how?" Ryan asked.

"It gives your enemies something new to worry about," she said. "And will send a large number of them too. Though mostly slavers, I'm afraid. *Lyagushki* have gills, though they are hard to see when not in use."

"Here come!" Jak shouted. His Python filled the bridge with a bright flash and brain-smashing noise.

Routed by the frogs' treacherous attack, a mob of slavers rushed up the stairs and poured into the bridge. The withering volley of blasterfire from Ryan and his four companions didn't slow them, except for those who fell and those who stumbled over them.

In an eyeblink the bridge was full of frantic bodies, reeking of sweat. It wasn't an assault. It was a pure stampede.

Ryan found himself grappled by a man with a full yellow beard chopped off square at his collarbone. His mouth and eyes were wide open. He was missing a front tooth and his breath smelled like a gaudy-house crapper after a cheap brew special.

The guy was bare-handed. He had Ryan by both wrists. His strength was that of a man driven by sheer adrenaline overload. Whether by accident or some residual design, he had his right hip turned against Ryan's body, forestalling the otherwise obvious knee to the balls.

Ryan head-butted him, flattening his nose against his fear-twisted face. Blood squirted hot onto his shirt. Ryan's quick glimpse of the slaver's face showed his nose had clearly been broken before, and those who had experienced it once or more were less susceptible to the shock and pain of it, which could totally freeze even a coldheart.

But it still hurt. Enough to make the man's wide blue eyes blink and the drowner's grip on Ryan's arms relax.

The one-eyed man wrenched his right hand free, then chopped the man's thick throat with the butt of his SIG-Sauer. The slaver reeled back, gagging and clutching his neck. Ryan shot him in the face, then fired two quick shots into the skinny black guy behind him.

There were at least a dozen slavers crowding into the pilothouse. Ryan drew his panga and started hacking.

A blaster roared. A child shrieked. A girl, by the voice—but too young for Milya, at least.

But that confirmed to Ryan he didn't dare shoot any more. He didn't want to shoot the other captives they'd freed, but if it came to a choice between them and his friends—or even Milya—that was just too bad for them. But he could just as easily blast Jak or J.B. in the scrum as he could a slaver.

And the slavers were beginning to collect themselves to fight more effectively. A punch caught Ryan on the blind left side of his face. His head rocked back. Another slaver slammed a longblaster butt into his belly while a third grabbed his blaster hand.

"Get down!" Milya screamed.

Ryan did. He just sat right down on the wet rubber mat. His weight pulled the weedy little slaver clutching his blaster arm with both fists down with him.

Brown eyes blinked from a ratlike face six inches from Ryan's nose. Then a burst of full-auto blasterfire erupted.

The rat-faced slaver squeaked like the rodent he resembled and fell straight down. Blood was spraying from wounds in his back.

Milya Frost stood at the front of the bridge with her back to her mother. She had recovered the AK-47 and was firing the blaster from the hip. She did her trainers credit, pumping out bursts short enough so that she could hold down the weapon's barrel with her skinny arms. She sprayed the mob of panicked slavers with steel-jacketed 7.62 mm death. They jerked and fell to the deck.

Then the bolt locked back. She began fumbling for a reload. There were still at least six slavers still standing, and they converged on her.

Ryan still had rounds in the magazine of his SIG-Sauer. He opened fire, as did Doc, Jak and J.B. All of them apparently had obeyed Milya's order in time—except the Armorer, who was still sitting and hadn't needed to.

The SIG-Sauer's slide locked back. The bearded, shave-headed slaver boss Ryan had seen board the *Serge Broom* with Milya loomed above him. His mightily mustached face was a twisted mask of blood and rage. He held a fire ax over his head with both hands, ready to split Ryan's breastbone like kindling.

Thunder crashed from Ryan's left. Yellow flashes lit that side of the slaver's face. He jerked as if dancing in place, and badly. Then he collapsed like an empty burlap sack.

Lady Katerina had turned from the helm. A pair of boxy black Glock blasters wisped blue smoke from her elegantly gloved fists.

"Gentlemen," she croaked in a voice both guttural and hollow, "brace yourselves."

Another slaver, this one carrying an M-16, burst out of the stairwell and took a frenzied step toward the bridge.

The vessel hit the rocks. The deck canted forward as momentum drove the stern upward. Ryan tumbled forward to slam against the control panel.

The earth-shattering crash of hull smashing against surf-pounded granite was joined by viscera-churning screeching and crackling as the shockwave rippled through the structure of the ship.

The stern hit the water with a hollow boom. Through the aft view ports, Ryan could see water rush upward in a white wave.

The ship began to swing its stern to starboard. The bow ground against the rocks. Looking up through the front windshield, Ryan saw the south cliffs rising out of sight like a black, implacable wall.

Her blasters still in hand, Katerina cradled Milya against her. The girl had dropped her longblaster and was sobbing wildly.

Ryan's first act was to reload his handblaster. Then he yelled, "Everybody fit to fight?"

Jak and Doc answered yes. A bit later so did J.B., to Ryan's vast relief.

"Where's Ricky?" he asked, pulling himself to a sitting position.

"Here," the youth called, climbing through the window Ryan had shot out. He had his longblaster slung and his Webley revolver in hand. "When Milya screamed to get down, there was a guy right under me. So I went out."

"Good move," Ryan said.

He heard a groan, followed by a long sigh. It ended in a gurgle. Ryan looked to see Doc, his hair wild, one wing of his shirt collar standing up, straightening and withdrawing his slim blade from the back of a pirate.

"Just making sure," he said.

Jak, as agile as a catamount and resilient as rubber, was already up checking the fallen slavers with a hunting knife in hand. Ryan saw him plunge it into a thick, grimy neck. The way blood spurted showed it was a well-chosen shot.

Climbing to his feet, Ryan surveyed the scene. The slavers were down. His companions were all accounted for. None of them showed obvious signs of punctures. But otherwise they looked the way he felt.

Which was as if his whole body had been used to pound the nails to build a mansion fit for a baron.

Four of the captives huddled to port of the helm, hugging each other and sobbing. The youngest, a black-haired girl of about eight, lay on her face, unmoving. Her blood had joined the mix of blood and dirt and water that lay an inch deep on the floor. The sixth, a black-haired boy of about sixteen, had vanished.

"Why didn't they shoot more?" Ricky asked.

"Blasters empty," Jak said. He straddled a burly back. As if to emphasize his words, he cut the fallen slaver's throat with an extra-vicious jerk of his arm.

"We're not exactly loaded down with ammo, either," Ryan stated.

"We brought some extra ammunition," said J.B.,

who now sat stuffing red plastic-hulled shells into his M-4000. "Just 9 mm, .45 caliber and 12 gauge, though. Didn't have any .44 Remington to hand. Sorry, Doc."

Doc flourished his blade. "This never needs reloading."

"I hear the frogs croaking in the stairs," J.B. said. "Not sure what's keeping them, truth to tell."

Lady Katerina kissed her daughter's reddened, tear-drenched face and pushed her away. "You must go. All of you. Now."

"What about you?" Ryan asked.

"Look at me," the baroness commanded. He did and his stomach turned. Her face was utterly unrecognizable now, distorted by the half-finished transformation from human to frog-mutie. "I have little time left. I wish to die as a woman."

"Mother!"

A hand whose fingers were joined by webs and whose tips sprouted black talons thrust her toward Ryan. Stunned by the rapidity of the transformation, Ryan barely caught the girl before she rebounded off his chest.

"What do you mean to do, my lady?" Doc asked.

Katerina's coat was already straining at the seams across the back as her torso swelled and hunched forward. She managed to force herself upright and tore open the front of it.

Beneath she wore a canvas vest. It had many pockets. In each one Ryan saw a small block of C-4 with a blasting cap inserted. Little loops of det cord joined them.

"Fireblast," he said.

Her smile was ghastly. "I shall soon go to embrace my family. Leave now!"

Chapter Thirty-Three

As Baroness Katerina promised, the storm was bashing the slaver ship to death against the foot of the cliffs.

The doomed ship leaned far to port as a storm-driven wave drove its keel up the rocks with a shriek like fingernails on a blackboard magnified a million times.

Ryan heard a scream of terror as another of the freed captives, a pretty blonde teenager, lost her grip on the ladder right above his head. He turned to see her vanish into gray boiling water below.

Grinding, the ship righted itself. Halfway down the ladder Ryan looked down at the deck.

Seven or eight frogs were in sight. They seemed to be searching for hiding slavers. Their short, sharply bowed legs seemed to enable them to keep their balance against the bucking of the deck better than Ryan could have kept his.

They hadn't been looking up, despite the blasterfire that roared from the pilothouse at irregular intervals as Lady Katerina shot muties—her kin—trying to get onto the bridge.

Ryan saw frog faces turned upward as the girl fell screaming to her death. The enormous bulging eyes could show no emotion. But the muties began to croak and point their claws at the fugitives, strung down the side of the superstructure like meat beads on a steel necklace.

From above Ryan heard a voice cry, "My people! I see it now!"

Lady Katerina croaked a series of syllables that hurt Ryan's throat to listen to. The only thing he could come close to deciphering any of it was what sounded like the letters *E* and *A* together, repeated several times.

"Fireblast!" Ryan yelled. "She's gone over!"

"No, she hasn't," J.B. called from above.

From the top of the superstructure, Ryan saw a white flash. He hugged the tower tightly as the pilothouse exploded in a ring of yellow flame. Arcing debris trails smoked far out over the churning water.

Ears ringing from the explosion, Ryan clambered down as fast as he could. When his boot heels were about six feet from the deck, he let go.

He landed, crouching, with his left hand on the cold steel deck for support. He had the SIG-Sauer in his right hand. Ignoring the pain where the muzzle of his slung Steyr Scout had gouged him in the kidneys, he double-tapped a frog staring down at him from six feet away. Then he turned and blasted the one who was trying to turn right behind him.

Full-auto fire ripped out from ten feet above Ryan's head. He recognized the snarl of J.B.'s Uzi.

Even while fighting for his life, Ryan winced in sympathy with J.B. at the pain his friend had to have endured, clinging to the frigid, rain-slick steel ladder with one arm while firing the heavy submachine gun with the other. To have done so with his recent chest wound and operation incisions just healed had to have hurt like a bitch.

In a moment, the frogs on the narrow space between superstructure and rail were down. Rain blanketed the view. For now, the muties had better things to do than investigate more random blasterfire, anyway.

In a matter of moments they were all safely on the deck. Ryan set Doc and J.B. facing aft with their blasters. Milya, sobbing constantly, took her place at their side with her AK reloaded with its last mag and ready. Ryan wondered how in the name of glowing nuke shit the slavers had ever caught her in the first place.

He watched forward as Jak and Ricky scouted toward the bow.

"What now, Ryan?" Doc asked. He sounded almost cheerful. Though he fought for his life as fiercely as any of them—and as well as most—he had a more philosophical attitude toward the leaving of it than his comrades did.

Ryan blew out a gusty breath, then had to throw out his blaster hand to brace himself against the cold metal of the superstructure as the most recent impact rocked the ship. The *Serge Broom* was dying, with neither dignity nor silence.

As much rust as she showed, Ryan was surprised the ship had stuck together as long as she had.

"We look for some of those lifeboats I so blithely promised Krysty we'd find waiting for us," he said.

"I see none, I fear," Doc said.

"Me, neither."

Ricky and Jak rounded the superstructure, running hard. "No boats up front!" Ricky called.

"But frogs!" Jak shouted. "Coming this way!"

"I see forms shambling through the rain toward us from astern, too," Doc added.

Ryan looked to sea. It was a constantly churning surge of death, as expected.

"I guess we go over the rail," he said.

"And swim?" Ricky asked.

A noise like a giant's backbone being broken vertebra by vertebra reverberated in their ears and in their bones.

"We're going to wind up doing that anyway," Ryan said. "Ship's breaking up. Only choice now is go down with the bitch, dive in ourselves, or travel in a mutie's belly."

"Ryan! Look over the rail!"

"Krysty?" he said aloud.

Then Ricky leaned way too far out over the rail, waving a hand furiously above his head and shrieking Krysty's name. Jak caught him by the back of his parka just in time to keep him going over as the ship rolled violently to port.

More judiciously—a bit, anyway—Ryan leaned over the rail.

There was a powerboat tossing in the waves hard beside the doomed freighter. A vaguely familiar-looking man was keeping it in position. And two very familiar female figures rode beside him in the cockpit, waving vigorously. Each held a loudspeaker.

"Hustle your butts down here!" Mildred yelled. "There's room for everybody!"

Ryan squeezed his eye shut. "If only we had a nukin' rope."

"Right here," J.B. called.

He was sitting on the deck with Doc holding him by the collar of his jacket.

He winced as obvious pain sliced through him, then with a grin of triumph he held up a blue-striped white nylon coil.

"Got two of them," he said. "Lady K had them packed."

Doc's handblaster boomed. A frog-mutie had approached within thirty feet from astern. It fell kicking to the deck.

"Stand them off!" Ryan shouted. "We're going home."

CAINE SENT THE launch speeding northeast, throwing up a white bow-wave, slaloming expertly to avoid getting slammed by the storm waves.

With a crack like a huge shinbone snapping, the *Serge Broom* at last broke in two on the rocks. The bow section started to settle where it was, only to be smashed repeatedly against the cliffs until the weight of the superstructure toppled it outward and it turned turtle. The longer stern section rolled to seaward; its broken-off end rapidly filling with seawater, it quickly sank, sliding down into the cove away from the sheer walls.

Huddled in the stern with Ryan, Krysty put her head against Ryan's shoulder and sighed.

"I wish more of the slaves had been able to get clear," she said.

He hugged her. "You two did what you could," he said. "Otherwise—well, that's life in the Deathlands."

She nodded. J.B. and Milya Frost rode in the chairs bolted into the cockpit. The rest were crowded into the space aft, including the two young women, both seventeen or eighteen, who were the only other liberated captives to make it to the craft. Those two clung together and said nothing.

J.B., holding his hat jammed on his head, had his neck craned around to watch as the ship went down.

"I guess that's a run of women blowing themselves up to save their loved ones," he said.

"What's that, J.B.?" Ryan asked. He knew about Lady Katerina, obviously, but his old friend had distinctly said women. The howl of the storm, the slap and crash of the waves, and the muted thunder of the engines weren't enough to make Ryan mistake that.

Sadly J.B. shook his head. "It's the past now," he said. "Let it lie and drive on."

A tumult of dirty white water was bubbling up from where the freighter's two sundered parts had vanished. Turned in her own chair, Milya uttered a lost-soul wail.

Mildred clambered over the partition into the cockpit to put a comforting arm around her.

"Might I suggest," Caine called, "that I put you ashore as close by as reasonable safety allows? So that you can recover your gear, which I presume you stashed?"

"What do you mean?" Ryan called. He was still not used to the servant's Brit accent. But the guy knew how to drive a speedboat under conditions that were nearly impossible to navigate. Ryan had to give him that.

"I can deliver Milya myself, if you will permit me. I shall take the other young ladies with me, as well, if you allow. We can give them proper homes, I daresay."

"He means," Krysty said, with just a final sniffle, "that if we go back to Stormbreak, the baron may not be happy about gaining a daughter but losing an adored wife."

"He seems a good man," Doc said, then added, "for a baron."

"Yeah," J.B. said. "And remember what they say about barons and gratitude."

"Good call, Caine," Ryan stated. "I think we'll just take you up on that deal, thanks very much."

"But Ryan!" Mildred exclaimed. "What about the rest of our payment? We busted our asses back there, and we can use the money!"

"And what good does jack do when the dirt's hitting you in the eyes, Mildred?"

"My friends," Caine said, "you need forgo nothing."
He turned and actually cracked a smile.

"If you will open the strongbox bolted behind the cockpit, you will see that Lady Katerina packed away the promised sum, as well as a bonus."

"She didn't miss much, Ryan," J.B. said. "I can testify to that."

"I reckon not," Ryan agreed.

"A remarkable woman," Caine said, his face once more turned forward. "Cursed by the evil deeds of men long dead. A great and powerful shame. We shall miss her terribly, not just her husband and daughter."

"Yeah," Ryan said. "Oh, and—J.B.?"

The Armorer cranked his head around. "Yeah?"

"Welcome back."

J.B. smiled.

"It's good to be home."

* * * * *

James Axler
Outlanders®

COSMIC RIFT

Dominate and Avenge

Untapped riches are being mined on Earth—a treasure trove of alien superscience strewn across the planet. High above, hidden in a quantum rift, the scavenger citizens of Authentiville have built a paradise from the trawled detritus of the God wars. A coup is poised to dethrone Authentiville's benevolent ruler and doom Earth, once again, to an epic battle against impossible odds. Cerberus must rally against a twisted—but quite human—new enemy who has mastered the secrets of inhuman power....

Available in November wherever books are sold.

TAKE 'EM FREE
2 action-packed novels
plus a mystery bonus

NO RISK

NO OBLIGATION
TO BUY

GE13

AleX Archer
BLOOD CURSED

A local superstition or one of history's monsters come to life?

Deep in the Bavarian forest, archaeologists unearth a medieval human skull with a brick stuffed in its mouth. When Annja Creed catches wind of the strange discovery, the TV host and archaeologist rushes to join the dig. But the superstitious locals fear the excavation has angered one of the chewing dead— those who rise from their graves to feast on human flesh and blood. Then a child goes missing. Suddenly ensnared in the Czech Republic's black market underworld, Annja must wield Joan of Arc's sword to protect the innocent....

Available in September wherever books are sold.